AF147709

The Food Of The Gods And How It Came To Earth

by
H.G. Wells

Double 9
BOOKS

The Food Of The Gods And How It Came To Earth
by H.G. Wells

Copyright © 2025

All Rights reserved.
No part of this publication may be reproduced,
stored in a retrieval system, or transmitted in any
form or by any means, electronic, mechanical,
photocopying or Otherwise, without the written
permission of the publisher.

The author/editor asserts the moral right to
be identified as the author/editor of this work.

ISBN: 978-93-57481-54-0

Published by

DOUBLE 9 BOOKS

2/13-B, Ansari Road
Daryaganj, New Delhi – 110002
info@double9books.com
www.double9books.com
Tel. 011-40042856

This book is under public domain

ABOUT THE AUTHOR

Herbert George Wells was born on 21 September, 1866. He was an English author. He wrote many books, brief tales, and works of social discourse, history, parody, account, and self-portrayal. Two of his books were written on recreational war games. In the present times, Wells is known for his sci-fi books and is frequently called the father of sci-fi".

In his own lifespan, he was regarded as a forward-looking, social critic who gave his scholarly abilities to the improvement of an ever-evolving vision on a worldwide scale. As a futurist, he composed various idealistic works and predicted the approach of an airplane, tanks, space travel, atomic weapons, satellite TV, and something that seemed similar to the World Wide Web. His sci-fis were based upon topics like time travel, allien intrusion, invisibility, and bio-engineering. Brian Aldiss alluded to Wells as the "Shakespeare of sci-fi", while American essayist Charles Fort alluded to him as a "wild ability".

Wells delivered his works persuading by imparting ordinary detail close by a solitary phenomenal suspicion for every work - named "Wells' regulation" - allowing Joseph Conrad to hail him in 1898 as "O Realist of the Fantastic!". His most striking sci-fi works incorporate The Time Machine (1895), which was his first novel, The Island of Doctor Moreau (1896), The Invisible Man (1897), The War of the Worlds (1898), and the tactical sci-fi The War in the Air (1907). Wells got nominated for the Nobel Prize in Literature several times.

Wells was professionally trained in biology and his reasoning on legal matters occurred in a context that referred to Darwin. He was a frank communist since early on, frequently (however not generally, as toward the start of the First World War) identifying with conservative perspectives. His later works turned out to be progressively political and instructional. Books, for example, Kipps and The History of Mr. Polly, which portray lower-working class life, prompted the idea that he was the deserved successor to Charles Dickens, however, Wells depicted a scope of social layers and tries to bring out the English society as a whole in Tono-Bungay (1909). Wells was diabetic and was the co-founder of the foundation 'The Diabetic Association' (referred to now as Diabetes UK) in 1934.

CONTENTS

BOOK I.
THE DAWN OF THE FOOD

CHAPTER THE FIRST.
THE DISCOVERY OF THE FOOD.

I.

In the middle years of the nineteenth century there first became abundant in this strange world of ours a class of men, men tending for the most part to become elderly, who are called, and who are very properly called, but who dislike extremely to be called — "Scientists." They dislike that word so much that from the columns of Nature, which was from the first their distinctive and characteristic paper, it is as carefully excluded as if it were — that other word which is the basis of all really bad language in this country. But the Great Public and its Press know better, and "Scientists" they are, and when they emerge to any sort of publicity, "distinguished scientists" and "eminent scientists" and "well-known scientists" is the very least we call them.

Certainly both Mr. Bensington and Professor Redwood quite merited any of these terms long before they came upon the marvellous discovery of which this story tells. Mr. Bensington was a Fellow of the Royal Society and a former president of the Chemical Society, and Professor Redwood was Professor of Physiology in the Bond Street College of the London University, and he had been grossly libelled by the anti-vivisectionists time after time. And they had led lives of academic distinction from their very earliest youth.

They were of course quite undistinguished looking men, as indeed all true Scientists are. There is more personal distinction about the mildest-mannered actor alive than there is about the entire Royal Society. Mr. Bensington was short and very, very bald, and he stooped slightly; he wore gold-rimmed spectacles and cloth boots that were abundantly cut open because of his numerous corns, and Professor Redwood was entirely ordinary in his appearance. Until they happened upon the Food of the Gods (as I must insist upon calling it) they led lives of such eminent and studious obscurity that it is hard to find anything whatever to tell the reader about them.

Mr. Bensington won his spurs (if one may use such an expression of a gentleman in boots of slashed cloth) by his splendid researches upon the More Toxic Alkaloids, and Professor Redwood rose to eminence—I do not clearly remember how he rose to eminence! I know he was very eminent, and that's all. Things of this sort grow. I fancy it was a voluminous work on Reaction Times with numerous plates of sphygmograph tracings (I write subject to correction) and an admirable new terminology, that did the thing for him.

The general public saw little or nothing of either of these gentlemen. Sometimes at places like the Royal Institution and the Society of Arts it did in a sort of way see Mr. Bensington, or at least his blushing baldness and something of his collar and coat, and hear fragments of a lecture or paper that he imagined himself to be reading audibly; and once I remember—one midday in the vanished past—when the British Association was at Dover, coming on Section C or D, or some such letter, which had taken up its quarters in a public-house, and following two, serious-looking ladies with paper parcels, out of mere curiosity, through a door labelled "Billiards" and "Pool" into a scandalous darkness, broken only by a magic-lantern circle of Redwood's tracings.

I watched the lantern slides come and go, and listened to a voice (I forget what it was saying) which I believe was the voice of Professor Redwood, and there was a sizzling from the lantern and another sound that kept me there, still out of curiosity, until the lights were unexpectedly turned up. And then I perceived that this sound was the sound of the munching of buns and sandwiches and things that the assembled British Associates had come there to eat under cover of the magic-lantern darkness.

And Redwood I remember went on talking all the time the lights were up and dabbing at the place where his diagram ought to have been visible on the screen—and so it was again so soon as the darkness was restored. I remember him then as a most ordinary, slightly nervous-looking dark man, with an air of being preoccupied with something else, and doing what he was doing just then under an unaccountable sense of duty.

I heard Bensington also once—in the old days—at an educational conference in Bloomsbury. Like most eminent chemists and botanists, Mr. Bensington was very authoritative upon teaching—though I am certain he would have been scared out of his wits by an average Board School class in half-an-hour—and so far as I can remember now, he was propounding an improvement of Professor Armstrong's Heuristic method, whereby at the cost of three or four hundred pounds' worth of apparatus, a total neglect of all other studies and the undivided attention of a teacher of exceptional gifts, an average child might with a peculiar sort of thumby thoroughness learn in the course of ten or twelve years almost as much chemistry as one could get in one of those objectionable shilling text-books that were then so common....

Quite ordinary persons you perceive, both of them, outside their science. Or if anything on the unpractical side of ordinary. And that you will find is the case with "scientists" as a class all the world over. What there is great of them is an annoyance to their fellow scientists and a mystery to the general public, and what is not is evident.

There is no doubt about what is not great, no race of men have such obvious littlenesses. They live in a narrow world so far as their human intercourse goes; their researches involve infinite attention and an almost monastic seclusion; and what is left over is not very much. To witness some queer, shy, misshapen, grey-headed, self-important, little discoverer of great discoveries, ridiculously adorned with the wide ribbon of some order of chivalry and holding a reception of his fellow-men, or to read the anguish of Nature at the "neglect of science" when the angel of the birthday honours passes the Royal Society by, or to listen to one indefatigable lichenologist commenting on the work of another indefatigable lichenologist, such things force one to realise the unfaltering littleness of men.

And withal the reef of Science that these little "scientists" built and are yet building is so wonderful, so portentous, so full of mysterious half-shapen promises for the mighty future of man! They do not seem to realise the things they are doing! No doubt long ago even

Mr. Bensington, when he chose this calling, when he consecrated his life to the alkaloids and their kindred compounds, had some inkling of the vision,—more than an inkling. Without some such inspiration, for such glories and positions only as a "scientist" may expect, what young man would have given his life to such work, as young men do? No, they must have seen the glory, they must have had the vision, but so near that it has blinded them. The splendour has blinded them, mercifully, so that for the rest of their lives they can hold the lights of knowledge in comfort—that we may see!

And perhaps it accounts for Redwood's touch of preoccupation, that—there can be no doubt of it now—he among his fellows was different, he was different inasmuch as something of the vision still lingered in his eyes.

II.

The Food of the Gods I call it, this substance that Mr. Bensington and Professor Redwood made between them; and having regard now to what it has already done and all that it is certainly going to do, there is surely no exaggeration in the name. So I shall continue to call it therefore throughout my story. But Mr. Bensington would no more have called it that in cold blood than he would have gone out from his flat in Sloane Street clad in regal scarlet and a wreath of laurel. The phrase was a mere first cry of astonishment from him. He called it the Food of the Gods, in his enthusiasm and for an hour or so at the most altogether. After that he decided he was being absurd. When he first thought of the thing he saw, as it were, a vista of enormous possibilities—literally enormous possibilities; but upon this dazzling vista, after one stare of amazement, he resolutely shut his eyes, even as a conscientious "scientist" should. After that, the Food of the Gods sounded blatant to the pitch of indecency. He was surprised he had used the expression. Yet for all that something of that clear-eyed moment hung about him and broke out ever and again....

"Really, you know," he said, rubbing his hands together and laughing nervously, "it has more than a theoretical interest.

"For example," he confided, bringing his face close to the Professor's and dropping to an undertone, "it would perhaps, if suitably handled, sell....

"Precisely," he said, walking away,—"as a Food. Or at least a food ingredient.

"Assuming of course that it is palatable. A thing we cannot know till we have prepared it."

He turned upon the hearthrug, and studied the carefully designed slits upon his cloth shoes.

"Name?" he said, looking up in response to an inquiry. "For my part I incline to the good old classical allusion. It—it makes Science res—. Gives it a touch of old-fashioned dignity. I have been thinking ... I don't know if you will think it absurd of me.... A little fancy is surely occasionally permissible.... Herakleophorbia. Eh? The nutrition of a possible Hercules? You know it might ...

"Of course if you think not—"

Redwood reflected with his eyes on the fire and made no objection.

"You think it would do?"

Redwood moved his head gravely.

"It might be Titanophorbia, you know. Food of Titans.... You prefer the former?

"You're quite sure you don't think it a little too—"

"No."

"Ah! I'm glad."

And so they called it Herakleophorbia throughout their investigations, and in their report,—the report that was never published, because of the unexpected developments that upset all their arrangements,—it is invariably written in that way. There were three kindred substances prepared before they hit on the one their speculations had foretolds and these they spoke of as Herakleophorbia I, Herakleophorbia II, and Herakleophorbia III. It is Herakleophorbia IV. which I—insisting upon Bensington's original name—call here the Food of the Gods.

III.

The idea was Mr. Bensington's. But as it was suggested to him by one of Professor Redwood's contributions to the Philosophical Transactions, he very properly consulted that gentleman before he carried it further. Besides which it was, as a research, a physiological. quite as much as a chemical inquiry.

Professor Redwood was one of those scientific men who are addicted to tracings and curves. You are familiar—if you are at all the sort of reader I like—with the sort of scientific paper I mean. It is a paper you cannot make head nor tail of, and at the end come five or six long folded diagrams that open out and show peculiar zigzag tracings, flashes of lightning overdone, or sinuous inexplicable things called "smoothed curves" set up on ordinates and rooting in abscissae—and things like that. You puzzle over the thing for a long time and end with the suspicion that not only do you not understand it but that the author does not understand it either. But really you know many of these scientific people understand the meaning of their own papers quite well: it is simply a defect of expression that raises the obstacle between us.

I am inclined to think that Redwood thought in tracings and curves. And after his monumental work upon Reaction Times (the unscientific reader is exhorted to stick to it for a little bit longer and everything will be as clear as daylight) Redwood began to turn out smoothed curves and sphygmographeries upon Growth, and it was one of his papers upon Growth that really gave Mr. Bensington his idea.

Redwood, you know, had been measuring growing things of all sorts, kittens, puppies, sunflowers, mushrooms, bean plants, and (until his wife put a stop to it) his baby, and he showed that growth went out not at a regular pace, or, as he put it, so,

but with bursts and intermissions of this sort,

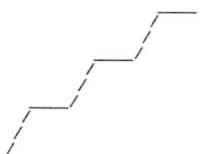

and that apparently nothing grew regularly and steadily, and so far as he could make out nothing could grow regularly and steadily: it was as if every living thing had just to accumulate force to grow, grew with vigour only for a time, and then had to wait for a space before it could go on growing again. And in the muffled and highly technical language of the really careful "scientist," Redwood suggested that the process of growth probably demanded the presence of a considerable quantity of some necessary substance in the blood that was only formed very slowly, and that when this substance was used up by growth, it was only very slowly replaced, and that meanwhile the organism had to mark time. He compared his unknown substance to oil in machinery. A growing animal was rather like an engine, he suggested, that can move a certain distance and must then be oiled before it can run again. ("But why shouldn't one oil the engine from without?" said Mr. Bensington, when he read the paper.) And all this, said Redwood, with the delightful nervous inconsecutiveness of his class, might very probably be found to throw a light upon the mystery of certain of the ductless glands. As though they had anything to do with it at all!

In a subsequent communication Redwood went further. He gave a perfect Brock's benefit of diagrams—exactly like rocket trajectories they were; and the gist of it—so far as it had any gist—was that the blood of puppies and kittens and the sap of sunflowers and the juice of mushrooms in what he called the "growing phase" differed in the proportion of certain elements from their blood and sap on the days when they were not particularly growing.

And when Mr. Bensington, after holding the diagrams sideways and upside down, began to see what this difference was, a great amazement came upon him. Because, you see, the difference might probably be due to the presence of just the very substance he had recently been trying to isolate in his researches upon such alkaloids as are most stimulating to the nervous system. He put down Redwood's paper on the patent reading-desk that swung inconveniently from his arm-chair, took off his gold-rimmed spectacles, breathed on them and wiped them very carefully.

"By Jove!" said Mr. Bensington.

Then replacing his spectacles again he turned to the patent reading-desk, which immediately, as his elbow came against its arm, gave a coquettish squeak and deposited the paper, with all its diagrams in a dispersed and crumpled state, on the floor. "By Jove!" said Mr. Bensington, straining his stomach over the arm-chair with a patient disregard of the habits of this convenience, and then, finding the pamphlet still out of reach, he went down on all fours in pursuit. It was on the floor that the idea of calling it the Food of the Gods came to him....

For you see, if he was right and Redwood was right, then by injecting or administering this new substance of his in food, he would do away with the "resting phase," and instead of growth going on in this fashion,

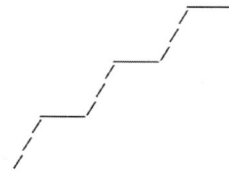

it would (if you follow me) go thus—

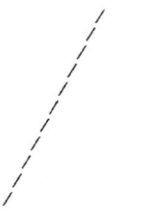

IV.

The night after his conversation with Redwood Mr. Bensington could scarcely sleep a wink. He did seem once to get into a sort of doze, but it was only for a moment, and then he dreamt he had dug a deep hole into the earth and poured in tons and tons of the Food of the Gods, and the earth was swelling and swelling, and all the boundaries of the countries were bursting, and the Royal Geographical Society was all at work like one great guild of tailors letting out the equator....

That of course was a ridiculous dream, but it shows the state of mental excitement into which Mr. Bensington got and the real value he attached to his idea, much better than any of the things he said or did when he was awake and on his guard. Or I should not have mentioned it, because as a general rule I do not think it is at all interesting for people to tell each other about their dreams.

By a singular coincidence Redwood also had a dream that night, and his dream was this:—

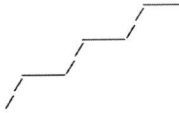

It was a diagram done in fire upon a long scroll of the abyss. And he (Redwood) was standing on a planet before a sort of black platform lecturing about the new sort of growth that was now possible, to the More than Royal Institution of Primordial Forces—forces which had always previously, even in the growth of races, empires, planetary systems, and worlds, gone so:—

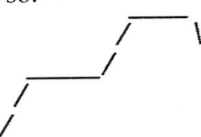

And even in some cases so:—

And he was explaining to them quite lucidly and convincingly that these slow, these even retrogressive methods would be very speedily quite put out of fashion by his discovery.

Ridiculous of course! But that too shows—

That either dream is to be regarded as in any way significant or prophetic beyond what I have categorically said, I do not for one moment suggest.

CHAPTER THE SECOND.
THE EXPERIMENTAL FARM.

I.

Mr. Bensington proposed originally to try this stuff, so soon as he was really able to prepare it, upon tadpoles. One always does try this sort of thing upon tadpoles to begin with; this being what tadpoles are for. And it was agreed that he should conduct the experiments and not Redwood, because Redwood's laboratory was occupied with the ballistic apparatus and animals necessary for an investigation into the Diurnal Variation in the Butting Frequency of the Young Bull Calf, an investigation that was yielding curves of an abnormal and very perplexing sort, and the presence of glass globes of tadpoles was extremely undesirable while this particular research was in progress.

But when Mr. Bensington conveyed to his cousin Jane something of what he had in mind, she put a prompt veto upon the importation of any considerable number of tadpoles, or any such experimental creatures, into their flat. She had no objection whatever to his use of one of the rooms of the flat for the purposes of a non-explosive chemistry that, so far as she was concerned, came to nothing; she let him have a gas furnace and a sink and a dust-tight cupboard of refuge from the weekly storm of cleaning she would not forego. And having known people addicted to drink, she regarded his solicitude for distinction in learned societies as an excellent substitute for the coarser form of depravity. But any sort of living things in quantity, "wriggly" as they were bound to be alive and "smelly" dead, she could not and would not abide. She said these things were certain to be unhealthy, and Bensington was notoriously a delicate man—it was nonsense to say he wasn't. And when Bensington tried to make the enormous importance of this possible discovery clear, she said that it was all very well, but if she consented to his making everything nasty and unwholesome in the place (and that was what it all came to) then she was certain he would be the first to complain.

And Mr. Bensington went up and down the room, regardless of his corns, and spoke to her quite firmly and angrily without the slightest effect. He said that nothing ought to stand in the way of the Advancement of Science, and she said that the Advancement of Science was one thing and having a lot of tadpoles in a flat was another; he said that in Germany it was an ascertained fact that a man with an idea like his would at once have twenty thousand properly-fitted cubic feet of laboratory placed at his disposal, and she said she was glad and always had been glad that she was not a German; he said that it would make him famous for ever, and she said it was much more likely to make him ill to have a lot of tadpoles in a flat like theirs; he said he was master in his own house, and she said that rather than wait on a lot of tadpoles she'd go as matron to a school; and then he asked her to be reasonable, and she asked him to be reasonable then and give up all this about tadpoles; and he said she might respect his ideas, and she said not if they were smelly she wouldn't, and then he gave way completely and said—in spite of the classical remarks of Huxley upon the subject—a bad word. Not a very bad word it was, but bad enough.

And after that she was greatly offended and had to be apologised to, and the prospect of ever trying the Food of the Gods upon tadpoles in their flat at any rate vanished completely in the apology.

So Bensington had to consider some other way of carrying out these experiments in feeding that would be necessary to demonstrate his discovery, so soon as he had his substance isolated and prepared. For some days he meditated upon the possibility of boarding out his tadpoles with some trustworthy person, and then the chance sight of the phrase in a newspaper turned his thoughts to an Experimental Farm.

And chicks. Directly he thought of it, he thought of it as a poultry farm. He was suddenly taken with a vision of wildly growing chicks. He conceived a picture of coops and runs, outsize and still more outsize coops, and runs progressively larger. Chicks are so accessible, so easily fed and observed, so much drier to handle and measure, that for his purpose tadpoles seemed to him now, in comparison with them, quite wild and uncontrollable beasts. He was quite puzzled to understand why he had not thought of chicks instead of tadpoles from the beginning. Among other things it would have saved all this trouble with his cousin Jane. And when he suggested this to Redwood, Redwood quite agreed with him.

Redwood said that in working so much upon needlessly small animals he was convinced experimental physiologists made a great mistake. It is exactly like making experiments in chemistry with an insufficient quantity of material; errors of observation and manipulation become disproportionately large. It was of extreme importance just at present that scientific men should assert their right to have their material big. That was why he was doing his present series of experiments at the Bond Street College upon Bull Calves, in spite of a certain amount of inconvenience to the students and professors of other subjects caused by their incidental levity in the corridors. But the curves he was getting were quite exceptionally interesting, and would, when published, amply justify his choice. For his own part, were it not for the inadequate endowment of science in this country, he would never, if he could avoid it, work on anything smaller than a whale. But a Public Vivarium on a sufficient scale to render this possible was, he feared, at present, in this country at any rate, a Utopian demand. In Germany—Etc.

As Redwood's Bull calves needed his daily attention, the selection and equipment of the Experimental Farm fell largely on Bensington. The entire cost also, was, it was understood, to be defrayed by Bensington, at least until a grant could be obtained. Accordingly he alternated his work in the laboratory of his flat with farm hunting up and down the lines that run southward out of London, and his peering spectacles, his simple baldness, and his lacerated cloth shoes filled the owners of numerous undesirable properties with vain hopes. And he advertised in several daily papers and Nature for a responsible couple (married), punctual, active, and used to poultry, to take entire charge of an Experimental Farm of three acres.

He found the place he seemed in need of at Hickleybrow, near Urshot, in Kent. It was a little queer isolated place, in a dell surrounded by old pine woods that were black and forbidding at night. A humped shoulder of down cut it off from the sunset, and a gaunt well with a shattered penthouse dwarfed the dwelling. The little house was creeperless, several windows were broken, and the cart shed had a black shadow at midday. It was a mile and a half from the end house of the village, and its loneliness was very doubtfully relieved by an ambiguous family of echoes.

The place impressed Bensington as being eminently adapted to the requirements of scientific research. He walked over the premises sketching out coops and runs with a sweeping arm, and he found the kitchen capable of accommodating a series of incubators and foster mothers with the very minimum of alteration. He took the place there and then; on his way back to London he stopped at Dunton Green and closed with an eligible couple that had answered his advertisements, and that same evening he succeeded in isolating a sufficient quantity of Herakleophorbia I. to more than justify these engagements.

The eligible couple who were destined under Mr. Bensington to be the first almoners on earth of the Food of the Gods, were not only very perceptibly aged, but also extremely dirty. This latter point Mr. Bensington did not observe, because nothing destroys the powers of general observation quite so much as a life of experimental science. They were named Skinner, Mr. and Mrs. Skinner, and Mr. Bensington interviewed them in a small room with hermetically sealed windows, a spotted overmantel looking-glass, and some ailing calceolarias.

Mrs. Skinner was a very little old woman, capless, with dirty white hair drawn back very very tightly from a face that had begun by being chiefly, and was now, through the loss of teeth and chin, and the wrinkling up of everything else, ending by being almost exclusively—nose. She was dressed in slate colour (so far as her dress had any colour) slashed in one place with red flannel. She let him in and talked to him guardedly and peered at him round and over her nose, while Mr. Skinner she alleged made some alteration in his toilette. She had one tooth that got into her articulations and she held her two long wrinkled hands nervously together. She told Mr. Bensington that she had managed fowls for years; and knew all about incubators; in fact, they themselves had run a Poultry Farm at one time, and it had only failed at last through the want of pupils. "It's the pupils as pay," said Mrs. Skinner.

Mr. Skinner, when he appeared, was a large-faced man, with a lisp and a squint that made him look over the top of your head, slashed slippers that appealed to Mr. Bensington's sympathies, and a manifest shortness of buttons. He held his coat and shirt together with one hand and traced patterns on the black-and-gold tablecloth with the index finger of the other, while his disengaged eye watched Mr. Bensington's sword of Damocles, so to speak, with an expression of sad detachment. "You don't want to run thith Farm for profit. No, Thir. Ith all the thame, Thir. Ekthperimenth! Prethithely."

He said they could go to the farm at once. He was doing nothing at Dunton Green except a little tailoring. "It ithn't the thmart plathe I thought it wath, and what I get ithent thkarthely worth having," he said, "tho that if it ith any convenienth to you for uth to come...."

And in a week Mr. and Mrs. Skinner were installed in the farm, and the jobbing carpenter from Hickleybrow was diversifying the task of erecting runs and henhouses with a systematic discussion of Mr. Bensington.

"I haven't theen much of 'im yet," said Mr. Skinner. "But as far as I can make 'im out 'e theems to be a thtewpid o' fool."

"I thought 'e seemed a bit Dotty," said the carpenter from Hickleybrow.

"'E fanthieth 'imself about poultry," said Mr. Skinner. "O my goodneth! You'd think nobody knew nothin' about poultry thept 'im."

"'E looks like a 'en," said the carpenter from Hickleybrow; "what with them spectacles of 'is."

Mr. Skinner came closer to the carpenter from Hickleybrow, and spoke in a confidential manner, and one sad eye regarded the distant village, and one was bright and wicked. "Got to be meathured every blethed day—every blethed 'en, 'e thays. Tho as to thee they grow properly. What oh ... eh? Every blethed 'en—every blethed day."

And Mr. Skinner put up his hand to laugh behind it in a refined and contagious manner, and humped his shoulders very much—and only the other eye of him failed to participate in his laughter. Then doubting if the carpenter had quite got the point of it, he repeated in a penetrating whisper; "Meathured!"

"'E's worse than our old guvnor; I'm dratted if 'e ain't," said the carpenter from Hickleybrow.

II.

Experimental work is the most tedious thing in the world (unless it be the reports of it in the Philosophical Transactions), and it seemed a long time to Mr. Bensington before his first dream of enormous possibilities was replaced by a crumb of realisation. He had taken the Experimental Farm in October, and it was May before the first inklings of success began. Herakleophorbia I. and II. and III. had to be tried, and failed; there was trouble with the rats of the Experimental Farm, and there was trouble with the Skinners. The only way to get Skinner to do anything he was told to do was to dismiss him. Then he would nib his unshaven chin—he was always unshaven most miraculously and yet never bearded—with a flattened hand, and look at Mr. Bensington with one eye, and over him with the other, and say, "Oo, of courthe, Thir—if you're theriouth!"

But at last success dawned. And its herald was a letter in the long slender handwriting of Mr. Skinner.

"The new Brood are out," wrote Mr. Skinner, "and don't quite like the look of them. Growing very rank—quite unlike what the similar lot was before your last directions was given. The last, before the cat got them, was a very nice, stocky chick, but these are Growing like thistles. I never saw. They peck so hard, striking above boot top, that am unable to give exact Measures as requested. They are regular Giants, and eating as such. We shall want more com very soon, for you never saw such chicks to eat. Bigger than Bantams. Going on at this rate, they ought to be a bird for show, rank as they are. Plymouth Rocks won't be in it. Had a scare last night thinking that cat was at them, and when I looked out at the window could have sworn I see her getting in under the wire. The chicks was all awake and pecking about hungry when I went out, but could not see anything of the cat. So gave them a peck of corn, and fastened up safe. Shall be glad to know if the Feeding to be continued as directed. Food you mixed is pretty near all gone, and do not like to mix any more myself on account of the accident with the pudding. With best wishes from us both, and soliciting continuance of esteemed favours,

"Respectfully yours,

"ALFRED NEWTON SKINNER."

The allusion towards the end referred to a milk pudding with which some Herakleophorbia II. had got itself mixed with painful and very nearly fatal results to the Skinners.

But Mr. Bensington, reading between the lines saw in this rankness of growth the attainment of his long sought goal. The next morning he alighted at Urshot station, and in the bag in his hand he carried, sealed in three tins, a supply of the Food of the Gods sufficient for all the chicks in Kent.

It was a bright and beautiful morning late in May, and his corns were so much better that he resolved to walk through Hickleybrow to his farm. It was three miles and a half altogether, through the park and villages and then along the green glades of the Hickleybrow preserves. The trees were all dusted with the green spangles of high spring, the hedges were full of stitchwort and campion and the woods of blue hyacinths and purple orchid; and everywhere there was a great noise of birds—thrushes, blackbirds, robins, finches, and many more—and in one warm corner of the park some bracken was unrolling, and there was a leaping and rushing of fallow deer.

These things brought back to Mr. Bensington his early and forgotten delight in life; before him the promise of his discovery grew bright and joyful, and it seemed to him that indeed he must have come upon the happiest day in his life. And when in the sunlit run by the sandy bank under the shadow of the pine trees he saw the chicks that had eaten the food he had mixed for them, gigantic and gawky, bigger already than many a hen that is married and settled and still growing, still in their first soft yellow plumage (just faintly marked with brown along the back), he knew indeed that his happiest day had come.

At Mr. Skinner's urgency he went into the runs but after he had been pecked through the cracks in his shoes once or twice he got out again, and watched these monsters through the wire netting. He peered close to the netting, and followed their movements as though he had never seen a chick before in his life.

"Whath they'll be when they're grown up ith impothible to think," said Mr. Skinner.

"Big as a horse," said Mr. Bensington.

"Pretty near," said Mr. Skinner.

"Several people could dine off a wing!" said Mr. Bensington. "They'd cut up into joints like butcher's meat."

"They won't go on growing at thith pathe though," said Mr. Skinner.

"No?" said Mr. Bensington.

"No," said Mr. Skinner. "I know thith thort. They begin rank, but they don't go on, bleth you! No."

There was a pause.

"Itth management," said Mr. Skinner modestly.

Mr. Bensington turned his glasses on him suddenly.

"We got 'em almoth ath big at the other plathe," said Mr. Skinner, with his better eye piously uplifted and letting himself go a little; "me and the mithith."

Mr. Bensington made his usual general inspection of the premises, but he speedily returned to the new run. It was, you know, in truth ever so much more than he had dared to expect. The course of science is so tortuous and so slow; after the clear promises and before the practical realisation arrives there comes almost always year after year of intricate contrivance, and here—here was the Foods of the Gods arriving after less than a year of testing! It seemed too good—too good. That Hope Deferred which is the daily food of the scientific imagination was to be his no more! So at least it seemed to him then. He came back and stared at these stupendous chicks of his, time after time.

"Let me see," he said. "They're ten days old. And by the side of an ordinary chick I should fancy—about six or seven times as big...."

"Itth about time we artht for a rithe in thkrew," said Mr. Skinner to his wife. "He'th ath pleathed ath Punth about the way we got thothe chickth on in the further run—pleathed ath Punth he ith."

He bent confidentially towards her. "Thinkth it'th that old food of hith," he said behind his hands and made a noise of suppressed laughter in his pharyngeal cavity....

Mr. Bensington was indeed a happy man that day. He was in no mood to find fault with details of management. The bright day certainly brought out the accumulating slovenliness of the Skinner couple more vividly than he had ever seen it before. But his comments were of the gentlest. The fencing of many of the runs was out of order, but he seemed to consider it quite satisfactory when Mr. Skinner explained that it was a "fokth or a dog or thomething" did it. He pointed out that the incubator had not been cleaned.

"That it asn't, Sir," said Mrs. Skinner with her arms folded, smiling coyly behind her nose. "We don't seem to have had time to clean it not since we been 'ere...."

He went upstairs to see some rat-holes that Skinner said would justify a trap—they certainly were enormous—and discovered that the room in which the Food of the Gods was mixed with meal and bran was in a quite disgraceful order. The Skinners were the sort of people who find a use for cracked saucers and old cans and pickle jars and mustard boxes, and the place was littered with these. In one corner a great pile of apples that Skinner had saved was decaying, and from a nail in the sloping part of the ceiling hung several rabbit skins, upon which he proposed to test his gift as a furrier. ("There ithn't mutth about furth and thingth that I don't know," said Skinner.)

Mr. Bensington certainly sniffed critically at this disorder, but he made no unnecessary fuss, and even when he found a wasp regaling itself in a gallipot half full of Herakleophorbia IV, he simply remarked mildly that his substance was better sealed from the damp than exposed to the air in that manner.

And he turned from these things at once to remark—what had been for some time in his mind—"I think, Skinner—you know, I shall kill one of these chicks—as a specimen. I think we will kill it this afternoon, and I will take it back with me to London."

He pretended to peer into another gallipot and then took off his spectacles to wipe them.

"I should like," he said, "I should like very much, to have some relic—some memento—of this particular brood at this particular day."

"By-the-bye," he said, "you don't give those little chicks meat?"

"Oh! no, Thir," said Skinner, "I can athure you, Thir, we know far too much about the management of fowlth of all dethcriptionth to do anything of that thort."

"Quite sure you don't throw your dinner refuse—I thought I noticed the bones of a rabbit scattered about the far corner of the run—"

But when they came to look at them they found they were the larger bones of a cat picked very clean and dry.

III.

"That's no chick," said Mr. Bensington's cousin Jane.

"Well, I should think I knew a chick when I saw it," said Mr.Bensington's cousin Jane hotly.

"It's too big for a chick, for one thing, and besides you can see perfectly well it isn't a chick.

"It's more like a bustard than a chick."

"For my part," said Redwood, reluctantly allowing Bensington to drag him into the argument, "I must confess that, considering all the evidence—"

"Oh I if you do that," said Mr. Bensington's cousin Jane, "instead of using your eyes like a sensible person—"

"Well, but really, Miss Bensington—!"

"Oh! Go on!" said Cousin Jane. "You men are all alike."

"Considering all the evidence, this certainly falls within the definition—no doubt it's abnormal and hypertrophied, but still— especially since it was hatched from the egg of a normal hen—Yes, I think, Miss Bensington, I must admit—this, so far as one can call it anything, is a sort of chick."

"You mean it's a chick?" said cousin Jane.

"I think it's a chick," said Redwood.

"What NONSENSE!" said Mr. Bensington's cousin Jane, and "Oh!" directed at Redwood's head, "I haven't patience with you," and then suddenly she turned about and went out of the room with a slam.

"And it's a very great relief for me to see it too, Bensington," said Redwood, when the reverberation of the slam had died away. "In spite of its being so big."

Without any urgency from Mr. Bensington he sat down in the low arm-chair by the fire and confessed to proceedings that even in an unscientific man would have been indiscreet. "You will think it very rash of me, Bensington, I know," he said, "but the fact is I put a little— not very much of it—but some—into Baby's bottle, very nearly a week ago!"

"But suppose—!" cried Mr. Bensington.

"I know," said Redwood, and glanced at the giant chick upon the plate on the table.

"It's turned out all right, thank goodness," and he felt in his pocket for his cigarettes.

He gave fragmentary details. "Poor little chap wasn't putting on weight... desperately anxious.—Winkles, a frightful duffer ... former pupil of mine ... no good.... Mrs. Redwood—unmitigated confidence in Winkles.... You know, man with a manner like a cliff—towering.... No confidence in me, of course.... Taught Winkles.... Scarcely allowed in the nursery.... Something had to be done.... Slipped in while the nurse was at breakfast ... got at the bottle."

"But he'll grow," said Mr. Bensington.

"He's growing. Twenty-seven ounces last week.... You should hear Winkles. It's management, he said."

"Dear me! That's what Skinner says!"

Redwood looked at the chick again. "The bother is to keep it up," he said. "They won't trust me in the nursery alone, because I tried to get a growth curve out of Georgina Phyllis—you know—and how I'm to give him a second dose—"

"Need you?"

"He's been crying two days—can't get on with his ordinary food again, anyhow. He wants some more now."

"Tell Winkles."

"Hang Winkles!" said Redwood.

"You might get at Winkles and give him powders to give the child—"

"That's about what I shall have to do," said Redwood, resting his chin on his fist and staring into the fire.

Bensington stood for a space smoothing the down on the breast of the giant chick. "They will be monstrous fowls," he said.

"They will," said Redwood, still with his eyes on the glow.

"Big as horses," said Bensington.

"Bigger," said Redwood. "That's just it!"

Bensington turned away from the specimen. "Redwood," he said, "these fowls are going to create a sensation."

Redwood nodded his head at the fire.

"And by Jove!" said Bensington, coming round suddenly with a flash in his spectacles, "so will your little boy!"

"That's just what I'm thinking of," said Redwood.

He sat back, sighed, threw his unconsumed cigarette into the fire and thrust his hands deep into his trousers pockets. "That's precisely what I'm thinking of. This Herakleophorbia is going to be queer stuff to handle. The pace that chick must have grown at—!"

"A little boy growing at that pace," said Mr. Bensington slowly, and stared at the chick as he spoke.

"I Say!" said Bensington, "he'll be Big."

"I shall give him diminishing doses," said Redwood. "Or at any rate Winkles will."

"It's rather too much of an experiment."

"Much."

"Yet still, you know, I must confess—... Some baby will sooner or later have to try it."

"Oh, we'll try it on some baby—certainly."

"Exactly so," said Bensington, and came and stood on the hearthrug and took off his spectacles to wipe them.

"Until I saw these chicks, Redwood, I don't think I began to realise—anything—of the possibilities of what we were making. It's only beginning to dawn upon me ... the possible consequences...."

And even then, you know, Mr. Bensington was far from any conception of the mine that little train would fire.

IV.

That happened early in June. For some weeks Bensington was kept from revisiting the Experimental Farm by a severe imaginary catarrh, and one necessary flying visit was made by Redwood. He returned an even more anxious-looking parent than he had gone. Altogether there were seven weeks of steady, uninterrupted growth....

And then the Wasps began their career.

It was late in July and nearly a week before the hens escaped from Hickleybrow that the first of the big wasps was killed. The report of it appeared in several papers, but I do not know whether the news reached Mr. Bensington, much less whether he connected it with the general laxity of method that prevailed in the Experimental Farm.

There can be but little doubt now, that while Mr. Skinner was plying Mr. Bensington's chicks with Herakleophorbia IV, a number of wasps were just as industriously—perhaps more industriously— carrying quantities of the same paste to their early summer broods in the sand-banks beyond the adjacent pine-woods. And there can be no dispute whatever that these early broods found just as much growth and benefit in the substance as Mr. Bensington's hens. It is in the nature of the wasp to attain to effective maturity before the domestic fowl—and in fact of all the creatures that were—through the generous carelessness of the Skinners—partaking of the benefits Mr. Bensington heaped upon his hens, the wasps were the first to make any sort of figure in the world.

It was a keeper named Godfrey, on the estate of Lieutenant-Colonel Rupert Hick, near Maidstone, who encountered and had the luck to kill the first of these monsters of whom history has any record. He was walking knee high in bracken across an open space in the beechwoods that diversify Lieutenant-Colonel Hick's park, and he was carrying his gun—very fortunately for him a double-barrelled gun—over his shoulder, when he first caught sight of the thing. It was, he says, coming down against the light, so that he could not see it very distinctly, and as it came it made a drone "like a motor car." He admits he was frightened. It was evidently as big or bigger than a barn owl, and, to his practised eye, its flight and particularly the misty whirl of its wings must have seemed weirdly unbirdlike. The instinct of self-defence, I fancy, mingled with long habit, when, as he says, he "let fly, right away."

The queerness of the experience probably affected his aim; at any rate most of his shot missed, and the thing merely dropped for a moment with an angry "Wuzzzz" that revealed the wasp at once, and then rose again, with all its stripes shining against the light. He says it turned on him. At any rate, he fired his second barrel at less than twenty yards and threw down his gun, ran a pace or so, and ducked to avoid it.

It flew, he is convinced, within a yard of him, struck the ground, rose again, came down again perhaps thirty yards away, and rolled over with its body wriggling and its sting stabbing out and back in its last agony. He emptied both barrels into it again before he ventured to go near.

When he came to measure the thing, he found it was twenty-seven and a half inches across its open wings, and its sting was three inches long. The abdomen was blown clean off from its body, but he estimated the length of the creature from head to sting as eighteen inches—which is very nearly correct. Its compound eyes were the size of penny pieces.

That is the first authenticated appearance of these giant wasps. The day after, a cyclist riding, feet up, down the hill between Sevenoaks and Tonbridge, very narrowly missed running over a second of these giants that was crawling across the roadway. His passage seemed to alarm it, and it rose with a noise like a sawmill. His bicycle jumped the footpath in the emotion of the moment, and when he could look back, the wasp was soaring away above the woods towards Westerham.

After riding unsteadily for a little time, he put on his brake, dismounted—he was trembling so violently that he fell over his machine in doing so—and sat down by the roadside to recover. He had intended to ride to Ashford, but he did not get beyond Tonbridge that day....

After that, curiously enough, there is no record of any big wasps being seen for three days. I find on consulting the meteorological record of those days that they were overcast and chilly with local showers, which may perhaps account for this intermission. Then on the fourth day came blue sky and brilliant sunshine and such an outburst of wasps as the world had surely never seen before.

How many big wasps came out that day it is impossible to guess. There are at least fifty accounts of their apparition. There was one victim, a grocer, who discovered one of these monsters in a sugar-cask and very rashly attacked it with a spade as it rose. He struck it to the ground for a moment, and it stung him through the boot as he struck at it again and cut its body in half. He was first dead of the two....

The most dramatic of the fifty appearances was certainly that of the wasp that visited the British Museum about midday, dropping out of the blue serene upon one of the innumerable pigeons that feed in the courtyard of that building, and flying up to the cornice to devour its victim at leisure. After that it crawled for a time over the museum roof, entered the dome of the reading-room by a skylight, buzzed about inside it for some little time—there was a stampede among the readers—and at last found another window and vanished again with a sudden silence from human observation.

Most of the other reports were of mere passings or descents. A picnic party was dispersed at Aldington Knoll and all its sweets and jam consumed, and a puppy was killed and torn to pieces near Whitstable under the very eyes of its mistress....

The streets that evening resounded with the cry, the newspaper placards gave themselves up exclusively in the biggest of letters to the "Gigantic Wasps in Kent." Agitated editors and assistant editors ran up and down tortuous staircases bawling things about "wasps." And Professor Redwood, emerging from his college in Bond Street at five, flushed from a heated discussion with his committee about the price of bull calves, bought an evening paper, opened it, changed colour, forgot about bull calves and committee forthwith, and took a hansom headlong for Bensington's flat.

V.

The flat was occupied, it seemed to him—to the exclusion of all other sensible objects—by Mr. Skinner and his voice, if indeed you can call either him or it a sensible object!

The voice was up very high slopping about among the notes of anguish. "Itth impothible for uth to thtop, Thir. We've thtopped on hoping thingth would get better and they've only got worth, Thir. It ithn't on'y the waptheth, Thir—thereth big earwigth, Thir—big ath that, Thir." (He indicated all his hand and about three inches of fat dirty wrist.) "They pretty near give Mithith Thkinner fitth, Thir. And the thtinging nettleth by the runth, Thir, they're growing, Thir, and the canary creeper, Thir, what we thowed near the think, Thir—it put itth tendril through the window in the night, Thir, and very nearly caught Mithith Thkinner by the legth, Thir. Itth that food of yourth, Thir. Wherever we thplathed it about, Thir, a bit, it'th thet everything growing ranker, Thir, than I ever thought anything could grow. Itth impothible to thtop a month, Thir. Itth more than our liveth are worth, Thir. Even if the waptheth don't thting uth, we thall be thuffocated by the creeper, Thir. You can't imagine, Thir—unleth you come down to thee, Thir—"

He turned his superior eye to the cornice above Redwood's head. "'Ow do we know the ratth 'aven't got it, Thir! That 'th what I think of motht, Thir. I 'aven't theen any big ratth, Thir, but 'ow do I know, Thir. We been frightened for dayth becauth of the earwigth we've theen—like lobthters they wath—two of 'em, Thir—and the frightful way the canary creeper wath growing, and directly I heard the waptheth—directly I 'eard 'em, Thir, I underthood. I didn't wait for nothing exthept to thow on a button I'd lortht, and then I came on up. Even now, Thir, I'm arf wild with angthiety, Thir. 'Ow do I know watth happenin' to Mithith Thkinner, Thir! Thereth the creeper growing all over the plathe like a thnake, Thir—thwelp me but you 'ave to watch it, Thir, and jump out of itth way!—and the earwigth gettin' bigger and bigger, and the waptheth—. She 'athen't even got a Blue Bag, Thir—if anything thould happen, Thir!"

"But the hens," said Mr. Bensington; "how are the hens?"

"We fed 'em up to yethterday, thwelp me," said Mr. Skinner, "But thith morning we didn't dare, Thir. The noithe of the waptheth wath—thomething awful, Thir. They wath coming ont—dothenth. Ath big ath 'enth. I thayth, to 'er, I thayth you juth thow me on a button or two, I thayth, for I can't go to London like thith, I thayth, and I'll go up to Mithter Benthington, I thayth, and ekthplain thingth to 'im. And you thtop in thith room till I come back to you, I thayth, and keep the windowth thhut juth ath tight ath ever you can, I thayth."

"If you hadn't been so confoundedly untidy—" began Redwood.

"Oh! don't thay that, Thir," said Skinner. "Not now, Thir. Not with me tho diththrethed, Thir, about Mithith Thkinner, Thir! Oh, don't, Thir! I 'aven't the 'eart to argue with you. Thwelp me, Thir, I 'aven't! Itth the ratth I keep a thinking of—'Ow do I know they 'aven't got at Mithith Thkinner while I been up 'ere?"

"And you haven't got a solitary measurement of all these beautiful growth curves!" said Redwood.

"I been too upthet, Thir," said Mr. Skinner. "If you knew what we been through—me and the mithith! All thith latht month. We 'aven't known what to make of it, Thir. What with the henth gettin' tho rank, and the earwigth, and the canary creeper. I dunno if I told you, Thir—the canary creeper ..."

"You've told us all that," said Redwood. "The thing is, Bensington, what are we to do?"

"What are we to do?" said Mr. Skinner.

"You'll have to go back to Mrs. Skinner," said Redwood. "You can't leave her there alone all night."

"Not alone, Thir, I don't. Not if there wath a dothen MithithThkinnerth. Itth Mithter Benthington—"

"Nonsense," said Redwood. "The wasps will be all right at night. And the earwigs will get out of your way—"

"But about the ratth?"

"There aren't any rats," said Redwood.

VI.

Mr. Skinner might have foregone his chief anxiety. Mrs. Skinner did not stop out her day.

About eleven the canary creeper, which had been quietly active all the morning, began to clamber over the window and darken it very greatly, and the darker it got the more and more clearly Mrs. Skinner perceived that her position would speedily become untenable. And also that she had lived many ages since Skinner went. She peered out of the darkling window, through the stirring tendrils, for some time, and then went very cautiously and opened the bedroom door and listened....

Everything seemed quiet, and so, tucking her skirts high about her, Mrs. Skinner made a bolt for the bedroom, and having first looked under the bed and locked herself in, proceeded with the methodical rapidity of an experienced woman to pack for departure. The bed had not been made, and the room was littered with pieces of the creeper that Skinner had hacked off in order to close the window overnight, but these disorders she did not heed. She packed in a decent sheet. She packed all her own wardrobe and a velveteen jacket that Skinner wore in his finer moments, and she packed a jar of pickles that had not been opened, and so far she was justified in her packing. But she also packed two of the hermetically closed tins containing Herakleophorbia IV. that Mr. Bensington had brought on his last visit. (She was honest, good woman—but she was a grandmother, and her heart had burned within her to see such good growth lavished on a lot of dratted chicks.)

And having packed all these things, she put on her bonnet, took off her apron, tied a new boot-lace round her umbrella, and after listening for a long time at door and window, opened the door and sallied out into a perilous world. The umbrella was under her arm and she clutched the bundle with two gnarled and resolute hands. It was her best Sunday bonnet, and the two poppies that reared their heads amidst its splendours of band and bead seemed instinct with the same tremulous courage that possessed her.

The features about the roots of her nose wrinkled with determination. She had had enough of it! All alone there! Skinner might come back there if he liked.

She went out by the front door, going that way not because she wanted to go to Hickleybrow (her goal was Cheasing Eyebright, where her married daughter resided), but because the back door was impassable on account of the canary creeper that had been growing so furiously ever since she upset the can of food near its roots. She listened for a space and closed the front door very carefully behind her.

At the corner of the house she paused and reconnoitred....

An extensive sandy scar upon the hillside beyond the pine-woods marked the nest of the giant Wasps, and this she studied very earnestly. The coming and going of the morning was over, not a wasp chanced to be in sight then, and except for a sound scarcely more perceptible than a steam wood-saw at work amidst the pines would have been, everything was still. As for earwigs, she could see not one. Down among the cabbage indeed something was stirring, but it might just as probably be a cat stalking birds. She watched this for a time.

She went a few paces past the corner, came in sight of the run containing the giant chicks and stopped again. "Ah!" she said, and shook her head slowly at the sight of them. They were at that time about the height of emus, but of course much thicker in the body—a larger thing altogether. They were all hens and five all told, now that the two cockerels had killed each other. She hesitated at their drooping attitudes. "Poor dears!" she said, and put down her bundle; "they've got no water. And they've 'ad no food these twenty-four hours! And such appetites, too, as they 'ave!" She put a lean finger to her lips and communed with herself.

Then this dirty old woman did what seems to me a quite heroic deed of mercy. She left her bundle and umbrella in the middle of the brick path and went to the well and drew no fewer than three pailfuls of water for the chickens' empty trough, and then while they were all crowding about that, she undid the door of the run very softly. After which she became extremely active, resumed her package, got over the hedge at the bottom of the garden, crossed the rank meadows (in order to avoid the wasps' nest) and toiled up the winding path towards Cheasing Eyebright.

She panted up the hill, and as she went she paused ever and again, to rest her bundle and get her breath and stare back at the little cottage beside the pine-wood below. And when at last, when she was near the crest of the hill, she saw afar off three several wasps dropping heavily westward, it helped her greatly on her way.

She soon got out of the open and in the high banked lane beyond (which seemed a safer place to her), and so up by Hickleybrow Coombe to the downs. There at the foot of the downs where a big tree gave an air of shelter she rested for a space on a stile.

Then on again very resolutely....

You figure her, I hope, with her white bundle, a sort of erect black ant, hurrying along the little white path-thread athwart the downland slopes under the hot sun of the summer afternoon. On she struggled after her resolute indefatigable nose, and the poppies in her bonnet quivered perpetually and her spring-side boots grew whiter and whiter with the downland dust. Flip-flap, flip-flap went her footfalls through the still heat of the day, and persistently, incurably, her umbrella sought to slip from under the elbow that retained it. The mouth wrinkle under her nose was pursed to an extreme resolution, and ever and again she told her umbrella to come up or gave her tightly clutched bundle a vindictive jerk. And at times her lips mumbled with fragments of some foreseen argument between herself and Skinner.

And far away, miles and miles away, a steeple and a hanger grew insensibly out of the vague blue to mark more and more distinctly the quiet corner where Cheasing Eyebright sheltered from the tumult of the world, recking little or nothing of the Herakleophorbia concealed in that white bundle that struggled so persistently towards its orderly retirement.

VII.

So far as I can gather, the pullets came into Hickleybrow about three o'clock in the afternoon. Their coming must have been a brisk affair, though nobody was out in the street to see it. The violent bellowing of little Skelmersdale seems to have been the first announcement of anything out of the way. Miss Durgan of the Post Office was at the window as usual, and saw the hen that had caught the unhappy child, in violent flight up the street with its victim, closely pursued by two others. You know that swinging stride of the emancipated athletic latter-day pullet! You know the keen insistence of the hungry hen! There was Plymouth Rock in these birds, I am told, and even without Herakleophorbia that is a gaunt and striding strain.

Probably Miss Durgan was not altogether taken by surprise. In spite of Mr. Bensington's insistence upon secrecy, rumours of the great chicken Mr. Skinner was producing had been about the village for some weeks. "Lor!" she cried, "it's what I expected."

She seems to have behaved with great presence of mind. She snatched up the sealed bag of letters that was waiting to go on to Urshot, and rushed out of the door at once. Almost simultaneously Mr. Skelmersdale himself appeared down the village, gripping a watering-pot by the spout, and very white in the face. And, of course, in a moment or so every one in the village was rushing to the door or window.

The spectacle of Miss Durgan all across the road, with the entire day's correspondence of Hickleybrow in her hand, gave pause to the pullet in possession of Master Skelmersdale. She halted through one instant's indecision and then turned for the open gates of Fulcher's yard. That instant was fatal. The second pullet ran in neatly, got possession of the child by a well-directed peck, and went over the wall into the vicarage garden.

"Charawk, chawk, chawk, chawk, chawk, chawk!" shrieked the hindmost hen, hit smartly by the watering-can Mr. Skelmersdale had thrown, and fluttered wildly over Mrs. Glue's cottage and so into the doctor's field, while the rest of those Gargantuan birds pursued the pullet, in possession of the child across the vicarage lawn.

"Good heavens!" cried the Curate, or (as some say) something much more manly, and ran, whirling his croquet mallet and shouting, to head off the chase.

"Stop, you wretch!" cried the curate, as though giant hens were the commonest facts in life.

And then, finding he could not possibly intercept her, he hurled his mallet with all his might and main, and out it shot in a gracious curve within a foot or so of Master Skelmersdale's head and through the glass lantern of the conservatory. Smash! The new conservatory! The Vicar's wife's beautiful new conservatory!

It frightened the hen. It might have frightened any one. She dropped her victim into a Portugal laurel (from which he was presently extracted, disordered but, save for his less delicate garments, uninjured), made a flapping leap for the roof of Fulcher's stables, put her foot through a weak place in the tiles, and descended, so to speak, out of the infinite into the contemplative quiet of Mr. Bumps the paralytic—who, it is now proved beyond all cavil, did, on this one occasion in his life, get down the entire length of his garden and indoors without any assistance whatever, bolt the door after him, and immediately relapse again into Christian resignation and helpless dependence upon his wife....

The rest of the pullets were headed off by the other croquet players, and went through the vicar's kitchen garden into the doctor's field, to which rendezvous the fifth also came at last, clucking disconsolately after an unsuccessful attempt to walk on the cucumber frames in Mr. Witherspoon's place.

They seem to have stood about in a hen-like manner for a time, and scratched a little and chirrawked meditatively, and then one pecked at and pecked over a hive of the doctor's bees, and after that they set off in a gawky, jerky, feathery, fitful sort of way across the fields towards Urshot, and Hickleybrow Street saw them no more. Near Urshot they really came upon commensurate food in a field of swedes; and pecked for a space with gusto, until their fame overtook them.

The chief immediate reaction of this astonishing irruption of gigantic poultry upon the human mind was to arouse an extraordinary passion to whoop and run and throw things, and in quite a little time almost all the available manhood of Hickleybrows and several ladies, were out with a remarkable assortment of flappish and whangable articles in hand—to commence the scooting of the giant hens. They drove them into Urshot, where there was a Rural Fete, and Urshot took them as the crowning glory of a happy day. They began to be shot at near Findon Beeches, but at first only with a rook rifle. Of course birds of that size could absorb an unlimited quantity of small shot without inconvenience. They scattered somewhere near Sevenoaks, and near Tonbridge one of them fled clucking for a time in excessive agitation, somewhat ahead of and parallel with the afternoon boat express—to the great astonishment of every one therein.

And about half-past five two of them were caught very cleverly by a circus proprietor at Tunbridge Wells, who lured them into a cage, rendered vacant through the death of a widowed dromedary, by scattering cakes and bread....

VIII.

When the unfortunate Skinner got out of the South-Eastern train at Urshot that evening it was already nearly dusk. The train was late, but not inordinately late—and Mr. Skinner remarked as much to the station-master. Perhaps he saw a certain pregnancy in the station-master's eye. After the briefest hesitation and with a confidential movement of his hand to the side of his mouth he asked if "anything" had happened that day.

"How d'yer mean?" said the station-master, a man with a hard, emphatic voice.

"Thethe 'ere waptheth and thingth."

"We 'aven't 'ad much time to think of waptheth," said the station-master agreeably. "We've been too busy with your brasted 'ens," and he broke the news of the pullets to Mr. Skinner as one might break the window of an adverse politician.

"You ain't 'eard anything of Mithith Thkinner?" asked Skinner, amidst that missile shower of pithy information and comment.

"No fear!" said the station-master—as though even he drew the line somewhere in the matter of knowledge.

"I mutht make inquireth bout thith," said Mr. Skinner, edging out of reach of the station-master's concluding generalisations about the responsibility attaching to the excessive nurture of hens....

Going through Urshot Mr. Skinner was hailed by a lime-burner from the pits over by Hankey and asked if he was looking for his hens.

"You ain't 'eard anything of Mithith Thkinner?" he asked.

The lime-burner—his exact phrases need not concern us—expressed his superior interest in hens....

It was already dark—as dark at least as a clear night in the English June can be—when Skinner—or his head at any rate—came into the bar of the Jolly Drovers and said: "Ello! You 'aven't 'eard anything of thith 'ere thtory bout my 'enth, 'ave you?"

"Oh, 'aven't we!" said Mr. Fulcher. "Why, part of the story's been and bust into my stable roof and one chapter smashed a 'ole in Missis Vicar's green 'ouse—I beg 'er pardon—Conservarratory."

Skinner came in. "I'd like thomething a little comforting," he said, "'ot gin and water'th about my figure," and everybody began to tell him things about the pullets.

"Grathuth me!" said Skinner.

"You 'aven't 'eard anything about Mithith Thkinner, 'ave you?" he asked in a pause.

"That we 'aven't!" said Mr. Witherspoon. "We 'aven't thought of 'er. We ain't thought nothing of either of you."

"Ain't you been 'ome to-day?" asked Fulcher over a tankard.

"If one of those brasted birds 'ave pecked 'er," began Mr. Witherspoons and left the full horror to their unaided imaginations....

It appeared to the meeting at the time that it would be an interesting end to an eventful day to go on with Skinner and see if anything had happened to Mrs. Skinner. One never knows what luck one may have when accidents are at large. But Skinner, standing at the bar and drinking his hot gin and water, with one eye roving over the things at the back of the bar and the other fixed on the Absolute, missed the psychological moment.

"I thuppothe there 'athen't been any trouble with any of thethe big waptheth to-day anywhere?" he asked, with an elaborate detachment of manner.

"Been too busy with your 'ens," said Fulcher.

"I thuppothe they've all gone in now anyhow," said Skinner.

"What—the 'ens?"

"I wath thinking of the waptheth more particularly," said Skinner.

And then, with, an air of circumspection that would have awakened suspicion in a week-old baby, and laying the accent heavily on most of the words he chose, he asked, "I thuppothe nobody 'athn't 'eard of any other big thingth, about, 'ave they? Big dogth or catth or anything of that thort? Theemth to me if thereth big henth and big waptheth comin' on—"

He laughed with a fine pretence of talking idly.

But a brooding expression came upon the faces of the Hickleybrow men. Fulcher was the first to give their condensing thought the concrete shape of words.

"A cat to match them 'ens—" said Fulcher.

"Ay!" said Witherspoon, "a cat to match they 'ens."

"'Twould be a tiger," said Fulcher.

"More'n a tiger," said Witherspoon....

When at last Skinner followed the lonely footpath over the swelling field that separated Hickleybrow from the sombre pine-shaded hollow in whose black shadows the gigantic canary-creeper grappled silently with the Experimental Farm, he followed it alone.

He was distinctly seen to rise against the sky-line, against the warm clear immensity of the northern sky—for so far public interest followed him—and to descend again into the night, into an obscurity from which it would seem he will nevermore emerge. He passed—into a mystery. No one knows to this day what happened to him after he crossed the brow. When later on the two Fulchers and Witherspoon, moved by their own imaginations, came up the hill and stared after him, the flight had swallowed him up altogether.

The three men stood close. There was not a sound out of the wooded blackness that hid the Farm from their eyes.

"It's all right," said young Fulcher, ending a silence.

"Don't see any lights," said Witherspoon.

"You wouldn't from here."

"It's misty," said the elder Fulcher.

They meditated for a space.

"'E'd 'ave come back if anything was wrong," said young Fulcher, and this seemed so obvious and conclusive that presently old Fulcher said, "Well," and the three went home to bed—thoughtfully I will admit....

A shepherd out by Huckster's Farm heard a squealing in the night that he thought was foxes, and in the morning one of his lambs had been killed, dragged halfway towards Hickleybrow and partially devoured....

The inexplicable part of it all is the absence of any indisputable remains of Skinner!

Many weeks after, amidst the charred ruins of the Experimental Farm, there was found something which may or may not have been a human shoulder-blade and in another part of the ruins a long bone greatly gnawed and equally doubtful. Near the stile going up towards Eyebright there was found a glass eye, and many people discovered thereupon that Skinner owed much of his personal charm to such a possession. It stared out upon the world with that same inevitable effect of detachment, that same severe melancholy that had been the redemption of his else worldly countenance.

And about the ruins industrious research discovered the metal rings and charred coverings of two linen buttons, three shanked buttons entire, and one of that metallic sort which is used in the less conspicuous sutures of the human Oeconomy. These remains have been accepted by persons in authority as conclusive of a destroyed and scattered Skinner, but for my own entire conviction, and in view of his distinctive idiosyncrasy, I must confess I should prefer fewer buttons and more bones.

The glass eye of course has an air of extreme conviction, but if it really is Skinner's—and even Mrs. Skinner did not certainly know if that immobile eye of his was glass—something has changed it from a liquid brown to a serene and confident blue. That shoulder-blade is an extremely doubtful document, and I would like to put it side by side with the gnawed scapulae of a few of the commoner domestic animals before I admitted its humanity.

And where were Skinner's boots, for example? Perverted and strange as a rat's appetite must be, is it conceivable that the same creatures that could leave a lamb only half eaten, would finish up Skinner—hair, bones, teeth, and boots?

I have closely questioned as many as I could of those who knew Skinner at all intimately, and they one and all agree that they cannot imagine anything eating him. He was the sort of man, as a retired seafaring person living in one of Mr. W.W. Jacobs' cottages at Dunton Green told me, with a guarded significance of manner not uncommon in those parts, who would "get washed up anyhow," and as regards the devouring element was "fit to put a fire out." He considered that Skinner would be as safe on a raft as anywhere. The retired seafaring man added that he wished to say nothing whatever against Skinner; facts were facts. And rather than have his clothes made by Skinner, the retired seafaring man remarked he would take his chance of being locked up. These observations certainly do not present Skinner in the light of an appetising object.

To be perfectly frank with the reader, I do not believe he ever went back to the Experimental Farm. I believe he hovered through long hesitations about the fields of the Hickleybrow glebe, and finally, when that squealing began, took the line of least resistance out of his perplexities into the Incognito.

And in the Incognito, whether of this or of some other world unknown to us, he obstinately and quite indisputably has remained to this day....

CHAPTER THE THIRD.
THE GIANT RATS.

I.

It was two nights after the disappearance of Mr. Skinner that the Podbourne doctor was out late near Hankey, driving in his buggy. He had been up all night assisting another undistinguished citizen into this curious world of ours, and his task accomplished, he was driving homeward in a drowsy mood enough. It was about two o'clock in the morning, and the waning moon was rising. The summer night had gone cold, and there was a low-lying whitish mist that made things indistinct. He was quite alone — for his coachman was ill in bed — and there was nothing to be seen on either hand but a drifting mystery of hedge running athwart the yellow glare of his lamps, and nothing to hear but the clitter-clatter of his horses and the gride and hedge echo of his wheels. His horse was as trustworthy as himself, and one does not wonder that he dozed....

You know that intermittent drowsing as one sits, the drooping of the head, the nodding to the rhythm of the wheels then chin upon the breast, and at once the sudden start up again.

Pitter, litter, patter.

"What was that?"

It seemed to the doctor he had heard a thin shrill squeal close at hand. For a moment he was quite awake. He said a word or two of undeserved rebuke to his horse, and looked about him. He tried to persuade himself that he had heard the distant squeal of a fox — or perhaps a young rabbit gripped by a ferret.

Swish, swish, swish, pitter, patter, swish — ...

What was that?

He felt he was getting fanciful. He shook his shoulders and told his horse to get on. He listened, and heard nothing.

Or was it nothing?

He had the queerest impression that something had just peeped over the hedge at him, a queer big head. With round ears! He peered hard, but he could see nothing.

"Nonsense," said he.

He sat up with an idea that he had dropped into a nightmare, gave his horse the slightest touch of the whip, spoke to it and peered again over the hedge. The glare of his lamp, however, together with the mist, rendered things indistinct, and he could distinguish nothing. It came into his head, he says, that there could be nothing there, because if there was his horse would have shied at it. Yet for all that his senses remained nervously awake.

Then he heard quite distinctly a soft pattering of feet in pursuit along the road.

He would not believe his ears about that. He could not look round, for the road had a sinuous curve just there. He whipped up his horse and glanced sideways again. And then he saw quite distinctly where a ray from his lamp leapt a low stretch of hedge, the curved back of—some big animal, he couldn't tell what, going along in quick convulsive leaps.

He says he thought of the old tales of witchcraft—the thing was so utterly unlike any animal he knew, and he tightened his hold on the reins for fear of the fear of his horse. Educated man as he was, he admits he asked himself if this could be something that his horse could not see.

Ahead, and drawing near in silhouette against the rising moon, was the outline of the little hamlet of Hankey, comforting, though it showed never a light, and he cracked his whip and spoke again, and then in a flash the rats were at him!

He had passed a gate, and as he did so, the foremost rat came leaping over into the road. The thing sprang upon him out of vagueness into the utmost clearness, the sharp, eager, round-eared face, the long body exaggerated by its movement; and what particularly struck him, the pink, webbed forefeet of the beast. What must have made it more horrible to him at the time was, that he had no idea the thing was any created beast he knew. He did not recognise it as a rat, because of the size. His horse gave a bound as the thing dropped into the road beside it. The little lane woke into tumult at the report of the whip and the doctor's shout. The whole thing suddenly went fast.

Rattle-clatter, clash, clatter.

The doctor, one gathers, stood up, shouted to his horse, and slashed with all his strength. The rat winced and swerved most reassuringly at his blow — in the glare of his lamp he could see the fur furrow under the lash — and he slashed again and again, heedless and unaware of the second pursuer that gained upon his off side.

He let the reins go, and glanced back to discover the third rat in pursuit behind....

His horse bounded forward. The buggy leapt high at a rut. For a frantic minute perhaps everything seemed to be going in leaps and bounds....

It was sheer good luck the horse came down in Hankey, and not either before or after the houses had been passed.

No one knows how the horse came down, whether it stumbled or whether the rat on the off side really got home with one of those slashing down strokes of the teeth (given with the full weight of the body); and the doctor never discovered that he himself was bitten until he was inside the brickmaker's house, much less did he discover when the bite occurred, though bitten he was and badly — a long slash like the slash of a double tomahawk that had cut two parallel ribbons of flesh from his left shoulder.

He was standing up in his buggy at one moment, and in the next he had leapt to the ground, with his ankle, though he did not know it, badly sprained, and he was cutting furiously at a third rat that was flying directly at him. He scarcely remembers the leap he must have made over the top of the wheel as the buggy came over, so obliteratingly hot and swift did his impressions rush upon him. I think myself the horse reared up with the rat biting again at its throat, and fell sideways, and carried the whole affair over; and that the doctor sprang, as it were, instinctively. As the buggy came down, the receiver of the lamp smashed, and suddenly poured a flare of blazing oil, a thud of white flame, into the struggle.

That was the first thing the brickmaker saw.

He had heard the clatter of the doctor's approach and — though the doctor's memory has nothing of this — wild shouting. He had got out of bed hastily, and as he did so came the terrific smash, and up shot the glare outside the rising blind. "It was brighter than day," he says. He stood, blind cord in hand, and stared out of the window at a nightmare transformation of the familiar road before him. The black figure of the doctor with its whirling whip danced out against the flame. The horse kicked indistinctly, half hidden by the blaze, with a rat at its throat. In the obscurity against the churchyard wall, the eyes of a second monster shone wickedly. Another—a mere dreadful blackness with red-lit eyes and flesh-coloured hands—clutched unsteadily on the wall coping to which it had leapt at the flash of the exploding lamp.

You know the keen face of a rat, those two sharp teeth, those pitiless eyes. Seen magnified to near six times its linear dimensions, and still more magnified by darkness and amazement and the leaping fancies of a fitful blaze, it must have been an ill sight for the brickmaker—still more than half asleep.

Then the doctor had grasped the opportunity, that momentary respite the flare afforded, and was out of the brickmaker's sight below battering the door with the butt of his whip....

The brickmaker would not let him in until he had got a light.

There are those who have blamed the man for that, but until I know my own courage better, I hesitate to join their number.

The doctor yelled and hammered....

The brickmaker says he was weeping with terror when at last the door was opened.

"Bolt," said the doctor, "bolt"—he could not say "bolt the door." He tried to help, and was of no service. The brickmaker fastened the door, and the doctor had to sit on the chair beside the clock for a space before he could go upstairs....

"I don't know what they are!" he repeated several times. "I don't know what they are"—with a high note on the "are."

The brickmaker would have got him whisky, but the doctor would not be left alone with nothing but a flickering light just then.

It was long before the brickmaker could get him to go upstairs....

And when the fire was out the giant rats came back, took the dead horse, dragged it across the churchyard into the brickfield and ate at it until it was dawn, none even then daring to disturb them....

II.

Redwood went round, to Bensington about eleven the next morning with the "second editions" of three evening papers in his hand.

Bensington looked up from a despondent meditation over the forgotten pages of the most distracting novel the Brompton Road librarian had been able to find him. "Anything fresh?" he asked.

"Two men stung near Chartham."

"They ought to let us smoke out that nest. They really did. It's their own fault."

"It's their own fault, certainly," said Redwood.

"Have you heard anything—about buying the farm?"

"The House Agent," said Redwood, "is a thing with a big mouth and made of dense wood. It pretends someone else is after the house— it always does, you know—and won't understand there's a hurry. 'This is a matter of life and death,' I said, 'don't you understand?' It drooped its eyes half shut and said, 'Then why don't you go the other two hundred pounds?' I'd rather live in a world of solid wasps than give in to the stonewalling stupidity of that offensive creature. I—"

He paused, feeling that a sentence like that might very easily be spoiled by its context.

"It's too much to hope," said Bensington, "that one of the wasps—"

"The wasp has no more idea of public utility than a—than a HouseAgent," said Redwood.

He talked for a little while about house agents and solicitors and people of that sort, in the unjust, unreasonable way that so many people do somehow get to talk of these business calculi ("Of all the cranky things in this cranky world, it is the most cranky to my mind of all, that while we expect honour, courage, efficiency, from a doctor or a soldier as a matter of course, a solicitor or a house agent is not only permitted but expected to display nothing but a sort of greedy, greasy, obstructive, over-reaching imbecility—" etc.)—and then, greatly relieved, he went to the window and stared out at the Sloane Street traffic.

Bensington had put the most exciting novel conceivable on the little table that carried his electric standard. He joined the fingers of his opposed hands very carefully and regarded them. "Redwood," he said. "Do they say much about Us?"

"Not so much as I should expect."

"They don't denounce us at all?"

"Not a bit. But, on the other hand, they don't back up what I point out must be done. I've written to the Times, you know, explaining the whole thing—"

"We take the Daily Chronicle," said Bensington.

"And the Times has a long leader on the subject—a very high-class, well-written leader, with three pieces of Times Latin—status quo is one—and it reads like the voice of Somebody Impersonal of the Greatest Importance suffering from Influenza Headache and talking through sheets and sheets of felt without getting any relief from it whatever. Reading between the lines, you know, it's pretty clear that the Times considers that it is useless to mince matters, and that something (indefinite of course) has to be done at once. Otherwise still more undesirable consequences—Times English, you know, for more wasps and stings. Thoroughly statesmanlike article!"

"And meanwhile this Bigness is spreading in all sorts of ugly ways."

"Precisely."

"I wonder if Skinner was right about those big rats—"

"Oh no! That would be too much," said Redwood.

He came and stood by Bensington's chair.

"By-the-bye," he said, with a slightly lowered voice, "how does she—?"

He indicated the closed door.

"Cousin Jane? She simply knows nothing about it. Doesn't connect us with it and won't read the articles. 'Gigantic wasps!' she says, 'I haven't patience to read the papers.'"

"That's very fortunate," said Redwood.

"I suppose—Mrs. Redwood—?"

"No," said Redwood, "just at present it happens—she's terribly worried about the child. You know, he keeps on."

"Growing?"

"Yes. Put on forty-one ounces in ten days. Weighs nearly four stone. And only six months old! Naturally rather alarming."

"Healthy?"

"Vigorous. His nurse is leaving because he kicks so forcibly. And everything, of course, shockingly outgrown. Everything, you know, has had to be made fresh, clothes and everything. Perambulator—light affair—broke one wheel, and the youngster had to be brought home on the milkman's hand-truck. Yes. Quite a crowd…. And we've put Georgina Phyllis back into his cot and put him into the bed of Georgina Phyllis. His mother—naturally alarmed. Proud at first and inclined to praise Winkles. Not now. Feels the thing can't be wholesome. You know."

"I imagined you were going to put him on diminishing doses."

"I tried it."

"Didn't it work?"

"Howls. In the ordinary way the cry of a child is loud and distressing; it is for the good of the species that this should be so—but since he has been on the Herakleophorbia treatment—-"

"Mm," said Bensington, regarding his fingers with more resignation than he had hitherto displayed.

"Practically the thing must come out. People will hear of this child, connect it up with our hens and things, and the whole thing will come round to my wife…. How she will take it I haven't the remotest idea."

"It is difficult," said Mr. Bensington, "to form any plan—certainly."

He removed his glasses and wiped them carefully.

"It is another instance," he generalised, "of the thing that is continually happening. We—if indeed I may presume to the adjective—scientific men—we work of course always for a theoretical result—a purely theoretical result. But, incidentally, we do set forces in operation—new forces. We mustn't control them—and nobody else can. Practically, Redwood, the thing is out of our hands. We supply the material—"

"And they," said Redwood, turning to the window, "get the experience."

"So far as this trouble down in Kent goes I am not disposed to worry further."

"Unless they worry us."

"Exactly. And if they like to muddle about with solicitors and pettifoggers and legal obstructions and weighty considerations of the tomfool order, until they have got a number of new gigantic species of vermin well established—Things always have been in a muddle, Redwood."

Redwood traced a twisted, tangled line in the air.

"And our real interest lies at present with your boy."

Redwood turned about and came and stared at his collaborator.

"What do you think of him, Bensington? You can look at this business with a greater detachment than I can. What am I to do about him?"

"Go on feeding him."

"On Herakleophorbia?"

"On Herakleophorbia."

"And then he'll grow."

"He'll grow, as far as I can calculate from the hens and the wasps, to the height of about five-and-thirty feet—with everything in proportion—-"

"And then what'll he do?"

"That," said Mr. Bensington, "is just what makes the whole thing so interesting."

"Confound it, man! Think of his clothes."

"And when he's grown up," said Redwood, "he'll only be one solitaryGulliver in a pigmy world."

Mr. Bensington's eye over his gold rim was pregnant.

"Why solitary?" he said, and repeated still more darkly, "Why solitary?"

"But you don't propose—-?"

"I said," said Mr. Bensington, with the self-complacency of a man who has produced a good significant saying, "Why solitary?"

"Meaning that one might bring up other children—-?"

"Meaning nothing beyond my inquiry."

Redwood began to walk about the room. "Of course," he said, "one might—But still! What are we coming to?"

Bensington evidently enjoyed his line of high intellectual detachment. "The thing that interests me most, Redwood, of all this, is to think that his brain at the top of him will also, so far as my reasoning goes, be five-and-thirty feet or so above our level.... What's the matter?"

Redwood stood at the window and stared at a news placard on a paper-cart that rattled up the street.

"What's the matter?" repeated Bensington, rising.

Redwood exclaimed violently.

"What is it?" said Bensington.

"Get a paper," said Redwood, moving doorward.

"Why?"

"Get a paper. Something—I didn't quite catch—Gigantic rats—!"

"Rats?"

"Yes, rats. Skinner was right after all!"

"What do you mean?"

"How the Deuce am I to know till I see a paper? Great Rats! Good Lord! I wonder if he's eaten!"

He glanced for his hat, and decided to go hatless.

As he rushed downstairs two steps at a time, he could hear along the street the mighty howlings, to and fro of the Hooligan paper-sellers making a Boom.

"'Orrible affair in Kent—'orrible affair in Kent. Doctor ... eaten by rats. 'Orrible affair—'orrible affair—rats—eaten by Stchewpendous rats. Full perticulars—'orrible affair."

III.

Cossar, the well-known civil engineer, found them in the great doorway of the flat mansions, Redwood holding out the damp pink paper, and Bensington on tiptoe reading over his arm. Cossar was a large-bodied man with gaunt inelegant limbs casually placed at convenient corners of his body, and a face like a carving abandoned at an early stage as altogether too unpromising for completion. His nose had been left square, and his lower jaw projected beyond his upper. He breathed audibly. Few people considered him handsome. His hair was entirely tangential, and his voice, which he used sparingly, was pitched high, and had commonly a quality of bitter protest. He wore a grey cloth jacket suit and a silk hat on all occasions. He plumbed an abysmal trouser pocket with a vast red hand, paid his cabman, and came panting resolutely up the steps, a copy of the pink paper clutched about the middle, like Jove's thunderbolt, in his hand.

"Skinner?" Bensington was saying, regardless of his approach.

"Nothing about him," said Redwood. "Bound to be eaten. Both of them.It's too terrible.... Hullo! Cossar!"

"This your stuff?" asked Cossar, waving the paper.

"Well, why don't you stop it?" he demanded.

"Can't be jiggered!" said Cossar.

"Buy the place?" he cried. "What nonsense! Burn it! I knew you chaps would fumble this. What are you to do? Why—what I tell you.

"You? Do? Why! Go up the street to the gunsmith's, of course. Why? For guns. Yes—there's only one shop. Get eight guns! Rifles. Not elephant guns—no! Too big. Not army rifles—too small. Say it's to kill—kill a bull. Say it's to shoot buffalo! See? Eh? Rats? No! How the deuce are they to understand that? Because we want eight. Get a lot of ammunition. Don't get guns without ammunition—No! Take the lot in a cab to—where's the place? Urshot? Charing Cross, then. There's a train—-Well, the first train that starts after two. Think you can do it? All right. License? Get eight at a post-office, of course. Gun licenses, you know. Not game. Why? It's rats, man.

"You—Bensington. Got a telephone? Yes. I'll ring up five of my chaps from Ealing. Why five? Because it's the right number!

"Where you going, Redwood? Get a hat! Nonsense. Have mine. You want guns, man—not hats. Got money? Enough? All right. So long.

"Where's the telephone, Bensington?"

Bensington wheeled about obediently and led the way.

Cossar used and replaced the instrument. "Then there's the wasps," he said. "Sulphur and nitre'll do that. Obviously. Plaster of Paris. You're a chemist. Where can I get sulphur by the ton in portable sacks? What for? Why, Lord bless my heart and soul!—to smoke out the nest, of course! I suppose it must be sulphur, eh? You're a chemist. Sulphur best, eh?"

"Yes, I should think sulphur."

"Nothing better?"

"Right. That's your job. That's all right. Get as much sulphur as you can—saltpetre to make it burn. Sent? Charing Cross. Right away. See they do it. Follow it up. Anything?"

He thought a moment.

"Plaster of Paris—any sort of plaster—bung up nest—holes—you know.That I'd better get."

"How much?"

"How much what?"

"Sulphur."

"Ton. See?"

Bensington tightened his glasses with a hand tremulous with determination. "Right," he said, very curtly.

"Money in your pocket?" asked Cossar.

"Hang cheques. They may not know you. Pay cash. Obviously. Where's your bank? All right. Stop on the way and get forty pounds—notes and gold."

Another meditation. "If we leave this job for public officials we shall have all Kent in tatters," said Cossar. "Now is there—anything? No! HI!"

He stretched a vast hand towards a cab that became convulsively eager to serve him ("Cab, Sir?" said the cabman. "Obviously," said Cossar); and Bensington, still hatless, paddled down the steps and prepared to mount.

"I think," he said, with his hand on the cab apron, and a sudden glance up at the windows of his flat, "I ought to tell my cousin Jane —"

"More time to tell her when you come back," said Cossar, thrusting him in with a vast hand expanded over his back....

"Clever chaps," remarked Cossar, "but no initiative whatever. Cousin Jane indeed! I know her. Rot, these Cousin Janes! Country infested with 'em. I suppose I shall have to spend the whole blessed night, seeing they do what they know perfectly well they ought to do all along. I wonder if it's Research makes 'em like that or Cousin Jane or what?"

He dismissed this obscure problem, meditated for a space upon his watch, and decided there would be just time to drop into a restaurant and get some lunch before he hunted up the plaster of Paris and took it to Charing Cross.

The train started at five minutes past three, and he arrived at Charing Cross at a quarter to three, to find Bensington in heated argument between two policemen and his van-driver outside, and Redwood in the luggage office involved in some technical obscurity about this ammunition. Everybody was pretending not to know anything or to have any authority, in the way dear to South-Eastern officials when they catch you in a hurry.

"Pity they can't shoot all these officials and get a new lot," remarked Cossar with a sigh. But the time was too limited for anything fundamental, and so he swept through these minor controversies, disinterred what may or may not have been the station-master from some obscure hiding-place, walked about the premises holding him and giving orders in his name, and was out of the station with everybody and everything aboard before that official was fully awake to the breaches in the most sacred routines and regulations that were being committed.

"Who was he?" said the high official, caressing the arm Cossar had gripped, and smiling with knit brows.

"'E was a gentleman, Sir," said a porter, "anyhow. 'Im and all 'is party travelled first class."

"Well, we got him and his stuff off pretty sharp—whoever he was," said the high official, rubbing his arm with something approaching satisfaction.

And as he walked slowly back, blinking in the unaccustomed daylight, towards that dignified retirement in which the higher officials at Charing Cross shelter from the importunity of the vulgar, he smiled still at his unaccustomed energy. It was a very gratifying revelation of his own possibilities, in spite of the stiffness of his arm. He wished some of those confounded arm-chair critics of railway management could have seen it.

IV.

By five o'clock that evening this amazing Cossar, with no appearance of hurry at all, had got all the stuff for his fight with insurgent Bigness out of Urshot and on the road to Hickleybrow. Two barrels of paraffin and a load of dry brushwood he had bought in Urshot; plentiful sacks of sulphur, eight big game guns and ammunition, three light breechloaders, with small-shot ammunition for the wasps, a hatchet, two billhooks, a pick and three spades, two coils of rope, some bottled beer, soda and whisky, one gross of packets of rat poison, and cold provisions for three days, had come down from London. All these things he had sent on in a coal trolley and a hay waggon in the most business-like way, except the guns and ammunition, which were stuck under the seat of the Red Lion waggonette appointed to bring on Redwood and the five picked men who had come up from Ealing at Cossar's summons.

Cossar conducted all these transactions with an invincible air of commonplace, in spite of the fact that Urshot was in a panic about the rats, and all the drivers had to be specially paid. All the shops were shut in the place, and scarcely a soul abroad in the street, and when he banged at a door a window was apt to open. He seemed to consider that the conduct of business from open windows was an entirely legitimate and obvious method. Finally he and Bensington got the Red Lion dog-cart and set off with the waggonette, to overtake the baggage. They did this a little beyond the cross-roads, and so reached Hickleybrow first.

Bensington, with a gun between his knees, sitting beside Cossar in the dog-cart, developed a long germinated amazement. All they were doing was, no doubt, as Cossar insisted, quite the obvious thing to do, only—! In England one so rarely does the obvious thing. He glanced from his neighbour's feet to the boldly sketched hands upon the reins. Cossar had apparently never driven before, and he was keeping the line of least resistance down the middle of the road by some no doubt quite obvious but certainly unusual light of his own.

"Why don't we all do the obvious?" thought Bensington. "How the world would travel if one did! I wonder for instance why I don't do such a lot of things I know would be all right to do—things I want to do. Is everybody like that, or is it peculiar to me!" He plunged into obscure speculation about the Will. He thought of the complex organised futilities of the daily life, and in contrast with them the plain and manifest things to do, the sweet and splendid things to do, that some incredible influences will never permit us to do. Cousin Jane? Cousin Jane he perceived was important in the question, in some subtle and difficult way. Why should we after all eat, drink, and sleep, remain unmarried, go here, abstain from going there, all out of deference to Cousin Jane? She became symbolical without ceasing to be incomprehensible!

A stile and a path across the fields caught his eye and reminded him of that other bright day, so recent in time, so remote in its emotions, when he had walked from Urshot to the Experimental Farm to see the giant chicks.

Fate plays with us.

"Tcheck, tcheck," said Cossar. "Get up."

It was a hot midday afternoon, not a breath of wind, and the dust was thick in the roads. Few people were about, but the deer beyond the park palings browsed in profound tranquillity. They saw a couple of big wasps stripping a gooseberry bush just outside Hickleybrow, and another was crawling up and down the front of the little grocer's shop in the village street trying to find an entry. The grocer was dimly visible within, with an ancient fowling-piece in hand, watching its endeavours. The driver of the waggonette pulled up outside the Jolly Drovers and informed Redwood that his part of the bargain was done. In this contention he was presently joined by the drivers of the waggon and the trolley. Not only did they maintain this, but they refused to let the horses be taken further.

"Them big rats is nuts on 'orses," the trolley driver kept on repeating.

Cossar surveyed the controversy for a moment.

"Get the things out of that waggonette," he said, and one of his men, a tall, fair, dirty engineer, obeyed.

"Gimme that shot gun," said Cossar.

He placed himself between the drivers. "We don't want you to drive," he said.

"You can say what you like," he conceded, "but we want these horses."

They began to argue, but he continued speaking.

"If you try and assault us I shall, in self-defence, let fly at your legs. The horses are going on."

He treated the incident as closed. "Get up on that waggon, Flack," he said to a thickset, wiry little man. "Boon, take the trolley."

The two drivers blustered to Redwood.

"You've done your duty to your employers," said Redwood. "You stop in this village until we come back. No one will blame you, seeing we've got guns. We've no wish to do anything unjust or violent, but this occasion is pressing. I'll pay if anything happens to the horses, never fear."

"That's all right," said Cossar, who rarely promised.

They left the waggonette behind, and the men who were not driving went afoot. Over each shoulder sloped a gun. It was the oddest little expedition for an English country road, more like a Yankee party, trekking west in the good old Indian days.

They went up the road, until at the crest by the stile they came into sight of the Experimental Farm. They found a little group of men there with a gun or so—the two Fulchers were among them—and one man, a stranger from Maidstone, stood out before the others and watched the place through an opera-glass.

These men turned about and stared at Redwood's party.

"Anything fresh?" said Cossar.

"The waspses keeps a comin' and a goin'," said old Fulcher. "Can't see as they bring anything."

"The canary creeper's got in among the pine trees now," said the man with the lorgnette. "It wasn't there this morning. You can see it grow while you watch it."

He took out a handkerchief and wiped his object-glasses with careful deliberation.

"I reckon you're going down there," ventured Skelmersdale.

"Will you come?" said Cossar.

Skelmersdale seemed to hesitate.

"It's an all-night job."

Skelmersdale decided that he wouldn't.

"Rats about?" asked Cossar.

"One was up in the pines this morning—rabbiting, we reckon.'

Cossar slouched on to overtake his party.

Bensington, regarding the Experimental Farm under his hand, was able to gauge now the vigour of the Food. His first impression was that the house was smaller than he had thought—very much smaller; his second was to perceive that all the vegetation between the house and the pine-wood had become extremely large. The roof over the well peeped amidst tussocks of grass a good eight feet high, and the canary creeper wrapped about the chimney stack and gesticulated with stiff tendrils towards the heavens. Its flowers were vivid yellow splashes, distinctly visible as separate specks this mile away. A great green cable had writhed across the big wire inclosures of the giant hens' run, and flung twining leaf stems about two outstanding pines. Fully half as tall as these was the grove of nettles running round behind the cart-shed. The whole prospect, as they drew nearer, became more and more suggestive of a raid of pigmies upon a dolls' house that has been left in a neglected corner of some great garden.

There was a busy coming and going from the wasps' nest, they saw. A swarm of black shapes interlaced in the air, above the rusty hill-front beyond the pine cluster, and ever and again one of these would dart up into the sky with incredible swiftness and soar off upon some distant quest. Their humming became audible at more than half a mile's distance from the Experimental Farm. Once a yellow-striped monster dropped towards them and hung for a space watching them with its great compound eyes, but at an ineffectual shot from Cossar it darted off again. Down in a corner of the field, away to the right, several were crawling about over some ragged bones that were probably the remains of the lamb the rats had brought from Huxter's Farm. The horses became very restless as they drew near these creatures. None of the party was an expert driver, and they had to put a man to lead each horse and encourage it with the voice.

They could see nothing of the rats as they came up to the house, and everything seemed perfectly still except for the rising and falling "whoozzzzzzZZZ, whoooo-zoo-oo" of the wasps' nest.

They led the horses into the yard, and one of Cossar's men, seeing the door open—the whole of the middle portion of the door had been gnawed out—walked into the house. Nobody missed him for the time, the rest being occupied with the barrels of paraffin, and the first intimation they had of his separation from them was the report of his gun and the whizz of his bullet. "Bang, bang," both barrels, and his first bullet it seems went through the cask of sulphur, smashed out a stave from the further side, and filled the air with yellow dust. Redwood had kept his gun in hand and let fly at something grey that leapt past him. He had a vision of the broad hind-quarters, the long scaly tail and long soles of the hind-feet of a rat, and fired his second barrel. He saw Bensington drop as the beast vanished round the corner.

Then for a time everybody was busy with a gun. For three minutes lives were cheap at the Experimental Farm, and the banging of guns filled the air. Redwood, careless of Bensington in his excitement, rushed in pursuit, and was knocked headlong by a mass of brick fragments, mortar, plaster, and rotten lath splinters that came flying out at him as a bullet whacked through the wall.

He found himself sitting on the ground with blood on his hands and lips, and a great stillness brooded over all about him.

Then a flattish voice from within the house remarked: "Gee-whizz!"

"Hullo!" said Redwood.

"Hullo there!" answered the voice.

And then: "Did you chaps get 'im?"

A sense of the duties of friendship returned to Redwood. "Is Mr.Bensington hurt?" he said.

The man inside heard imperfectly. "No one ain't to blame if I ain't," said the voice inside.

It became clearer to Redwood that he must have shot Bensington. He forgot the cuts upon his face, arose and came back to find Bensington seated on the ground and rubbing his shoulder. Bensington looked over his glasses. "We peppered him, Redwood," he said, and then: "He tried to jump over me, and knocked me down. But I let him have it with both barrels, and my! how it has hurt my shoulder, to be sure."

A man appeared in the doorway. "I got him once in the chest and once in the side," he said.

"Where's the waggons?" said Cossar, appearing amidst a thicket of gigantic canary-creeper leaves.

It became evident, to Redwood's amazement, first, that no one had been shot, and, secondly, that the trolley and waggon had shifted fifty yards, and were now standing with interlocked wheels amidst the tangled distortions of Skinner's kitchen garden. The horses had stopped their plunging. Half-way towards them, the burst barrel of sulphur lay in the path with a cloud of sulphur dust above it. He indicated this to Cossar and walked towards it. "Has any one seen that rat?" shouted Cossar, following. "I got him in between the ribs once, and once in the face as he turned on me."

They were joined by two men, as they worried at the locked wheels.

"I killed that rat," said one of the men.

"Have they got him?" asked Cossar.

"Jim Bates has found him, beyond the hedge. I got him jest as he came round the corner.... Whack behind the shoulder...."

When things were a little ship-shape again Redwood went and stared at the huge misshapen corpse. The brute lay on its side, with its body slightly bent. Its rodent teeth overhanging its receding lower jaw gave its face a look of colossal feebleness, of weak avidity. It seemed not in the least ferocious or terrible. Its fore-paws reminded him of lank emaciated hands. Except for one neat round hole with a scorched rim on either side of its neck, the creature was absolutely intact. He meditated over this fact for some time. "There must have been two rats," he said at last, turning away.

"Yes. And the one that everybody hit—got away."

"I am certain that my own shot—"

A canary-creeper leaf tendril, engaged in that mysterious search for a holdfast which constitutes a tendril's career, bent itself engagingly towards his neck and made him step aside hastily.

"Whoo-z-z z-z-z-z-Z-Z-Z," from the distant wasps' nest, "whoo oo zoo-oo."

<h2 style="text-align:center">V.</h2>

This incident left the party alert but not unstrung.

They got their stores into the house, which had evidently been ransacked by the rats after the flight of Mrs. Skinner, and four of the men took the two horses back to Hickleybrow. They dragged the dead rat through the hedge and into a position commanded by the windows of the house, and incidentally came upon a cluster of giant earwigs in the ditch. These creatures dispersed hastily, but Cossar reached out incalculable limbs and managed to kill several with his boots and gun-butt. Then two of the men hacked through several of the main stems of the canary creeper—huge cylinders they were, a couple of feet in diameter, that came out by the sink at the back; and while Cossar set the house in order for the night, Bensington, Redwood, and one of the assistant electricians went cautiously round by the fowl runs in search of the rat-holes.

They skirted the giant nettles widely, for these huge weeds threatened them with poison-thorns a good inch long. Then round beyond the gnawed, dismantled stile they came abruptly on the huge cavernous throat of the most westerly of the giant rat-holes, an evil-smelling profundity, that drew them up into a line together.

"I hope they'll come out," said Redwood, with a glance at the penthouse of the well.

"If they don't—" reflected Bensington.

"They will," said Redwood.

They meditated.

"We shall have to rig up some sort of flare if we do go in," saidRedwood.

They went up a little path of white sand through the pine-wood and halted presently within sight of the wasp-holes.

The sun was setting now, and the wasps were coming home for good; their wings in the golden light made twirling haloes about them. The three men peered out from under the trees—they did not care to go right to the edge of the wood—and watched these tremendous insects drop and crawl for a little and enter and disappear. "They will be still in a couple of hours from now," said Redwood.... "This is like being a boy again."

"We can't miss those holes," said Bensington, "even if the night is dark. By-the-bye—about the light—"

"Full moon," said the electrician. "I looked it up."

They went back and consulted with Cossar.

He said that "obviously" they must get the sulphur, nitre, and plaster of Paris through the wood before twilight, and for that they broke bulk and carried the sacks. After the necessary shouting of the preliminary directions, never a word was spoken, and as the buzzing of the wasps' nest died away there was scarcely a sound in the world but the noise of footsteps, the heavy breathing of burthened men, and the thud of the sacks. They all took turns at that labour except Mr. Bensington, who was manifestly unfit. He took post in the Skinners' bedroom with a rifle, to watch the carcase of the dead rat, and of the others, they took turns to rest from sack-carrying and to keep watch two at a time upon the rat-holes behind the nettle grove. The pollen sacs of the nettles were ripe, and every now and then the vigil would be enlivened by the dehiscence of these, the bursting of the sacs sounding exactly like the crack of a pistol, and the pollen grains as big as buckshot pattered all about them.

Mr. Bensington sat at his window on a hard horse-hair-stuffed arm-chair, covered by a grubby antimacassar that had given a touch of social distinction to the Skinners' sitting-room for many years. His unaccustomed rifle rested on the sill, and his spectacles anon watched the dark bulk of the dead rat in the thickening twilight, anon wandered about him in curious meditation. There was a faint smell of paraffin without, for one of the casks leaked, and it mingled with a less unpleasant odour arising from the hacked and crushed creeper.

Within, when he turned his head, a blend of faint domestic scents, beer, cheese, rotten apples, and old boots as the leading motifs, was full of reminiscences of the vanished Skinners. He regarded the dim room for a space. The furniture had been greatly disordered — perhaps by some inquisitive rat — but a coat upon a clothes-peg on the door, a razor and some dirty scraps of paper, and a piece of soap that had hardened through years of disuse into a horny cube, were redolent of Skinner's distinctive personality. It came to Bensington's mind with a complete novelty of realisation that in all probability the man had been killed and eaten, at least in part, by the monster that now lay dead there in the darkling.

To think of all that a harmless-looking discovery in chemistry may lead to!

Here he was in homely England and yet in infinite danger, sitting out alone with a gun in a twilit, ruined house, remote from every comfort, his shoulder dreadfully bruised from a gun-kick, and — by Jove!

He grasped now how profoundly the order of the universe had changed for him. He had come right away to this amazing experience, without even saying a word to his cousin Jane!

What must she be thinking of him?

He tried to imagine it and he could not. He had an extraordinary feeling that she and he were parted for ever and would never meet again. He felt he had taken a step and come into a world of new immensities. What other monsters might not those deepening shadows hide? The tips of the giant nettles came out sharp and black against the pale green and amber of the western sky. Everything was very still — very still indeed. He wondered why he could not hear the others away there round the corner of the house. The shadow in the cart-shed was now an abysmal black.

* * * * *

Bang ... Bang ... Bang.

A sequence of echoes and a shout.

A long silence.

Bang and a diminuendo of echoes.

Stillness.

Then, thank goodness! Redwood and Cossar were coming out of the inaudible darknesses, and Redwood was calling "Bensington!"

"Bensington! We've bagged another of the rats!"

"Cossar's bagged another of the rats!"

VI.

When the Expedition had finished refreshment, the night had fully come. The stars were at their brightest, and a growing pallor towards Hankey heralded the moon. The watch on the rat-holes had been maintained, but the watchers had shifted to the hill slope above the holes, feeling this a safer firing-point. They squatted there in a rather abundant dew, fighting the damp with whisky. The others rested in the house, and the three leaders discussed the night's work with the men. The moon rose towards midnight, and as soon as it was clear of the downs, every one except the rat-hole sentinels started off in single file, led by Cossar, towards the wasps' nest.

So far as the wasps' nest went, they found their task exceptionally easy—astonishingly easy. Except that it was a longer labour, it was no graver affair than any common wasps' nest might have been. Danger there was, no doubt, danger to life, but it never so much as thrust its head out of that portentous hillside. They stuffed in the sulphur and nitre, they bunged the holes soundly, and fired their trains. Then with a common impulse all the party but Cossar turned and ran athwart the long shadows of the pines, and, finding Cossar had stayed behind, came to a halt together in a knot, a hundred yards away, convenient to a ditch that offered cover. Just for a minute or two the moonlit night, all black and white, was heavy with a suffocated buzz, that rose and mingled to a roar, a deep abundant note, and culminated and died, and then almost incredibly the night was still.

"By Jove!" said Bensington, almost in a whisper, "it's done!"

All stood intent. The hillside above the black point-lace of the pine shadows seemed as bright as day and as colourless as snow. The setting plaster in the holes positively shone. Cossar's loose framework moved towards them.

"So far—" said Cossar.

Crack—bang!

A shot from near the house and then—stillness.

"What's that?" said Bensington.

"One of the rats put its head out," suggested one of the men.

"By-the-bye, we left our guns up there," said Redwood.

"By the sacks."

Every one began to walk towards the hill again.

"That must be the rats," said Bensington.

"Obviously," said Cossar, gnawing his finger nails.

Bang!

"Hullo?" said one of the men.

Then abruptly came a shout, two shots, a loud shout that was almost a scream, three shots in rapid succession and a splintering of wood. All these sounds were very clear and very small in the immense stillness of the night. Then for some moments nothing but a minute muffled confusion from the direction of the rat-holes, and then again a wild yell ... Each man found himself running hard for the guns.

Two shots.

Bensington found himself, gun in hand, going hard through the pine trees after a number of receding backs. It is curious that the thought uppermost in his mind at that moment was the wish that his cousin Jane could see him. His bulbous slashed boots flew out in wild strides, and his face was distorted into a permanent grin, because that wrinkled his nose and kept his glasses in place. Also he held the muzzle of his gun projecting straight before him as he flew through the chequered moonlight. The man who had run away met them full tilt—he had dropped his gun.

"Hullo," said Cossar, and caught him in his arms. "What's this?"

"They came out together," said the man.

"The rats?"

"Yes, six of them."

"Where's Flack?"

"Down."

"What's he say?" panted Bensington, coming up, unheeded.

"Flack's down?"

"He fell down."

"They came out one after the other."

"What?"

"Made a rush. I fired both barrels first."

"You left Flack?"

"They were on to us."

"Come on," said Cossar. "You come with us. Where's Flack? Show us."

The whole party moved forward. Further details of the engagement dropped from the man who had run away. The others clustered about him, except Cossar, who led.

"Where are they?"

"Back in their holes, perhaps. I cleared. They made a rush for their holes."

"What do you mean? Did you get behind them?"

"We got down by their holes. Saw 'em come out, you know, and tried to cut 'em off. They lolloped out—like rabbits. We ran down and let fly. They ran about wild after our first shot and suddenly came at us. Went for us."

"How many?"

"Six or seven."

Cossar led the way to the edge of the pine-wood and halted.

"D'yer mean they got Flack?" asked some one.

"One of 'em was on to him."

"Didn't you shoot?"

"How could I?"

"Every one loaded?" said Cossar over his shoulder.

There was a confirmatory movement.

"But Flack—" said one.

"D'yer mean—Flack—" said another.

"There's no time to lose," said Cossar, and shouted "Flack!" as he led the way. The whole force advanced towards the rat-holes, the man who had run away a little to the rear. They went forward through the rank exaggerated weeds and skirted the body of the second dead rat. They were extended in a bunchy line, each man with his gun pointing forward, and they peered about them in the clear moonlight for some crumpled, ominous shape, some crouching form. They found the gun of the man who had run away very speedily.

"Flack!" cried Cossar. "Flack!"

"He ran past the nettles and fell down," volunteered the man who ran away.

"Where?"

"Round about there."

"Where did he fall?"

He hesitated and led them athwart the long black shadows for a space and turned judicially. "About here, I think."

"Well, he's not here now."

"But his gun—-?"

"Confound it!" swore Cossar, "where's everything got to?" He strode a step towards the black shadows on the hillside that masked the holes and stood staring. Then he swore again. "If they have dragged him in—-!"

So they hung for a space tossing each other the fragments of thoughts. Bensington's glasses flashed like diamonds as he looked from one to the other. The men's faces changed from cold clearness to mysterious obscurity as they turned them to or from the moon. Every one spoke, no one completed a sentence. Then abruptly Cossar chose his line. He flapped limbs this way and that and expelled orders in pellets. It was obvious he wanted lamps. Every one except Cossar was moving towards the house.

"You're going into the holes?" asked Redwood.

"Obviously," said Cossar.

He made it clear once more that the lamps of the cart and trolley were to be got and brought to him.

Bensington, grasping this, started off along the path by the well. He glanced over his shoulder, and saw Cossar's gigantic figure standing out as if he were regarding the holes pensively. At the sight Bensington halted for a moment and half turned. They were all leaving Cossar—-!

Cossar was able to take care of himself, of course!

Suddenly Bensington saw something that made him shout a windless "HI!" In a second three rats had projected themselves from the dark tangle of the creeper towards Cossar. For three seconds Cossar stood unaware of them, and then he had become the most active thing in the world. He didn't fire his gun. Apparently he had no time to aim, or to think of aiming; he ducked a leaping rat, Bensington saw, and then smashed at the back of its head with the butt of his gun. The monster gave one leap and fell over itself.

Cossar's form went right down out of sight among the reedy grass, and then he rose again, running towards another of the rats and whirling his gun overhead. A faint shout came to Bensington's ears, and then he perceived the remaining two rats bolting divergently, and Cossar in pursuit towards the holes.

The whole thing was an affair of misty shadows; all three fighting monsters were exaggerated and made unreal by the delusive clearness of the light. At moments Cossar was colossal, at moments invisible. The rats flashed athwart the eye in sudden unexpected leaps, or ran with a movement of the feet so swift, they seemed to run on wheels. It was all over in half a minute. No one saw it but Bensington. He could hear the others behind him still receding towards the house. He shouted something inarticulate and then ran back towards Cossar, while the rats vanished. He came up to him outside the holes. In the moonlight the distribution of shadows that constituted Cossar's visage intimated calm. "Hullo," said Cossar, "back already? Where's the lamps? They're all back now in their holes. One I broke the neck of as it ran past me ... See? There!" And he pointed a gaunt finger.

Bensington was too astonished for conversation ...

The lamps seemed an interminable time in coming. At last they appeared, first one unwinking luminous eye, preceded by a swaying yellow glare, and then, winking now and then, and then shining out again, two others. About them came little figures with little voices, and then enormous shadows. This group made as it were a spot of inflammation upon the gigantic dreamland of moonshine.

"Flack," said the voices. "Flack."

An illuminating sentence floated up. "Locked himself in the attic."

Cossar was continually more wonderful. He produced great handfuls of cotton wool and stuffed them in his ears—Bensington wondered why. Then he loaded his gun with a quarter charge of powder. Who else could have thought of that? Wonderland culminated with the disappearance of Cossar's twin realms of boot sole up the central hole.

Cossar was on all fours with two guns, one trailing on each side from a string under his chin, and his most trusted assistant, a little dark man with a grave face, was to go in stooping behind him, holding a lantern over his head. Everything had been made as sane and obvious and proper as a lunatic's dream. The wool, it seems, was on account of the concussion of the rifle; the man had some too. Obviously! So long as the rats turned tail on Cossar no harm could come to him, and directly they headed for him he would see their eyes and fire between them. Since they would have to come down the cylinder of the hole, Cossar could hardly fail to hit them. It was, Cossar insisted, the obvious method, a little tedious perhaps, but absolutely certain. As the assistant stooped to enter, Bensington saw that the end of a ball of twine had been tied to the tail of his coat. By this he was to draw in the rope if it should be needed to drag out the bodies of the rats.

Bensington perceived that the object he held in his hand was Cossar's silk hat.

How had it got there?

It would be something to remember him by, anyhow.

At each of the adjacent holes stood a little group with a lantern on the ground shining up the hole, and with one man kneeling and aiming at the round void before him, waiting for anything that might emerge.

There was an interminable suspense.

Then they heard Cossar's first shot, like an explosion in a mine....

Every one's nerves and muscles tightened at that, and bang! bang! bang! the rats had tried a bolt, and two more were dead. Then the man who held the ball of twine reported a twitching. "He's killed one in there," said Bensington, "and he wants the rope."

He watched the rope creep into the hole, and it seemed as though it had become animated by a serpentine intelligence—for the darkness made the twine invisible. At last it stopped crawling, and there was a long pause. Then what seemed to Bensington the queerest monster of all crept slowly from the hole, and resolved itself into the little engineer emerging backwards. After him, and ploughing deep furrows, Cossar's boots thrust out, and then came his lantern-illuminated back....

Only one rat was left alive now, and this poor, doomed wretch cowered in the inmost recesses until Cossar and the lantern went in again and slew it, and finally Cossar, that human ferret, went through all the runs to make sure.

"We got 'em," he said to his nearly awe-stricken company at last. "And if I hadn't been a mud-headed mucker I should have stripped to the waist. Obviously. Feel my sleeves, Bensington! I'm wet through with perspiration. Jolly hard to think of everything. Only a halfway-up of whisky can save me from a cold."

VII.

There were moments during that wonderful night when it seemed to Bensington that he was planned by nature for a life of fantastic adventure. This was particularly the case for an hour or so after he had taken a stiff whisky. "Shan't go back to Sloane Street," he confided to the tall, fair, dirty engineer.

"You won't, eh?"

"No fear," said Bensington, nodding darkly.

The exertion of dragging the seven dead rats to the funeral pyre by the nettle grove left him bathed in perspiration, and Cossar pointed out the obvious physical reaction of whisky to save him from the otherwise inevitable chill. There was a sort of brigand's supper in the old bricked kitchen, with the row of dead rats lying in the moonlight against the hen-runs outside, and after thirty minutes or so of rest, Cossar roused them all to the labours that were still to do. "Obviously," as he said, they had to "wipe the place out. No litter—no scandal. See?" He stirred them up to the idea of making destruction complete. They smashed and splintered every fragment of wood in the house; they built trails of chopped wood wherever big vegetation was springing; they made a pyre for the rat bodies and soaked them in paraffin.

Bensington worked like a conscientious navvy. He had a sort of climax of exhilaration and energy towards two o'clock. When in the work of destruction he wielded an axe the bravest fled his neighbourhood. Afterwards he was a little sobered by the temporary loss of his spectacles, which were found for him at last in his side coat-pocket.

Men went to and fro about him—grimy, energetic men. Cossar moved amongst them like a god.

Bensington drank that delight of human fellowship that comes to happy armies, to sturdy expeditions—never to those who live the life of the sober citizen in cities. After Cossar had taken his axe away and set him to carry wood he went to and fro, saying they were all "good fellows." He kept on—long after he was aware of fatigue.

At last all was ready, and the broaching of the paraffin began. The moon, robbed now of all its meagre night retinue of stars, shone high above the dawn.

"Burn everything," said Cossar, going to and fro—"burn the ground and make a clean sweep of it. See?"

Bensington became aware of him, looking now very gaunt and horrible in the pale beginnings of the daylight, hurrying past with his lower jaw projected and a flaring torch of touchwood in his hand.

"Come away!" said some one, pulling Bensington's arm.

The still dawn—no birds were singing there—was suddenly full of a tumultuous crackling; a little dull red flame ran about the base of the pyre, changed to blue upon the ground, and set out to clamber, leaf by leaf, up the stem of a giant nettle. A singing sound mingled with the crackling....

They snatched their guns from the corner of the Skinners' living-room, and then every one was running. Cossar came after them with heavy strides....

Then they were standing looking back at the Experimental Farm. It was boiling up; the smoke and flames poured out like a crowd in a panic, from doors and windows and from a thousand cracks and crevices in the roof. Trust Cossar to build a fire! A great column of smoke, shot with blood-red tongues and darting flashes, rushed up into the sky. It was like some huge giant suddenly standing up, straining upward and abruptly spreading his great arms out across the sky. It cast the night back upon them, utterly hiding and obliterating the incandescence of the sun that rose behind it. All Hickleybrow was soon aware of that stupendous pillar of smoke, and came out upon the crest, in various deshabille, to watch them coming.

Behind, like some fantastic fungus, this smoke pillar swayed and fluctuated, up, up, into the sky — making the Downs seem low and all other objects petty, and in the foreground, led by Cossar, the makers of this mischief followed the path, eight little black figures coming wearily, guns shouldered, across the meadow.

As Bensington looked back there came into his jaded brain, and echoed there, a familiar formula. What was it? "You have lit to-day —? You have lit to-day —?" Then he remembered Latimer's words: "We have lit this day such a candle in England as no man may ever put out again —"

What a man Cossar was, to be sure! He admired his back view for a space, and was proud to have held that hat. Proud! Although he was an eminent investigator and Cossar only engaged in applied science.

Suddenly he fell shivering and yawning enormously and wishing he was warmly tucked away in bed in his little flat that looked out upon Sloane Street. (It didn't do even to think of Cousin Jane.) His legs became cotton strands, his feet lead. He wondered if any one would get them coffee in Hickleybrow. He had never been up all night for three-and-thirty years.

VIII.

And while these eight adventurers fought with rats about the Experimental Farm, nine miles away, in the village of Cheasing Eyebright, an old lady with an excessive nose struggled with great difficulties by the light of a flickering candle. She gripped a sardine tin opener in one gnarled hand, and in the other she held a tin of Herakleophorbia, which she had resolved to open or die. She struggled indefatigably, grunting at each fresh effort, while through the flimsy partition the voice of the Caddles infant wailed.

"Bless 'is poor 'art," said Mrs. Skinner; and then, with her solitary tooth biting her lip in an ecstasy of determination, "Come up!"

And presently, "Jab!" a fresh supply of the Food of the Gods was let loose to wreak its powers of giantry upon the world.

CHAPTER THE FOURTH.
THE GIANT CHILDREN.

I.

For a time at least the spreading circle of residual consequences about the Experimental Farm must pass out of the focus of our narrative—how for a long time a power of bigness, in fungus and toadstool, in grass and weed, radiated from that charred but not absolutely obliterated centre. Nor can we tell here at any length how these mournful spinsters, the two surviving hens, made a wonder of and a show, spent their remaining years in eggless celebrity. The reader who is hungry for fuller details in these matters is referred to the newspapers of the period—to the voluminous, indiscriminate files of the modern Recording Angel. Our business lies with Mr. Bensington at the focus of the disturbance.

He had come back to London to find himself a quite terribly famous man. In a night the whole world had changed with respect to him. Everybody understood. Cousin Jane, it seemed, knew all about it; the people in the streets knew all about it; the newspapers all and more. To meet Cousin Jane was terrible, of course, but when it was over not so terrible after all. The good woman had limits even to her power over facts; it was clear that she had communed with herself and accepted the Food as something in the nature of things.

She took the line of huffy dutifulness. She disapproved highly, it was evident, but she did not prohibit. The flight of Bensington, as she must have considered it, may have shaken her, and her worst was to treat him with bitter persistence for a cold he had not caught and fatigue he had long since forgotten, and to buy him a new sort of hygienic all-wool combination underwear that was apt to get involved and turned partially inside out and partially not, and as difficult to get into for an absent-minded man, as—Society. And so for a space, and as far as this convenience left him leisure, he still continued to participate in the development of this new element in human history, the Food of the Gods.

The public mind, following its own mysterious laws of selection, had chosen him as the one and only responsible Inventor and Promoter of this new wonder; it would hear nothing of Redwood, and without a protest it allowed Cossar to follow his natural impulse into a terribly prolific obscurity. Before he was aware of the drift of these things, Mr. Bensington was, so to speak, stark and dissected upon the hoardings. His baldness, his curious general pinkness, and his golden spectacles had become a national possession. Resolute young men with large expensive-looking cameras and a general air of complete authorisation took possession of the flat for brief but fruitful periods, let off flash lights in it that filled it for days with dense, intolerable vapour, and retired to fill the pages of the syndicated magazines with their admirable photographs of Mr. Bensington complete and at home in his second-best jacket and his slashed shoes. Other resolute-mannered persons of various ages and sexes dropped in and told him things about Boomfood—it was Punch first called the stuff "Boomfood"—and afterwards reproduced what they had said as his own original contribution to the Interview. The thing became quite an obsession with Broadbeam, the Popular Humourist. He scented another confounded thing he could not understand, and he fretted dreadfully in his efforts to "laugh the thing down." One saw him in clubs, a great clumsy presence with the evidences of his midnight oil burning manifest upon his large unwholesome face, explaining to every one he could buttonhole: "These Scientific chaps, you know, haven't a Sense of Humour, you know. That's what it is. This Science— kills it." His jests at Bensington became malignant libels....

An enterprising press-cutting agency sent Bensington a long article about himself from a sixpenny weekly, entitled "A New Terror," and offered to supply one hundred such disturbances for a guinea, and two extremely charming young ladies, totally unknown to him, called, and, to the speechless indignation of Cousin Jane, had tea with him and afterwards sent him their birthday books for his signature. He was speedily quite hardened to seeing his name associated with the most incongruous ideas in the public press, and to discover in the reviews articles written about Boomfood and himself in a tone of the utmost intimacy by people he had never heard of. And whatever delusions he may have cherished in the days of his obscurity about the pleasantness of Fame were dispelled utterly and for ever.

At first—except for Broadbeam—the tone of the public mind was quite free from any touch of hostility. It did not seem to occur to the public mind as anything but a mere playful supposition that any more Herakleophorbia was going to escape again. And it did not seem to occur to the public mind that the growing little band of babies now being fed on the food would presently be growing more "up" than most of us ever grow. The sort of thing that pleased the public mind was caricatures of eminent politicians after a course of Boom-feeding, uses of the idea on hoardings, and such edifying exhibitions as the dead wasps that had escaped the fire and the remaining hens.

Beyond that the public did not care to look, until very strenuous efforts were made to turn its eyes to the remoter consequences, and even then for a while its enthusiasm for action was partial. "There's always somethin' New," said the public—a public so glutted with novelty that it would hear of the earth being split as one splits an apple without surprise, and, "I wonder what they'll do next."

But there were one or two people outside the public, as it were, who did already take that further glance, and some it seems were frightened by what they saw there. There was young Caterham, for example, cousin of the Earl of Pewterstone, and one of the most promising of English politicians, who, taking the risk of being thought a faddist, wrote a long article in the Nineteenth Century and After to suggest its total suppression. And—in certain of his moods, there was Bensington.

"They don't seem to realise—" he said to Cossar.

"No, they don't."

"And do we? Sometimes, when I think of what it means—This poor child ofRedwood's—And, of course, your three... Forty feet high, perhaps!After all, ought we to go on with it?"

"Go on with it!" cried Cossar, convulsed with inelegant astonishment and pitching his note higher than ever. "Of course you'll go on with it! What d'you think you were made for? Just to loaf about between meal-times?

"Serious consequences," he screamed, "of course! Enormous. Obviously. Ob-viously. Why, man, it's the only chance you'll ever get of a serious consequence! And you want to shirk it!" For a moment his indignation was speechless, "It's downright Wicked!" he said at last, and repeated explosively, "Wicked!"

But Bensington worked in his laboratory now with more emotion than zest. He couldn't, tell whether he wanted serious consequences to his life or not; he was a man of quiet tastes. It was a marvellous discovery, of course, quite marvellous—but—He had already become the proprietor of several acres of scorched, discredited property near Hickleybrow, at a price of nearly £90 an acre, and at times he was disposed to think this as serious a consequence of speculative chemistry as any unambitious man, could wish. Of course he was Famous—terribly Famous. More than satisfying, altogether more than satisfying, was the Fame he had attained.

But the habit of Research was strong in him....

And at moments, rare moments in the laboratory chiefly, he would find something else than habit and Cossar's arguments to urge him to his work. This little spectacled man, poised perhaps with his slashed shoes wrapped about the legs of his high stool and his hand upon the tweezer of his balance weights, would have again a flash of that adolescent vision, would have a momentary perception of the eternal unfolding of the seed that had been sown in his brain, would see as it were in the sky, behind the grotesque shapes and accidents of the present, the coming world of giants and all the mighty things the future has in store—vague and splendid, like some glittering palace seen suddenly in the passing of a sunbeam far away.... And presently it would be with him as though that distant splendour had never shone upon his brain, and he would perceive nothing ahead but sinister shadows, vast declivities and darknesses, inhospitable immensities, cold, wild, and terrible things.

II.

Amidst the complex and confused happenings, the impacts from the great outer world that constituted Mr. Bensington's fame, a shining and active figure presently became conspicuous—became almost, as it were, a leader and marshal of these externalities in Mr. Bensington's eyes. This was Dr. Winkles, that convincing young practitioner, who has already appeared in this story as the means whereby Redwood was able to convey the Food to his son. Even before the great outbreak, it was evident that the mysterious powders Redwood had given him had awakened this gentleman's interest immensely, and so soon as the first wasps came he was putting two and two together.

He was the sort of doctor that is in manners, in morals, in methods and appearance, most succinctly and finally expressed by the word "rising." He was large and fair, with a hard, alert, superficial, aluminium-coloured eye, and hair like chalk mud, even-featured and muscular about the clean-shaven mouth, erect in figure and energetic in movement, quick and spinning on the heel, and he wore long frock coats, black silk ties and plain gold studs and chains and his silk hats had a special shape and brim that made him look wiser and better than anybody. He looked as young or old as anybody grown up. And after that first wonderful outbreak he took to Bensington and Redwood and the Food of the Gods with such a convincing air of proprietorship, that at times, in spite of the testimony of the Press to the contrary, Bensington was disposed to regard him as the original inventor of the whole affair.

"These accidents," said Winkles, when Bensington hinted at the dangers of further escapes, "are nothing. Nothing. The discovery is everything. Properly developed, suitably handled, sanely controlled, we have—we have something very portentous indeed in this food of ours.... We must keep our eye on it ... We mustn't let it out of control again, and—we mustn't let it rest."

He certainly did not mean to do that. He was at Bensington's now almost every day. Bensington, glancing from the window, would see the faultless equipage come spanking up Sloane Street and after an incredibly brief interval Winkles would enter the room with a light, strong motion, and pervade it, and protrude some newspaper and supply information and make remarks.

"Well," he would say, rubbing his hands, "how are we getting on?" and so pass to the current discussion about it.

"Do you see," he would say, for example, "that Caterham has been talking about our stuff at the Church Association?"

"Dear me!" said Bensington, "that's a cousin of the Prime Minister, isn't it?"

"Yes," said Winkles, "a very able young man—very able. Quite wrong-headed; you know, violently reactionary—but thoroughly able. And he's evidently disposed to make capital out of this stuff of ours. Takes a very emphatic line. Talks of our proposal to use it in the elementary schools—-"

"Our proposal to use it in the elementary schools!"

"I said something about that the other day—quite in passing—little affair at a Polytechnic. Trying to make it clear the stuff was really highly beneficial. Not in the slightest degree dangerous, in spite of those first little accidents. Which cannot possibly occur again…. You know it would be rather good stuff—But he's taken it up."

"What did you say?"

"Mere obvious nothings. But as you see—-! Takes it up with perfect gravity. Treats the thing as an attack. Says there is already a sufficient waste of public money in elementary schools without this. Tells the old stories about piano lessons again—you know. No one; he says, wishes to prevent the children of the lower classes obtaining an education suited to their condition, but to give them a food of this sort will be to destroy their sense of proportion utterly. Expands the topic. What Good will it do, he asks, to make poor people six-and-thirty feet high? He really believes, you know, that they will be thirty-six feet high."

"So they would be," said Bensington, "if you gave them our food at all regularly. But nobody said anything—-"

"I said something."

"But, my dear Winkles—!"

"They'll be Bigger, of course," interrupted Winkles, with an air of knowing all about it, and discouraging the crude ideas of Bensington. "Bigger indisputably. But listen to what he says! Will it make them happier? That's his point. Curious, isn't it? Will it make them better? Will they be more respectful to properly constituted authority? Is it fair to the children themselves?? Curious how anxious his sort are for justice—so far as any future arrangements go. Even nowadays, he says, the cost, of feeding and clothing children is more than many of their parents can contrive, and if this sort of thing is to be permitted—! Eh?

"You see he makes my mere passing suggestion into a positive proposal. And then he calculates how much a pair of breeches for a growing lad of twenty feet high or so will cost. Just as though he really believed—Ten pounds, he reckons, for the merest decency. Curious this Caterham! So concrete! The honest, and struggling ratepayer will have to contribute to that, he says. He says we have to consider the Rights of the Parent. It's all here. Two columns. Every Parent has a right to have, his children brought up in his own Size....

"Then comes the question of school accommodation, cost of enlarged desks and forms for our already too greatly burthened National Schools. And to get what?—a proletariat of hungry giants. Winds up with a very serious passage, says even if this wild suggestion—mere passing fancy of mine, you know, and misinterpreted at that—this wild suggestion about the schools comes to nothing, that doesn't end the matter. This is a strange food, so strange as to seem to him almost wicked. It has been scattered recklessly—so he says—and it may be scattered again. Once you've taken it, it's poison unless you go on with it. 'So it is,' said Bensington. And in short he proposes the formation of a National Society for the Preservation of the Proper Proportions of Things. Odd? Eh? People are hanging on to the idea like anything."

"But what do they propose to do?"

Winkles shrugged his shoulders and threw out his hands. "Form a Society," he said, "and fuss. They want to make it illegal to manufacture this Herakleophorbia—or at any rate to circulate the knowledge of it. I've written about a bit to show that Caterham's idea of the stuff is very much exaggerated—very much exaggerated indeed, but that doesn't seem to check it. Curious how people are turning against it. And the National Temperance Association, by-the-bye, has founded a branch for Temperance in Growth."

"Mm," said Bensington and stroked his nose.

"After all that has happened there's bound to be this uproar. On the face of it the thing's—startling."

Winkles walked about the room for a time, hesitated, and departed.

It became evident there was something at the back of his mind, some aspect of crucial importance to him, that he waited to display. One day, when Redwood and Bensington were at the flat together he gave them a glimpse of this something in reserve.

"How's it all going?" he said; rubbing his hands together.

"We're getting together a sort of report."

"For the Royal Society?"

"Yes."

"Hm," said. Winkles, very profoundly, and walked to the hearth-rug."Hm. But—Here's the point. Ought you?"

"Ought we—what?"

"Ought you to publish?"

"We're not in the Middle Ages," said Redwood.

"I know."

"As Cossar says, swapping wisdom—that's the true scientific method."

"In most cases, certainly. But—This is exceptional."

"We shall put the whole thing before the Royal Society in the proper way," said Redwood.

Winkles returned to that on a later occasion.

"It's in many ways an Exceptional discovery."

"That doesn't matter," said Redwood.

"It's the sort of knowledge that could easily be subject to grave abuse—grave dangers, as Caterham puts it."

Redwood said nothing.

"Even carelessness, you know—"

"If we were to form a committee of trustworthy people to control the manufacture of Boomfood—Herakleophorbia, I should say—we might—"

He paused, and Redwood, with a certain private discomfort, pretended that he did not see any sort of interrogation....

Outside the apartments of Redwood and Bensington, Winkle, in spite of the incompleteness of his instructions, became a leading authority upon Boomfood. He wrote letters defending its use; he made notes and articles explaining its possibilities; he jumped up irrelevantly at the meetings of the scientific and medical associations to talk about it; he identified himself with it. He published a pamphlet called "The Truth about Boomfood," in which he minimised the whole of the Hickleybrow affair almost to nothing. He said that it was absurd to say Boomfood would make people thirty-seven feet high. That was "obviously exaggerated." It would make them Bigger, of course, but that was all....

Within that intimate circle of two it was chiefly evident that Winkles was extremely anxious to help in the making of Herakleophorbia, help in correcting any proofs there might be of any paper there might be in preparation upon the subject—do anything indeed that might lead up to his participation in the details of the making of Herakleophorbia. He was continually telling them both that he felt it was a Big Thing, that it had big possibilities. If only they were—"safeguarded in some way." And at last one day he asked outright to be told just how it was made.

"I've been thinking over what you said," said Redwood.

"Well?" said Winkles brightly.

"It's the sort of knowledge that could easily be subject to grave abuse," said Redwood.

"But I don't see how that applies," said Winkles.

"It does," said Redwood.

Winkles thought it over for a day or so. Then he came to Redwood and said that he doubted if he ought to give powders about which he knew nothing to Redwood's little boy; it seemed to him it was uncommonly like taking responsibility in the dark. That made Redwood thoughtful.

"You've seen that the Society for the Total Suppression of Boomfood claims to have several thousand members," said Winkles, changing the subject. "They've drafted a Bill," said Winkles. "They've got young Caterham to take it up—readily enough. They're in earnest. They're forming local committees to influence candidates. They want to make it penal to prepare and store Herakleophorbia without special license, and felony—matter of imprisonment without option—to administer Boomfood—that's what they call it, you know—to any person under one-and-twenty. But there's collateral societies, you know. All sorts of people. The Society for the Preservation of Ancient Statures is going to have Mr. Frederic Harrison on the council, they say. You know he's written an essay about it; says it is vulgar, and entirely inharmonious with that Revelation of Humanity that is found in the teachings of

Comte. It is the sort of thing the Eighteenth Century couldn't have produced even in its worst moments. The idea of the Food never entered the head of Comte—which shows how wicked it really is. No one, he says, who really understood Comte...."

"But you don't mean to say—" said Redwood, alarmed out of his disdain for Winkles.

"They'll not do all that," said Winkles. "But public opinion is public opinion, and votes are votes. Everybody can see you are up to a disturbing thing. And the human instinct is all against disturbance, you know. Nobody seems to believe Caterham's idea of people thirty-seven feet high, who won't be able to get inside a church, or a meeting-house, or any social or human institution. But for all that they're not so easy in their minds about it. They see there's something—something more than a common discovery—"

"There is," said Redwood, "in every discovery."

"Anyhow, they're getting—restive. Caterham keeps harping on what may happen if it gets loose again. I say over and over again, it won't, and it can't. But—there it is!"

And he bounced about the room for a little while as if he meant to reopen the topic of the secret, and then thought better of it and went.

The two scientific men looked at one another. For a space only their eyes spoke.

"If the worst comes to the worst," said Redwood at last, in a strenuously calm voice, "I shall give the Food to my little Teddy with my own hands."

III.

It was only a few days after this that Redwood opened his paper to find that the Prime Minister had promised a Royal Commission on Boomfood. This sent him, newspaper in hand, round to Bensington's flat.

"Winkles, I believe, is making mischief for the stuff. He plays into the hands of Caterham. He keeps on talking about it, and what it is going to do, and alarming people. If he goes on, I really believe he'll hamper our inquiries. Even as it is—with this trouble about my little boy—"

Bensington wished Winkles wouldn't.

"Do you notice how he has dropped into the way of calling it Boomfood?"

"I don't like that name," said Bensington, with a glance over his glasses.

"It is just so exactly what it is—to Winkles."

"Why does he keep on about it? It isn't his!"

"It's something called Booming," said Redwood. "I don't understand. If it isn't his, everybody is getting to think it is. Not that that matters."

"In the event of this ignorant, this ridiculous agitation becoming—Serious," began Bensington.

"My little boy can't get on without the stuff," said Redwood. "I don't see how I can help myself now. If the worst comes to the worst—'

A slight bouncing noise proclaimed the presence of Winkles. He became visible in the middle of the room rubbing his hands together.

"I wish you'd knock," said Bensington, looking vicious over the gold rims.

Winkles was apologetic. Then he turned to Redwood. "I'm glad to find you here," he began; "the fact is—"

"Have you seen about this Royal Commission?" interrupted Redwood.

"Yes," said Winkles, thrown out. "Yes."

"What do you think of it?"

"Excellent thing," said Winkles. "Bound to stop most of this clamour. Ventilate the whole affair. Shut up Caterham. But that's not what I came round for, Redwood. The fact is—"

"I don't like this Royal Commission," said Bensington.

"I can assure you it will be all right. I may say—I don't think it's a breach of confidence—that very possibly I may have a place on the Commission—"

"Oom," said Redwood, looking into the fire.

"I can put the whole thing right. I can make it perfectly clear, first, that the stuff is controllable, and, secondly, that nothing short of a miracle is needed before anything like that catastrophe at Hickleybrow can possibly happen again. That is just what is wanted, an authoritative assurance. Of course, I could speak with more confidence if I knew—But that's quite by the way. And just at present there's something else, another little matter, upon which I'm wanting to consult you. Ahem. The fact is—Well—I happen to be in a slight difficulty, and you can help me out."

Redwood raised his eyebrows, and was secretly glad.

"The matter is—highly confidential."

"Go on," said Redwood. "Don't worry about that."

"I have recently been entrusted with a child—the child of—of anExalted Personage."

Winkles coughed.

"You're getting on," said Redwood.

"I must confess it's largely your powders—and the reputation of my success with your little boy—There is, I cannot disguise, a strong feeling against its use. And yet I find that among the more intelligent—One must go quietly in these things, you know—little by little. Still, in the case of Her Serene High—I mean this new little patient of mine. As a matter of fact—the suggestion came from the parent. Or I should never—"

He struck Redwood as being embarrassed.

"I thought you had a doubt of the advisability of using these powders," said Redwood.

"Merely a passing doubt."

"You don't propose to discontinue—"

"In the case of your little boy? Certainly not!"

"So far as I can see, it would be murder."

"I wouldn't do it for the world."

"You shall have the powders," said Redwood.

"I suppose you couldn't—"

"No fear," said Redwood. "There isn't a recipe. It's no good, Winkles, if you'll pardon my frankness. I'll make you the powders myself."

"Just as well, perhaps," said Winkles, after a momentary hard stare at Redwood—"just as well." And then: "I can assure you I really don't mind in the least."

IV.

When Winkles had gone Bensington came and stood on the hearth-rug and looked down at Redwood.

"Her Serene Highness!" he remarked.

"Her Serene Highness!" said Redwood.

"It's the Princess of Weser Dreiburg!"

"No further than a third cousin."

"Redwood," said Bensington; "it's a curious thing to say, I know, but—do you think Winkles understands?"

"What?"

"Just what it is we have made."

"Does he really understand," said Bensington, dropping his voice and keeping his eye doorward, "that in the Family—the Family of his new patient—"

"Go on," said Redwood.

"Who have always been if anything a little under—under—"

"The Average?"

"Yes. And so very tactfully undistinguished in any way, he is going to produce a royal personage—an outsize royal personage—of that size. You know, Redwood, I'm not sure whether there is not something almost—treasonable ..."

He transferred his eyes from the door to Redwood.

Redwood flung a momentary gesture—index finger erect—at the fire. "ByJove!" he said, "he doesn't know!"

"That man," said Redwood, "doesn't know anything. That was his most exasperating quality as a student. Nothing. He passed all his examinations, he had all his facts—and he had just as much knowledge—as a rotating bookshelf containing the Times Encyclopedia. And he doesn't know anything now. He's Winkles, and incapable of really assimilating anything not immediately and directly related to his superficial self. He is utterly void of imagination and, as a consequence, incapable of knowledge. No one could possibly pass so many examinations and be so well dressed, so well done, and so successful as a doctor without that precise incapacity. That's it. And in spite of all he's seen and heard and been told, there he is—he has no idea whatever of what he has set going. He has got a Boom on, he's working it well on Boomfood, and some one has let him in to this new Royal Baby—and that's Boomier than ever! And the fact that Weser Dreiburg will presently have to face the gigantic problem of a thirty-odd-foot Princess not only hasn't entered his head, but couldn't—it couldn't!"

"There'll be a fearful row," said Bensington.

"In a year or so."

"So soon as they really see she is going on growing."

"Unless after their fashion—they hush it up."

"It's a lot to hush up."

"Rather!"

"I wonder what they'll do?"

"They never do anything—Royal tact."

"They're bound to do something."

"Perhaps she will."

"O Lord! Yes."

"They'll suppress her. Such things have been known."

Redwood burst into desperate laughter. "The redundant royalty—the bouncing babe in the Iron Mask!" he said. "They'll have to put her in the tallest tower of the old Weser Dreiburg castle and make holes in the ceilings as she grows from floor to floor! Well, I'm in the very same pickle. And Cossar and his three boys. And—Well, well."

"There'll be a fearful row," Bensington repeated, not joining in the laughter. "A fearful row."

"I suppose," he argued, "you've really thought it out thoroughly, Redwood. You're quite sure it wouldn't be wiser to warn Winkles, wean your little boy gradually, and—and rely upon the Theoretical Triumph?"

"I wish to goodness you'd spend half an hour in my nursery when the Food's a little late," said Redwood, with a note of exasperation in his voice; "then you wouldn't talk like that, Bensington. Besides—Fancy warning Winkles... No! The tide of this thing has caught us unawares, and whether we're frightened or whether we're not—we've got to swim!"

"I suppose we have," said Bensington, staring at his toes. "Yes. We've got to swim. And your boy will have to swim, and Cossar's boys—he's given it to all three of them. Nothing partial abou: Cossar—all or nothing! And Her Serene Highness. And everything. We are going on making the Food. Cossar also. We're only just in the dawn of the beginning, Redwood. It's evident all sorts of things are to follow. Monstrous great things. But I can't imagine them, Redwood. Except—"

He scanned his finger nails. He looked up at Redwood with eyes bland through his glasses.

"I've half a mind," he adventured, "that Caterham is right. At times. It's going to destroy the Proportions of Things. It's going to dislocate—What isn't it going to dislocate?"

"Whatever it dislocates," said Redwood, "my little boy must have theFood."

They heard some one falling rapidly upstairs. Then Cossar put his head into the fiat. "Hullo!" he said at their expressions, and entering, "Well?"

They told him about the Princess.

"Difficult question!" he remarked. "Not a bit of it. She'll grow. Your boy'll grow. All the others you give it to 'll grow. Everythirg. Like anything. What's difficult about that? That's all right. A child could tell you that. Where's the bother?"

They tried to make it clear to him.

"Not go on with it!" he shrieked. "But—! You can't help yourselves now. It's what you're for. It's what Winkles is for. It's all right. Often wondered what Winkles was for. Now it's obvious. What's the trouble?

"Disturbance? Obviously. Upset things? Upset everythirg. Finally—upset every human concern. Plain as a pikestaff. They're going to try and stop it, but they're too late. It's their way to be too late. You go on and start as much of it as you can. Thank God He has a use for you!"

"But the conflict!" said Bensington, "the stress! I don't know if you have imagined—"

"You ought to have been some sort of little vegetable, Bensington," said Cossar—"that's what you ought to have been. Something growing over a rockery. Here you are, fearfully and wonderfully made, and all you think you're made for is just to sit about and take your vittles. D'you think this world was made for old women to mop about in? Well, anyhow, you can't help yourselves now—you've got to go on."

"I suppose we must," said Redwood. "Slowly—"

"No!" said Cossar, in a huge shout. "No! Make as much as you can and as soon as you can. Spread it about!"

He was inspired to a stroke of wit. He parodied one of Redwood's curves with a vast upward sweep of his arm.

"Redwood!" he said, to point the allusion, "make it SO!"

V.

There is, it seems, an upward limit to the pride of maternity, and this in the case of Mrs. Redwood was reached when her offspring completed his sixth month of terrestrial existence, broke down his high-class bassinet-perambulator, and was brought home, bawling, in the milk-truck. Young Redwood at that time weighed fifty-nine and a half pounds, measured forty-eight inches in height, and gripped about sixty pounds. He was carried upstairs to the nursery by the cook and housemaid. After that, discovery was only a question of days. One afternoon Redwood came home from his laboratory to find his unfortunate wife deep in the fascinating pages of The Mighty Atom, and at the sight of him she put the book aside and ran violently forward and burst into tears on his shoulder.

"Tell me what you have done to him," she wailed. "Tell me what you have done." Redwood took her hand and led her to the sofa, while he tried to think of a satisfactory line of defence.

"It's all right, my dear," he said; "it's all right. You're only a little overwrought. It's that cheap perambulator. I've arranged for a bath-chair man to come round with something stouter to-morrow—"

Mrs. Redwood looked at him tearfully over the top of her handkerchief.

"A baby in a bath-chair?" she sobbed.

"Well, why not?"

"It's like a cripple."

"It's like a young giant, my dear, and you've no cause to be ashamed of him."

"You've done something to him, Dandy," she said. "I can see it in your face."

"Well, it hasn't stopped his growth, anyhow," said Redwood heartlessly.

"I knew," said Mrs. Redwood, and clenched her pocket-handkerchief ball fashion in one hand. She looked at him with a sudden change to severity. "What have you done to our child, Dandy?"

"What's wrong with him?"

"He's so big. He's a monster."

"Nonsense. He's as straight and clean a baby as ever a woman had. What's wrong with him?"

"Look at his size."

"That's all right. Look at the puny little brutes about us! He's the finest baby—"

"He's too fine," said Mrs. Redwood.

"It won't go on," said Redwood reassuringly; "it's just a start he's taken."

But he knew perfectly well it would go on. And it did. By the time this baby was twelve months old he tottered just one inch under five feet high and scaled eight stone three; he was as big in fact as a St. Peter's in Vaticano cherub, and his affectionate clutch at the hair and features of visitors became the talk of West Kensington. They had an invalid's chair to carry him up and down to his nursery, and his special nurse, a muscular young person just out of training, used to take him for his airings in a Panhard 8 h.p. hill-climbing perambulator specially made to meet his requirement. It was lucky in every way that Redwood had his expert witness connection in addition to his professorship.

When one got over the shock of little Redwood's enormous size, he was, I am told by people who used to see him almost daily teufteufing slowly about Hyde Park, a singularly bright and pretty baby. He rarely cried or needed a comforter. Commonly he clutched a big rattle, and sometimes he went along hailing the bus-drivers and policemen along the road outside the railings as "Dadda!" and "Babba!" in a sociable, democratic way.

"There goes that there great Boomfood baby," the bus-driver used to say.

"Looks 'ealthy," the forward passenger would remark.

"Bottle fed," the bus-driver would explain. "They say it 'olds a gallon and 'ad to be specially made for 'im."

"Very 'ealthy child any'ow," the forward passenger would conclude.

When Mrs. Redwood realized that his growth was indeed going on indefinitely and logically—and this she really did for the first time when the motor-perambulator arrived—she gave way to a passion of grief. She declared she never wished to enter her nursery again, wished she was dead, wished the child was dead, wished everybody was dead, wished she had never married Redwood, wished no one ever married anybody, Ajaxed a little, and retired to her own room, where she lived almost exclusively on chicken broth for three days. When Redwood came to remonstrate with her, she banged pillows about and wept and tangled her hair.

"He's all right," said Redwood. "He's all the better for being big. You wouldn't like him smaller than other people's children."

"I want him to be like other children, neither smaller nor bigger. I wanted him to be a nice little boy, just as Georgina Phyllis is a nice little girl, and I wanted to bring him up nicely in a nice way, and here he is"—and the unfortunate woman's voice broke—"wearing number four grown-up shoes and being wheeled about by—booboo!—Petroleum!

"I can never love him," she wailed, "never! He's too much for me! I can never be a mother to him, such as I meant to be!"

But at last, they contrived to get her into the nursery, and there was Edward Monson Redwood ("Pantagruel" was only a later nickname) swinging in a specially strengthened rocking-chair and smiling and talking "goo" and "wow." And the heart of Mrs. Redwood warmed again to her child, and she went and held him in her arms and wept.

"They've done something to you," she sobbed, "and you'll grow and grow, dear; but whatever I can do to bring you up nice I'll do for you, whatever your father may say."

And Redwood, who had helped to bring her to the door, went down the passage much relieved. (Eh! but it's a base job this being a man—with women as they are!)

VI.

Before the year was out there were, in addition to Redwood's pioneer vehicle, quite a number of motor-perambulators to be seen in the west of London. I am told there were as many as eleven; but the most careful inquiries yield trustworthy evidence of only six within the Metropolitan area at that time. It would seem the stuff acted differently upon different types of constitution. At first Herakleophorbia was not adapted to injection, and there can be no doubt that quite a considerable proportion of human beings are incapable of absorbing this substance in the normal course of digestion. It was given, for example, to Winkles' youngest boy; but he seems to have been as incapable of growth as, if Redwood was right, his father was incapable of knowledge. Others again, according to the Society for the Total Suppression of Boomfood, became in some inexplicable way corrupted by it, and perished at the onset of infantile disorders. The Cossar boys took to it with amazing avidity.

Of course a thing of this kind never comes with absolute simplicity of application into the life of man; growth in particular is a complex thing, and all generalisations must needs be a little inaccurate. But the general law of the Food would seem to be this, that when it could be taken into the system in any way it stimulated it in very nearly the same degree in all cases. It increased the amount of growth from six to seven times, and it did not go beyond that, whatever amount of the Food in excess was taken. Excess of Herakleophorbia indeed beyond the necessary minimum led, it was found, to morbid disturbances of nutrition, to cancer and tumours, ossifications, and the like. And once growth upon the large scale had begun, it was soon evident that it could only continue upon that scale, and that the continuous administration of Herakleophorbia in small but sufficient doses was imperative.

If it was discontinued while growth was still going on, there was first a vague restlessness and distress, then a period of voracity—as in the case of the young rats at Hankey—and then the growing creature had a sort of exaggerated anaemia and sickened and died. Plants suffered in a similar way. This, however, applied only to the growth period. So soon as adolescence was attained—in plants this was represented by the formation of the first flower-buds—the need and appetite for Herakleophorbia diminished, and so soon as the plant or animal was fully adult, it became altogether independent of any further supply of the food. It was, as it were, completely established on the new scale. It was so completely established on the new scale that, as the thistles about Hickleybrow and the grass of the down side already demonstrated, its seed produced giant offspring after its kind.

And presently little Redwood, pioneer of the new race, first child of all who ate the food, was crawling about his nursery, smashing furniture, biting like a horse, pinching like a vice, and bawling gigantic baby talk at his "Nanny" and "Mammy" and the rather scared and awe-stricken "Daddy," who had set this mischief going.

The child was born with good intentions. "Padda be good, be good," he used to say as the breakables flew before him. "Padda" was his rendering of Pantagruel, the nickname Redwood imposed on him. And Cossar, disregarding certain Ancient Lights that presently led to trouble, did, after a conflict with the local building regulations, get building on a vacant piece of ground adjacent to Redwood's home, a comfortable well-lit playroom, schoolroom, and nursery for their four boys—sixty feet square about this room was, and forty feet high.

Redwood fell in love with that great nursery as he and Cossar built it, and his interest in curves faded, as he had never dreamt it could fade, before the pressing needs of his son. "There is much," he said, "in fitting a nursery. Much.

"The walls, the things in it, they will all speak to this new mind of ours, a little more, a little less eloquently, and teach it, or fail to teach it a thousand things."

"Obviously," said Cossar, reaching hastily for his hat.

They worked together harmoniously, but Redwood supplied most of the educational theory required ...

They had the walls and woodwork painted with a cheerful vigour; for the most part a slightly warmed white prevailed, but there were bands of bright clean colour to enforce the simple lines of construction. "Clean colours we must have," said Redwood, and in one place had a neat horizontal band of squares, in which crimson and purple, orange and lemon, blues and greens, in many hues and many shades, did themselves honour. These squares the giant children should arrange and rearrange to their pleasure. "Decorations must follow," said Redwood; "let them first get the range of all the tints, and then this may go away. There is no reason why one should bias them in favour of any particular colour or design."

Then, "The place must be full of interest," said Redwood. "Interest is food for a child, and blankness torture and starvation. He must have pictures galore." There were no pictures hung about the room for any permanent service, however, but blank frames were provided into which new pictures would come and pass thence into a portfolio so soon as their fresh interest had passed. There was one window that looked down the length of a street, and in addition, for an added interest, Redwood had contrived above the roof of the nursery a camera obscura that watched the Kensington High Street and not a little of the Gardens.

In one corner that most worthy implement, an Abacus, four feet square, a specially strengthened piece of ironmongery with rounded corners, awaited the young giants' incipient computations. There were few woolly lambs and such-like idols, but instead Cossar, without explanation, had brought one day in three four-wheelers a great number of toys (all just too big for the coming children to swallow) that could be piled up, arranged in rows, rolled about, bitten, made to flap and rattle, smacked together, felt over, pulled out, opened, closed, and mauled and experimented with to an interminable extent. There were many bricks of wood in diverse colours, oblong and cuboid, bricks of polished china, bricks of transparent glass and bricks of india-rubber; there were slabs and slates; there were cones, truncated cones, and cylinders; there were oblate and prolate spheroids, balls of varied substances, solid and hollow, many boxes of diverse size and shape, with hinged lids and screw lids and fitting lids, and one or two to catch and lock; there were bands of elastic and leather, and a number of rough and sturdy little objects of a size together that could stand up steadily and suggest the shape of a man. "Give 'em these," said Cossar. "One at a time."

These things Redwood arranged in a locker in one corner. Along one side of the room, at a convenient height for a six-or eight-foot child, there was a blackboard, on which the youngsters might flourish in white and coloured chalk, and near by a sort of drawing block, from which sheet after sheet might be torn, and on which they could draw in charcoal, and a little desk there was, furnished with great carpenter's pencils of varying hardness and a copious supply of paper, on which the boys might first scribble and then draw more neatly. And moreover Redwood gave orders, so far ahead did his imagination go, for specially large tubes of liquid paint and boxes of pastels against the time when they should be needed. He laid in a cask or so of plasticine and modelling clay. "At first he and his tutor shall model together," he said, "and when he is more skilful he shall copy casts and perhaps animals. And that reminds me, I must also have made for him a box of tools!

"Then books. I shall have to look out a lot of books to put in his way, and they'll have to be big type. Now what sort of books will he need? There is his imagination to be fed. That, after all, is the crown of every education. The crown—as sound habits of mind and conduct are the throne. No imagination at all is brutality; a base imagination is lust and cowardice; but a noble imagination is God walking the earth again. He must dream too of a dainty fairy-land and of all the quaint little things of life, in due time. But he must feed chiefly on the splendid real; he shall have stories of travel through all the world, travels and adventures and how the world was won; he shall have stories of beasts, great books splendidly and clearly done of animals and birds and plants and creeping things, great books about the deeps of the sky and the mystery of the sea; he shall have histories and maps of all the empires the world has seen, pictures and stories of all the tribes and habits and customs of men. And he must have books and pictures to quicken his sense of beauty, subtle Japanese pictures to make him love the subtler beauties of bird and tendril and falling flower, and western pictures too, pictures of gracious men and women, sweet groupings, and broad views of land and sea. He shall have books on the building of houses and palaces; he shall plan rooms and invent cities —

"I think I must give him a little theatre.

"Then there is music!"

Redwood thought that over, and decided that his son might best begin with a very pure-sounding harmonicon of one octave, to which afterwards there could be an extension. "He shall play with this first, sing to it and give names to the notes," said Redwood, "and afterwards—?"

He stared up at the window-sill overhead and measured the size of the room with his eye.

"They'll have to build his piano in here," he said. "Bring it in in pieces."

He hovered about amidst his preparations, a pensive, dark, little figure. If you could have seen him there he would have looked to you like a ten-inch man amidst common nursery things. A great rug—indeed it was a Turkey carpet—four hundred square feet of it, upon which young Redwood was soon to crawl—stretched to the grill-guarded electric radiator that was to warm the whole place. A man from Cossar's hung amidst scaffolding overhead, fixing the great frame that was to hold the transitory pictures. A blotting-paper book for plant specimens as big as a house door leant against the wall, and from it projected a gigantic stalk, a leaf edge or so and one flower of chickweed, all of that gigantic size that was soon to make Urshot famous throughout the botanical world ...

A sort of incredulity came to Redwood as he stood among these things.

"If it really is going on—" said Redwood, staring up at the remote ceiling.

From far away came a sound like the bellowing of a Mafficking bull, almost as if in answer.

"It's going on all right," said Redwood. "Evidently."

There followed resounding blows upon a table, followed by a vast crowing shout, "Gooloo! Boozoo! Bzz ..."

"The best thing I can do," said Redwood, following out some divergent line of thought, "is to teach him myself."

That beating became more insistent. For a moment it seemed to Redwood that it caught the rhythm of an engine's throbbing—the engine he could have imagined of some great train of events that bore down upon him. Then a descendant flight of sharper beats broke up that effect, and were repeated.

"Come in," he cried, perceiving that some one rapped, and the door that was big enough for a cathedral opened slowly a little way. The new winch ceased to creak, and Bensington appeared in the crack, gleaming benevolently under his protruded baldness and over his glasses.

"I've ventured round to see," he whispered in a confidentially furtive manner.

"Come in," said Redwood, and he did, shutting the door behind him.

He walked forward, hands behind his back, advanced a few steps, and peered up with a bird-like movement at the dimensions about him. He rubbed his chin thoughtfully.

"Every time I come in," he said, with a subdued note in his voice, "it strikes me as—'Big.'"

"Yes," said Redwood, surveying it all again also, as if in an endeavour to keep hold of the visible impression. "Yes. They're going to be big too, you know."

"I know," said Bensington, with a note that was nearly awe. "Very big."

They looked at one another, almost, as it were, apprehensively.

"Very big indeed," said Bensington, stroking the bridge of his nose, and with one eye that watched Redwood doubtfully for a confirmatory expression. "All of them, you know—fearfully big. I don't seem able to imagine—even with this—just how big they're all going to be."

CHAPTER THE FIFTH.
THE MINIMIFICENCE OF MR. BENSINGTON.

I.

It was while the Royal Commission on Boomfood was preparing its report that Herakleophorbia really began to demonstrate its capacity for leakage. And the earliness of this second outbreak was the more unfortunate, from the point of view of Cossar at any rate, since the draft report still in existence shows that the Commission had, under the tutelage of that most able member, Doctor Stephen Winkles (F.R.S. M.D. F.R.C.P. D. Sc. J.P. D.L. etc.), already quite made up its mind that accidental leakages were impossible, and was prepared to recommend that to entrust the preparation of Boomfood to a qualified committee (Winkles chiefly), with an entire control over its sale, was quite enough to satisfy all reasonable objections to its free diffusion. This committee was to have an absolute monopoly. And it is, no doubt, to be considered as a part of the irony of life that the first and most alarming of this second series of leakages occurred within fifty yards of a little cottage at Keston occupied during the summer months by Doctor Winkles.

There can be little doubt now that Redwood's refusal to acquaint Winkles with the composition of Herakleophorbia IV. had aroused in that gentleman a novel and intense desire towards analytical chemistry. He was not a very expert manipulator, and for that reason probably he saw fit to do his work not in the excellently equipped laboratories that were at his disposal in London, but without consulting any one, and almost with an air of secrecy, in a rough little garden laboratory at the Keston establishment. He does not seem to have shown either very great energy or very great ability in this quest; indeed one gathers he dropped the inquiry after working at it intermittently for about a month.

This garden laboratory, in which the work was done, was very roughly equipped, supplied by a standpipe tap with water, and draining into a pipe that ran down into a swampy rush-bordered pool under an alder tree in a secluded corner of the common just outside the garden hedge. The pipe was cracked, and the residuum of the Food of the Gods escaped through the crack into a little puddle amidst clumps of rushes, just in time for the spring awakening.

Everything was astir with life in that scummy little corner. There was frog spawn adrift, tremulous with tadpoles just bursting their gelatinous envelopes; there were little pond snails creeping out into life, and under the green skin of the rush stems the larvae of a big Water Beetle were struggling out of their egg cases. I doubt if the reader knows the larva of the beetle called (I know not why) Dytiscus. It is a jointed, queer-looking thing, very muscular and sudden in its movements, and given to swimming head downward with its tail out of water; the length of a man's top thumb joint it is, and more—two inches, that is for those who have not eaten the Food—and it has two sharp jaws that meet in front of its head—tubular jaws with sharp points—through which its habit is to suck its victim's blood ...

The first things to get at the drifting grains of the Food were the little tadpoles and the little water snails; the little wriggling tadpoles in particular, once they had the taste of it, took to it with zest. But scarcely did one of them begin to grow into a conspicuous position in that little tadpole world and try a smaller brother or so as an aid to a vegetarian dietary, when nip! one of the Beetle larva had its curved bloodsucking prongs gripping into his heart, and with that red stream went Herakleophorbia IV, in a state of solution, into the being of a new client. The only thing that had a chance with these monsters to get any share of the Food were the rushes and slimy green scum in the water and the seedling weeds in the mud at the bottom. A clean up of the study presently washed a fresh spate of the Food into the puddle, and overflowed it, and carried all this sinister expansion of the struggle for life into the adjacent pool under the roots of the alder...

The first person to discover what was going on was a Mr. Lukey Carrington, a special science teacher under the London Education Board, and, in his leisure, a specialist in fresh-water algae, and he is certainly not to be envied his discovery. He had come down to Keston Common for the day to fill a number of specimen tubes for subsequent examination, and he came, with a dozen or so of corked tubes clanking faintly in his pocket, over the sandy crest and down towards the pool, spiked walking stick in hand. A garden lad standing on the top of the kitchen steps clipping Doctor Winkles' hedge saw him in this unfrequented corner, and found him and his occupation sufficiently inexplicable and interesting to watch him pretty closely.

He saw Mr. Carrington stoop down by the side of the pool, with his hand against the old alder stem, and peer into the water, but of course he could not appreciate the surprise and pleasure with which Mr. Carrington beheld the big unfamiliar-looking blobs and threads of the algal scum at the bottom. There were no tadpoles visible—they had all been killed by that time—and it would seem Mr. Carrington saw nothing at all unusual except the excessive vegetation. He bared his arm to the elbow, leant forward, and dipped deep in pursuit of a specimen. His seeking hand went down. Instantly there flashed out of the cool shadow under the tree roots something—

Flash! It had buried its fangs deep into his arm—a bizarre shape it was, a foot long and more, brown and jointed like a scorpion.

Its ugly apparition and the sharp amazing painfulness of its bite were too much for Mr. Carrington's equilibrium. He felt himself going, and yelled aloud. Over he toppled, face foremost, splash! into the pool.

The boy saw him vanish, and heard the splashing of his struggle in the water. The unfortunate man emerged again into the boy's field of vision, hatless and streaming with water, and screaming!

Never before had the boy heard screams from a man.

This astonishing stranger appeared to be tearing at something on the side of his face. There appeared streaks of blood there. He flung out his arms as if in despair, leapt in the air like a frantic creature, ran violently ten or twelve yards, and then fell and rolled on the ground and over and out of sight of the boy. The lad was down the steps and through the hedge in a trice—happily with the garden shears still in hand. As he came crashing through the gorse bushes, he says he was half minded to turn back, fearing he had to deal with a lunatic, but the possession of the shears reassured him. "I could 'ave jabbed his eyes," he explained, "anyhow." Directly Mr. Carrington caught sight of him, his demeanour became at once that of a sane but desperate man. He struggled to his feet, stumbled, stood up, and came to meet the boy.

"Look!" he cried, "I can't get 'em off!"

And with a qualm of horror the boy saw that, attached to Mr. Carrington's cheek, to his bare arm, and to his thigh, and lashing furiously with their lithe brown muscular bodies, were three of these horrible larvae, their great jaws buried deep in his flesh and sucking for dear life. They had the grip of bulldogs, and Mr. Carrington's efforts to detach the monsters from his face had only served to lacerate the flesh to which it had attached itself, and streak face and neck and coat with living scarlet.

"I'll cut 'im," cried the boy; "'old on, Sir."

And with the zest of his age in such proceedings, he severed one by one the heads from the bodies of Mr. Carrington's assailants. "Yup," said the boy with a wincing face as each one fell before him. Even then, so tough and determined was their grip that the severed heads remained for a space, still fiercely biting home and still sucking, with the blood streaming out of their necks behind. But the boy stopped that with a few more slashes of his scissors—in one of which Mr. Carrington was implicated.

"I couldn't get 'em off!" repeated Carrington, and stood for a space, swaying and bleeding profusely. He dabbed feeble hands at his injuries and examined the result upon his palms. Then he gave way at the knees and fell headlong in a dead faint at the boy's feet, between the still leaping bodies of his defeated foes. Very luckily it didn't occur to the boy to splash water on his face—for there were still more of these horrors under the alder roots—and instead he passed back by the pond and went into the garden with the intention of calling assistance. And there he met the gardener coachman and told him of the whole affair.

When they got back to Mr. Carrington he was sitting up, dazed and weak, but able to warn them against the danger in the pool.

II.

Such were the circumstances by which the world had its first notification that the Food was loose again. In another week Keston Common was in full operation as what naturalists call a centre of distribution. This time there were no wasps or rats, no earwigs and no nettles, but there were at least three water-spiders, several dragon-fly larvae which presently became dragon-flies, dazzling all Kent with their hovering sapphire bodies, and a nasty gelatinous, scummy growth that swelled over the pond margin, and sent its slimy green masses surging halfway up the garden path to Doctor Winkles's house. And there began a growth of rushes and equisetum and potamogeton that ended only with the drying of the pond.

It speedily became evident to the public mind that this time there was not simply one centre of distribution, but quite a number of centres. There was one at Ealing—there can be no doubt now—and from that came the plague of flies and red spider; there was one at Sunbury, productive of ferocious great eels, that could come ashore and kill sheep; and there was one in Bloomsbury that gave the world a new strain of cockroaches of a quite terrible sort—an old house it was in Bloomsbury, and much inhabited by undesirable things. Abruptly the world found itself confronted with the Hickleybrow experiences all over again, with all sorts of queer exaggerations of familiar monsters in the place of the giant hens and rats and wasps. Each centre burst out with its own characteristic local fauna and flora....

We know now that every one of these centres corresponded to one of the patients of Doctor Winkles, but that was by no means apparent at the time. Doctor Winkles was the last person to incur any odium in the matter. There was a panic quite naturally, a passionate indignation, but it was indignation not against Doctor Winkles but against the Food, and not so much against the Food as against the unfortunate Bensington, whom from the very first the popular imagination had insisted upon regarding as the sole and only person responsible for this new thing.

The attempt to lynch him that followed is just one of those explosive events that bulk largely in history and are in reality the least significant of occurrences.

The history of the outbreak is a mystery. The nucleus of the crowd certainly came from an Anti-Boomfood meeting in Hyde Park organised by extremists of the Caterham party, but there seems no one in the world who actually first proposed, no one who ever first hinted a suggestion of the outrage at which so many people assisted. It is a problem for M. Gustave le Bon—a mystery in the psychology of crowds. The fact emerges that about three o'clock on Sunday afternoon a remarkably big and ugly London crowd, entirely out of hand, came rolling down Thursday Street intent on Bensington's exemplary death as a warning to all scientific investigators, and that it came nearer accomplishing its object than any London crowd has ever come since the Hyde Park railings came down in remote middle Victorian times. This crowd came so close to its object indeed, that for the space of an hour or more a word would have settled the unfortunate gentleman's fate.

The first intimation he had of the thing was the noise of the people outside. He went to the window and peered, realising nothing of what impended. For a minute perhaps he watched them seething about the entrance, disposing of an ineffectual dozen of policemen who barred their way, before he fully realised his own importance in the affair. It came upon him in a flash—that that roaring, swaying multitude was after him. He was all alone in the flat—fortunately perhaps—his cousin Jane having gone down to Ealing to have tea with a relation on her mother's side, and he had no more idea of how to behave under such circumstances than he had of the etiquette of the Day of Judgment. He was still dashing about the flat asking his furniture what he should do, turning keys in locks and then unlocking them again, making darts at door and window and bedroom—when the floor clerk came to him.

"There isn't a moment, Sir," he said. "They've got your number from the board in the hall! They're coming straight up!"

He ran Mr. Bensington out into the passage, already echoing with the approaching tumult from the great staircase, locked the door behind them, and led the way into the opposite flat by means of his duplicate key.

"It's our only chance now," he said.

He flung up a window which opened on a ventilating shaft, and showed that the wall was set with iron staples that made the rudest and most perilous of wall ladders to serve as a fire escape from the upper flats. He shoved Mr. Bensington out of the window, showed him how to cling on, and pursued him up the ladder, goading and jabbing his legs with a bunch of keys whenever he desisted from climbing. It seemed to Bensington at times that he must climb that vertical ladder for evermore. Above, the parapet was inaccessibly remote, a mile perhaps, below—He did not care to think of things below.

"Steady on!" cried the clerk, and gripped his ankle. It was quite horrible having his ankle gripped like that, and Mr. Bensington tightened his hold on the iron staple above to a drowning clutch, and gave a faint squeal of terror.

It became evident the clerk had broken a window, and then it seemed he had leapt a vast distance sideways, and there came the noise of a window-frame sliding in its sash. He was bawling things.

Mr. Bensington moved his head round cautiously until he could see the clerk. "Come down six steps," the clerk commanded.

All this moving about seemed very foolish, but very, very cautiously Mr.Bensington lowered a foot.

"Don't pull me!" he cried, as the clerk made to help him from the open window.

It seemed to him that to reach the window from the ladder would be a very respectable feat for a flying fox, and it was rather with the idea of a decent suicide than in any hope of accomplishing it that he made the step at last, and quite ruthlessly the clerk pulled him in. "You'll have to stop here," said the clerk; "my keys are no good here. It's an American lock. I'll get out and slam the door behind me and see if I can find the man of this floor. You'll be locked in. Don't go to the window, that's all. It's the ugliest crowd I've ever seen. If only they think you're out they'll probably content themselves by breaking up your stuff—"

"The indicator said In," said Bensington.

"The devil it did! Well, anyhow, I'd better not be found—"

He vanished with a slam of the door.

Bensington was left to his own initiative again.

It took him under the bed.

There presently he was found by Cossar.

Bensington was almost comatose with terror when he was found, for Cossar had burst the door in with his shoulder by jumping at it across the breadth of the passage.

"Come out of it, Bensington," he said. "It's all right. It's me. We've got to get out of this. They're setting the place on fire. The porters are all clearing out. The servants are gone. It's lucky I caught the man who knew.

"Look here!"

Bensington, peering from under the bed, became aware of some unaccountable garments on Cossar's arm, and, of all things, a black bonnet in his hand!

"They're having a clear out," said Cossar, "If they don't set the place on fire they'll come here. Troops may not be here for an hour yet. Fifty per cent. Hooligans in the crowd, and the more furnished flats they go into the better they'll like it. Obviously.... They mean a clear out. You put this skirt and bonnet on, Bensington, and clear out with me."

"D'you mean—?" began Bensington, protruding a head, tortoise fashion.

"I mean, put 'em on and come! Obviously," And with a sudden vehemence he dragged Bensington from under the bed, and began to dress him for his new impersonation of an elderly woman of the people.

He rolled up his trousers and made him kick off his slippers, took off his collar and tie and coat and vest, slipped a black skirt over his head, and put on a red flannel bodice and a body over the same. He made him take off his all too characteristic spectacles, and clapped the bonnet on his head. "You might have been born an old woman," he said as he tied the strings. Then came the spring-side boots—a terrible wrench for corns—and the shawl, and the disguise was complete. "Up and down," said Cossar, and Bensington obeyed.

"You'll do," said Cossar.

And in this guise it was, stumbling awkwardly over his unaccustomed skirts, shouting womanly imprecations upon his own head in a weird falsetto to sustain his part, and to the roaring note of a crowd bent upon lynching him, that the original discoverer of Herakleophorbia IV. proceeded down the corridor of Chesterfield Mansions, mingled with that inflamed disorderly multitude, and passed out altogether from the thread of events that constitutes our story.

Never once after that escape did he meddle again with the stupendous development of the Food of the Gods he of all men had done most to begin.

III.

This little man who started the whole thing passes out of the story, and after a time he passed altogether out of the world of things, visible and tellable. But because he started the whole thing it is seemly to give his exit an intercalary page of attention. One may picture him in his later days as Tunbridge Wells came to know him. For it was at Tunbridge Wells he reappeared after a temporary obscurity, so soon as he fully realised how transitory, how quite exceptional and unmeaning that fury of rioting was. He reappeared under the wing of Cousin Jane, treating himself for nervous shock to the exclusion of all other interests, and totally indifferent, as it seemed, to the battles that were raging then about those new centres of distribution, and about the baby Children of the Food.

He took up his quarters at the Mount Glory Hydrotherapeutic Hotel, where there are quite extraordinary facilities for baths, Carbonated Baths, Creosote Baths, Galvanic and Faradic Treatment, Massage, Pine Baths, Starch and Hemlock Baths, Radium Baths, Light Baths, Heat Baths, Bran and Needle Baths, Tar and Birdsdown Baths, — all sorts of baths; and he devoted his mind to the development of that system of curative treatment that was still imperfect when he died. And sometimes he would go down in a hired vehicle and a sealskin trimmed coat, and sometimes, when his feet permitted, he would walk to the Pantiles, and there he would sip chalybeate water under the eye of his cousin Jane.

His stooping shoulders, his pink appearance, his beaming glasses, became a "feature" of Tunbridge Wells. No one was the least bit unkind to him, and indeed the place and the Hotel seemed very glad to have the distinction of his presence. Nothing could rob him of that distinction now. And though he preferred not to follow the development of his great invention in the daily papers, yet when he crossed the Lounge of the Hotel or walked down the Pantiles and heard the whisper, "There he is! That's him!" it was not dissatisfaction that softened his mouth and gleamed for a moment in his eye.

This little figure, this minute little figure, launched the Food of the Gods upon the world! One does not know which is the most amazing, the greatness or the littleness of these scientific and philosophical men. You figure him there on the Pantiles, in the overcoat trimmed with fur. He stands under that chinaware window where the spring spouts, and holds and sips the glass of chalybeate water in his hand. One bright eye over the gilt rim is fixed, with an expression of inscrutable severity, on Cousin Jane, "Mm," he says, and sips.

So we make our souvenir, so we focus and photograph this discoverer of ours for the last time, and leave him, a mere dot in our foreground, and pass to the greater picture that, has developed about him, to the story of his Food, how the scattered Giant Children grew up day by day into a world that was all too small for them, and how the net of Boomfood Laws and Boomfood Conventions, which the Boomfood Commission was weaving even then, drew closer and closer upon them with every year of their growth, Until—

BOOK II.
THE FOOD IN THE VILLAGE.

CHAPTER THE FIRST.
THE COMING OF THE FOOD.

I.

Our theme, which began so compactly in Mr. Bensington's study, has already spread and branched, until it points this way and that, and henceforth our whole story is one of dissemination. To follow the Food of the Gods further is to trace the ramifications of a perpetually branching tree; in a little while, in the quarter of a lifetime, the Food had trickled and increased from its first spring in the little farm near Hickleybrow until it had spread,—it and the report and shadow of its power,—throughout the world. It spread beyond England very speedily. Soon in America, all over the continent of Europe, in Japan, in Australia, at last all over the world, the thing was working towards its appointed end. Always it worked slowly, by indirect courses and against resistance. It was bigness insurgent. In spite of prejudice, in spite of law and regulation, in spite of all that obstinate conservatism that lies at the base of the formal order of mankind, the Food of the Gods, once it had been set going, pursued its subtle and invincible progress.

The children of the Food grew steadily through all these years; that was the cardinal fact of the time. But it is the leakages make history. The children who had eaten grew, and soon there were other children growing; and all the best intentions in the world could not stop further leakages and still further leakages. The Food insisted on escaping with the pertinacity of a thing alive. Flour treated with the stuff crumbled in dry weather almost as if by intention into an impalpable powder, and would lift and travel before the lightest breeze. Now it would be some fresh insect won its way to a temporary fatal new development, now some fresh outbreak from the sewers of rats and such-like vermin. For some days the village of Pangbourne in Berkshire fought with giant ants. Three men were bitten and died. There would be a panic, there would be a struggle, and the salient evil would be fought down again, leaving always something behind, in the obscurer things of life—changed for ever. Then again another acute and startling outbreak, a swift upgrowth of monstrous weedy thickets, a drifting dissemination about the world of inhumanly growing thistles, of cockroaches men fought with shot guns, or a plague of mighty flies.

There were some strange and desperate struggles in obscure places. TheFood begot heroes in the cause of littleness …

And men took such happenings into their lives, and met them by the expedients of the moment, and told one another there was "no change in the essential order of things." After the first great panic, Caterham, in spite of his power of eloquence, became a secondary figure in the political world, remained in men's minds as the exponent of an extreme view.

Only slowly did he win a way towards a central position in affairs. "There was no change in the essential order of things,"—that eminent leader of modern thought, Doctor Winkles, was very clear upon this,—and the exponents of what was called in those days Progressive Liberalism grew quite sentimental upon the essential insincerity of their progress. Their dreams, it would appear, ran wholly on little nations, little languages, little households, each self-supported on its little farm. A fashion for the small and neat set in. To be big was to be "vulgar," and dainty, neat, mignon, miniature, "minutely perfect," became the key-words of critical approval…. ˙

Meanwhile, quietly, taking their time as children must, the children of the Food, growing into a world that changed to receive them, gathered strength and stature and knowledge, became individual and purposeful, rose slowly towards the dimensions of their destiny. Presently they seemed a natural part of the world; all these stirrings of bigness seemed a natural part of the world, and men wondered how things had been before their time. There came to men's ears stories of things the giant boys could do, and they said "Wonderful!"—without a spark of wonder. The popular papers would tell of the three sons of Cossar, and how these amazing children would lift great cannons, hurl masses of iron for hundreds of yards, and leap two hundred feet. They were said to be digging a well, deeper than any well or mine that man had ever made, seeking, it was said, for treasures hidden in the earth since ever the earth began.

These Children, said the popular magazines, will level mountains, bridge seas, tunnel your earth to a honeycomb. "Wonderful!" said the little folks, "isn't it? What a lot of conveniences we shall have!" and went about their business as though there was no such thing as the Food of the Gods on earth. And indeed these things were no more than the first hints and promises of the powers of the Children of the Food. It was still no more than child's play with them, no more than the first use of a strength in which no purpose had arisen. They did not know themselves for what they were. They were children — slow-growing children of a new race. The giant strength grew day by day — the giant will had still to grow into purpose and an aim.

Looking at it in a shortened perspective of time, those years of transition have the quality of a single consecutive occurrence; but indeed no one saw the coming of Bigness in the world, as no one in all the world till centuries had passed saw, as one happening, the Decline and Fall of Rome. They who lived in those days were too much among these developments to see them together as a single thing. It seemed even to wise men that the Food was giving the world nothing but a crop of unmanageable, disconnected irrelevancies, that might shake and trouble indeed, but could do no more to the established order and fabric of mankind.

To one observer at least the most wonderful thing throughout that period of accumulating stress is the invincible inertia of the great mass of people, their quiet persistence in all that ignored the enormous presences, the promise of still more enormous things, that grew among them. Just as many a stream will be at its smoothest, will look most tranquil, running deep and strong, at the very verge of a cataract, so all that is most conservative in man seemed settling quietly into a serene ascendency during these latter days. Reaction became popular: there was talk of the bankruptcy of science, of the dying of Progress, of the advent of the Mandarins, — talk of such things amidst the echoing footsteps of the Children of the Food. The fussy pointless Revolutions of the old time, a vast crowd of silly little people chasing some silly little monarch and the like, had indeed died out and passed away; but Change had not died out. It was only Change that had changed. The New was coming in its own fashion and beyond the common understanding of the world.

To tell fully of its coming would be to write a great history, but everywhere there was a parallel chain of happenings. To tell therefore of the manner of its coming in one place is to tell something of the whole. It chanced one stray seed of Immensity fell into the pretty, petty village of Cheasing Eyebright in Kent, and from the story of its queer germination there and of the tragic futility that ensued, one may attempt—following one thread, as it were—to show the direction in which the whole great interwoven fabric of the thing rolled off the loom of Time.

II.

Cheasing Eyebright had of course a Vicar. There are vicars and vicars, and of all sorts I love an innovating vicar—a piebald progressive professional reactionary—the least. But the Vicar of Cheasing Eyebright was one of the least innovating of vicars, a most worthy, plump, ripe, and conservative-minded little man. It is becoming to go back a little in our story to tell of him. He matched his village, and one may figure them best together as they used to be, on the sunset evening when Mrs. Skinner—you will remember her flight!—brought the Food with her all unsuspected into these rustic serenities.

The village was looking its very best just then, under that western light. It lay down along the valley beneath the beechwoods of the Hanger, a beading of thatched and red-tiled cottages—cottages with trellised porches and pyracanthus-lined faces, that clustered closer and closer as the road dropped from the yew trees by the church towards the bridge. The vicarage peeped not too ostentatiously between the trees beyond the inn, an early Georgian front ripened by time, and the spire of the church rose happily in the depression made by the valley in the outline of the hills. A winding stream, a thin intermittency of sky blue and foam, glittered amidst a thick margin of reeds and loosestrife and overhanging willows, along the centre of a sinuous pennant of meadow. The whole prospect had that curiously English quality of ripened cultivation—that look of still completeness—that apes perfection, under the sunset warmth.

And the Vicar too looked mellow. He looked habitually and essentially mellow, as though he had been a mellow baby born into a mellow class, a ripe and juicy little boy. One could see, even before he mentioned it, that he had gone to an ivy-clad public school in its anecdotage, with magnificent traditions, aristocratic associations, and no chemical laboratories, and proceeded thence to a venerable college in the very ripest Gothic. Few books he had younger than a thousand years; of these, Yarrow and Ellis and good pre-Methodist sermons made the bulk. He was a man of moderate height, a little shortened in appearance by his equatorial dimensions, and a face that had been mellow from the first was now climacterically ripe. The beard of a David hid his redundancy of chin; he wore no watch chain out of refinements and his modest clerical garments were made by a West End tailor.... And he sat with a hand on either shin, blinking at his village in beatific approval. He waved a plump palm towards it. His burthen sang out again. What more could any one desire?

"We are fortunately situated," he said, putting the thing tamely.

"We are in a fastness of the hills," he expanded.

He explained himself at length. "We are out of it all."

For they had been talking, he and his friend, of the Horrors of the Age, of Democracy, and Secular Education, and Sky Scrapers, and Motor Cars, and the American Invasion, the Scrappy Reading of the Public, and the disappearance of any Taste at all.

"We are out of it all," he repeated, and even as he spoke the footsteps of some one coming smote upon his ear, and he rolled over and regarded her.

You figure the old woman's steadfastly tremulous advance, the bundle clutched in her gnarled lank hand, her nose (which was her countenance) wrinkled with breathless resolution. You see the poppies nodding fatefully on her bonnet, and the dust-white spring-sided boots beneath her skimpy skirts, pointing with an irrevocable slow alternation east and west. Beneath her arm, a restive captive, waggled and slipped a scarcely valuable umbrella. What was there to tell the Vicar that this grotesque old figure was—so far as his village was concerned at any rate—no less than Fruitful Chance and the Unforeseen, the Hag weak men call Fate. But for us, you understand, no more than Mrs. Skinner.

As she was too much encumbered for a curtsey, she pretended not to see him and his friend at all, and so passed, flip-flop, within three yards of them, onward down towards the village. The Vicar watched her slow transit in silence, and ripened a remark the while....

The incident seemed to him of no importance whatever. Old womankind, aere perennius, has carried bundles since the world began. What difference has it made?

"We are out of it all," said the Vicar. "We live in an atmosphere of simple and permanent things, Birth and Toil, simple seed-time and simple harvest. The Uproar passes us by." He was always very great upon what he called the permanent things. "Things change," he would say, "but Humanity—aere perennius."

Thus the Vicar. He loved a classical quotation subtly misapplied. Below, Mrs. Skinner, inelegant but resolute, had involved herself curiously with Wilmerding's stile.

III.

No one knows what the Vicar made of the Giant Puff-Balls.

No doubt he was among the first to discover them. They were scattered at intervals up and down the path between the near down and the village end—a path he frequented daily in his constitutional round. Altogether, of these abnormal fungi there were, from first to last, quite thirty. The Vicar seems to have stared at each severally, and to have prodded most of them with his stick once or twice. One he attempted to measure with his arms, but it burst at his Ixion embrace.

He spoke to several people about them, and said they were "marvellous!" and he related to at least seven different persons the well-known story of the flagstone that was lifted from the cellar floor by a growth of fungi beneath. He looked up his Sowerby to see if it was Lycoperdon coelatum or giganteum—like all his kind since Gilbert White became famous, he Gilbert-Whited. He cherished a theory that giganteum is unfairly named.

One does not know if he observed that those white spheres lay in the very track that old woman of yesterday had followed, or if he noted that the last of the series swelled not a score of yards from the gate of the Caddles' cottage. If he observed these things, he made no attempt to place his observation on record. His observation in matters botanical was what the inferior sort of scientific people call a "trained observation"—you look for certain definite things and neglect everything else. And he did nothing to link this phenomenon with the remarkable expansion of the Caddles' baby that had been going on now for some weeks, indeed ever since Caddles walked over one Sunday afternoon a month or more ago to see his mother-in-law and hear Mr. Skinner (since defunct) brag about his management of hens.

IV.

The growth of the puff-balls following on the expansion of the Caddles' baby really ought to have opened the Vicar's eyes. The latter fact had already come right into his arms at the christening—almost over-poweringly....

The youngster bawled with deafening violence when the cold water that sealed its divine inheritance and its right to the name of "Albert Edward Caddles" fell upon its brow. It was already beyond maternal porterage, and Caddles, staggering indeed, but grinning triumphantly at quantitatively inferior parents, bore it back to the free-sitting occupied by his party.

"I never saw such a child!" said the Vicar. This was the first public intimation that the Caddles' baby, which had begun its earthly career a little under seven pounds, did after all intend to be a credit to its parents. Very soon it was clear it meant to be not only a credit but a glory. And within a month their glory shone so brightly as to be, in connection with people in the Caddles' position, improper.

The butcher weighed the infant eleven times. He was a man of few words, and he soon got through with them. The first time he said, "E's a good un;" the next time he said, "My word!" the third time he said, "Well, mum," and after that he simply blew enormously each time, scratched his head, and looked at his scales with an unprecedented mistrust. Every one came to see the Big Baby—so it was called by universal consent—and most of them said, "E's a Bouncer," and almost all remarked to him, "Did they?" Miss Fletcher came and said she "never did," which was perfectly true.

Lady Wondershoot, the village tyrant, arrived the day after the third weighing, and inspected the phenomenon narrowly through glasses that filled it with howling terror. "It's an unusually Big child," she told its mother, in a loud instructive voice. "You ought to take unusual care of it, Caddles. Of course it won't go on like this, being bottle fed, but we must do what we can for it. I'll send you down some more flannel."

The doctor came and measured the child with a tape, and put the figures in a notebook, and old Mr. Drift-hassock, who fanned by Up Marden, brought a manure traveller two miles out of their way to look at it. The traveller asked the child's age three times over, and said finally that he was blowed. He left it to be inferred how and why he was blowed; apparently it was the child's size blowed him. He also said it ought to be put into a baby show. And all day long, out of school hours, little children kept coming and saying, "Please, Mrs. Caddles, mum, may we have a look at your baby, please, mum?" until Mrs. Caddles had to put a stop to it. And amidst all these scenes of amazement came Mrs. Skinner, and stood and smiled, standing somewhat in the background, with each sharp elbow in a lank gnarled hand, and smiling, smiling under and about her nose, with a smile of infinite profundity.

"It makes even that old wretch of a grandmother look quite pleasant," said Lady Wondershoot. "Though I'm sorry she's come back to the village."

Of course, as with almost all cottagers' babies, the eleemosynary element had already come in, but the child soon made it clear by colossal bawling, that so far as the filling of its bottle went, it hadn't come in yet nearly enough.

The baby was entitled to a nine days' wonder, and every one wondered happily over its amazing growth for twice that time and more. And then you know, instead of its dropping into the background and giving place to other marvels, it went on growing more than ever!

Lady Wondershoot heard Mrs. Greenfield, her housekeeper, with infinite amazement.

"Caddles downstairs again. No food for the child! My dear Greenfield, it's impossible. The creature eats like a hippopotamus! I'm sure it can't be true."

"I'm sure I hope you're not being imposed upon, my lady," said Mrs.Greenfield.

"It's so difficult to tell with these people," said Lady Wondershoot."Now I do wish, my good Greenfield, that you'd just go down thereyourself this afternoon and see—see it have its bottle. Big as it is,I cannot imagine that it needs more than six pints a day."

"It hasn't no business to, my lady," said Mrs. Greenfield.

The hand of Lady Wondershoot quivered, with that C.O.S. sort of emotion, that suspicious rage that stirs in all true aristocrats, at the thought that possibly the meaner classes are after all—as mean as their betters, and—where the sting lies—scoring points in the game.

But Mrs. Greenfield could observe no evidence of peculation, and the order for an increasing daily supply to the Caddles' nursery was issued. Scarcely had the first instalment gone, when Caddles was back again at the great house in a state abjectly apologetic.

"We took the greates' care of 'em, Mrs. Greenfield, I do assure you, mum, but he's regular bust 'em! They flew with such vilence, mum, that one button broke a pane of the window, mum, and one hit me a regular stinger jest 'ere, mum."

Lady Wondershoot, when she heard that this amazing child had positively burst out of its beautiful charity clothes, decided that she must speak to Caddles herself. He appeared in her presence with his hair hastily wetted and smoothed by hand, breathless, and clinging to his hat brim as though it was a life-belt, and he stumbled at the carpet edge out of sheer distress of mind.

Lady Wondershoot liked bullying Caddles. Caddles was her ideal lower-class person, dishonest, faithful, abject, industrious, and inconceivably incapable of responsibility. She told him it was a serious matter, the way his child was going on. "It's 'is appetite, my ladyship," said Caddles, with a rising note.

"Check 'im, my ladyship, you can't," said Caddles. "There 'e lies, my ladyship, and kicks out 'e does, and 'owls, that distressin'. We 'aven't the 'eart, my ladyship. If we 'ad—the neighbours would interfere...."

Lady Wondershoot consulted the parish doctor.

"What I want to know," said Lady Wondershoot, "is it right this child should have such an extraordinary quantity of milk?"

"The proper allowance for a child of that age," said the parish doctor, "is a pint and a half to two pints in the twenty-four hours. I don't see that you are called upon to provide more. If you do, it is your own generosity. Of course we might try the legitimate quantity for a few days. But the child, I must admit, seems for some reason to be physiologically different. Possibly what is called a Sport. A case of General Hypertrophy."

"It isn't fair to the other parish children," said Lady Wondershoot. "I am certain we shall have complaints if this goes on."

"I don't see that any one can be expected to give more than the recognised allowance. We might insist on its doing with that, or if it wouldn't, send it as a case into the Infirmary."

"I suppose," said Lady Wondershoot, reflecting, "that apart from the size and the appetite, you don't find anything else abnormal— nothing monstrous?"

"No. No, I don't. But no doubt if this growth goes on, we shall find grave moral and intellectual deficiencies. One might almost prophesy that from Max Nordau's law. A most gifted and celebrated philosopher, Lady Wondershoot. He discovered that the abnormal is—abnormal, a most valuable discovery, and well worth bearing in mind. I find it of the utmost help in practice. When I come upon anything abnormal, I say at once, This is abnormal." His eyes became profound, his voice dropped, his manner verged upon the intimately confidential. He raised one hand stiffly. "And I treat it in that spirit," he said.

V.

"Tut, tut!" said the Vicar to his breakfast things—the day after the coming of Mrs. Skinner. "Tut, tut! what's this?" and poised his glasses at his paper with a general air of remonstrance.

"Giant wasps! What's the world coming to? American journalists, I suppose! Hang these Novelties! Giant gooseberries are good enough for me.

"Nonsense!" said the Vicar, and drank off his coffee at a gulp, eyes steadfast on the paper, and smacked his lips incredulously.

"Bosh!" said the Vicar, rejecting the hint altogether.

But the next day there was more of it, and the light came.

Not all at once, however. When he went for his constitutional that day he was still chuckling at the absurd story his paper would have had him believe. Wasps indeed—killing a dog! Incidentally as he passed by the site of that first crop of puff-balls he remarked that the grass was growing very rank there, but he did not connect that in any way with the matter of his amusement. "We should certainly have heard something of it," he said; "Whitstable can't be twenty miles from here."

Beyond he found another puff-ball, one of the second crop, rising like a roc's egg out of the abnormally coarsened turf.

The thing came upon him in a flash.

He did not take his usual round that morning. Instead he turned aside by the second stile and came round to the Caddles' cottage. "Where's that baby?" he demanded, and at the sight of it, "Goodness me!"

He went up the village blessing his heart, and met the doctor full tilt coming down. He grasped his arm. "What does this mean?" he said. "Have you seen the paper these last few days?"

The doctor said he had.

"Well, what's the matter with that child? What's the matter with everything—wasps, puff-balls, babies, eh? What's making them grow so big? This is most unexpected. In Kent too! If it was America now—"

"It's a little difficult to say just what it is," said the doctor. "So far as I can grasp the symptoms—"

"Yes?"

"It's Hypertrophy—General Hypertrophy."

"Hypertrophy?"

"Yes. General—affecting all the bodily structures—all the organism. I may say that in my own mind, between ourselves, I'm very nearly convinced it's that.... But one has to be careful."

"Ah," said the Vicar, a good deal relieved to find the doctor equal to the situation. "But how is it it's breaking out in this fashion, all over the place?"

"That again," said the doctor, "is difficult to say."

"Urshot. Here. It's a pretty clear case of spreading."

"Yes," said the doctor. "Yes. I think so. It has a strong resemblance at any rate to some sort of epidemic. Probably Epidemic Hypertrophy will meet the case."

"Epidemic!" said the Vicar. "You don't mean it's contagious?"

The doctor smiled gently and rubbed one hand against the other. "That I couldn't say," he said.

"But—-!" cried the Vicar, round-eyed. "If it's catching—it—it affects us!"

He made a stride up the road and turned about.

"I've just been there," he cried. "Hadn't I better—-? I'll go home at once and have a bath and fumigate my clothes."

The doctor regarded his retreating back for a moment, and then turned about and went towards his own house....

But on the way he reflected that one case had been in the village a month without any one catching the disease, and after a pause of hesitation decided to be as brave as a doctor should be and take the risks like a man.

And indeed he was well advised by his second thoughts. Growth was the last thing that could ever happen to him again. He could have eaten—and the Vicar could have eaten—Herakleophorbia by the truckful. For growth had done with them. Growth had done with these two gentlemen for evermore.

VI.

It was a day or so after this conversation—a day or so, that is, after the burning of the Experimental Farm—that Winkles came to Redwood and showed him an insulting letter. It was an anonymous letter, and an author should respect his character's secrets. "You are only taking credit for a natural phenomenon," said the letter, "and trying to advertise yourself by your letter to the Times. You and your Boomfood! Let me tell you, this absurdly named food of yours has only the most accidental connection with those big wasps and rats. The plain fact is there is an epidemic of Hypertrophy—Contagious Hypertrophy—which you have about as much claim to control as you have to control the solar system. The thing is as old as the hills. There was Hypertrophy in the family of Anak. Quite outside your range, at Cheasing Eyebright, at the present time there is a baby—"

"Shaky up and down writing. Old gentleman apparently," said Redwood."But it's odd a baby—"

He read a few lines further, and had an inspiration.

"By Jove!" said he. "That's my missing Mrs. Skinner!"

He descended upon her suddenly in the afternoon of the following day.

She was engaged in pulling onions in the little garden before her daughter's cottage when she saw him coming through the garden gate. She stood for a moment "consternated," as the country folks say, and then folded her arms, and with the little bunch of onions held defensively under her left elbow, awaited his approach. Her mouth opened and shut several times; she mumbled her remaining tooth, and once quite suddenly she curtsied, like the blink of an arc-light.

"I thought I should find you," said Redwood.

"I thought you might, sir," she said, without joy.

"Where's Skinner?"

"'E ain't never written to me, Sir, not once, nor come nigh of me sinceI came here. Sir."

"Don't you know what's become of him?"

"Him not having written, no, Sir," and she edged a step towards the left with an imperfect idea of cutting off Redwood from the barn door.

"No one knows what has become of him," said Redwood.

"I dessay 'e knows," said Mrs. Skinner.

"He doesn't tell."

"He was always a great one for looking after 'imself and leaving them that was near and dear to 'im in trouble, was Skinner. Though clever as could be," said Mrs. Skinner....

"Where's this child?" asked Redwood abruptly.

She begged his pardon.

"This child I hear about, the child you've been giving our stuff to—the child that weighs two stone."

Mrs. Skinner's hands worked, and she dropped the onions. "Reely, Sir," she protested, "I don't hardly know, Sir, what you mean. My daughter, Sir, Mrs. Caddles, 'as a baby, Sir." And she made an agitated curtsey and tried to look innocently inquiring by tilting her nose to one side.

"You'd better let me see that baby, Mrs. Skinner," said Redwood.

Mrs. Skinner unmasked an eye at him as she led the way towards the barn. "Of course, Sir, there may 'ave been a little, in a little can of Nicey I give his father to bring over from the farm, or a little perhaps what I happened to bring about with me, so to speak. Me packing in a hurry and all ..."

"Um!" said Redwood, after he had cluckered to the infant for a space."Oom!"

He told Mrs. Caddles the baby was a very fine child indeed, a thing that was getting well home to her intelligence—and he ignored her altogether after that. Presently she left the barn—through sheer insignificance.

"Now you've started him, you'll have to keep on with him, you know," he said to Mrs. Skinner.

He turned on her abruptly. "Don't splash it about this time," he said.

"Splash it about, Sir?"

"Oh! you know."

She indicated knowledge by convulsive gestures.

"You haven't told these people here? The parents, the squire and so on at the big house, the doctor, no one?"

Mrs. Skinner shook her head.

"I wouldn't," said Redwood....

He went to the door of the barn and surveyed the world about him. The door of the barn looked between the end of the cottage and some disused piggeries through a five-barred gate upon the highroad. Beyond was a high, red brick-wall rich with ivy and wallflower and pennywort, and set along the top with broken glass. Beyond the corner of the wall, a sunlit notice-board amidst green and yellow branches reared itself above the rich tones of the first fallen leaves and announced that "Trespassers in these Woods will be Prosecuted." The dark shadow of a gap in the hedge threw a stretch of barbed wire into relief.

"Um," said Redwood, then in a deeper note, "Oom!"

There came a clatter of horses and the sound of wheels, and Lady Wondershoot's greys came into view. He marked the faces of coachman and footman as the equipage approached. The coachman was a very fine specimen, full and fruity, and he drove with a sort of sacramental dignity. Others might doubt their calling and position in the world, he at any rate was sure—he drove her ladyship. The footman sat beside him with folded arms and a face of inflexible certainties. Then the great lady herself became visible, in a hat and mantle disdainfully inelegant, peering through her glasses. Two young ladies protruded necks and peered also.

The Vicar passing on the other side swept off the hat from his David's brow unheeded....

Redwood remained standing in the doorway for a long time after the carriage had passed, his hands folded behind him. His eyes went to the green, grey upland of down, and into the cloud-curdled sky, and came back to the glass-set wall. He turned upon the cool shadows within, and amidst spots and blurs of colour regarded the giant child amidst that Rembrandtesque gloom, naked except for a swathing of flannel, seated upon a huge truss of straw and playing with its toes.

"I begin to see what we have done," he said.

He mused, and young Caddles and his own child and Cossar's brood mingled in his musing.

He laughed abruptly. "Good Lord!" he said at some passing thought.

He roused himself presently and addressed Mrs. Skinner. "Anyhow he mustn't be tortured by a break in his food. That at least we can prevent. I shall send you a can every six months. That ought to do for him all right."

Mrs. Skinner mumbled something about "if you think so, Sir," and "probably got packed by mistake.... Thought no harm in giving him a little," and so by the aid of various aspen gestures indicated that she understood.

So the child went on growing.

And growing.

"Practically," said Lady Wondershoot, "he's eaten up every calf in the place. If I have any more of this sort of thing from that man Caddles—"

VII.

But even so secluded a place as Cheasing Eyebright could not rest for long in the theory of Hypertrophy—Contagious or not—in view of the growing hubbub about the Food. In a little while there were painful explanations for Mrs. Skinner—explanations that reduced her to speechless mumblings of her remaining tooth—explanations that probed her and ransacked her and exposed her—until at last she was driven to take refuge from a universal convergence of blame in the dignity of inconsolable widowhood. She turned her eye—which she constrained to be watery—upon the angry Lady of the Manor, and wiped suds from her hands.

"You forget, my lady, what I'm bearing up under."

And she followed up this warning note with a slightly defiant:

"It's 'IM I think of, my lady, night and day."

She compressed her lips, and her voice flattened and faltered: "Bein' et, my lady."

And having established herself on these grounds, she repeated the affirmation her ladyship had refused before. "I 'ad no more idea what I was giving the child, my lady, than any one could 'ave...."

Her ladyship turned her mind in more hopeful directions, wigging Caddles of course tremendously by the way. Emissaries, full of diplomatic threatenings, entered the whirling lives of Bensington and Redwood. They presented themselves as Parish Councillors, stolid and clinging phonographically to prearranged statements. "We hold you responsible, Mister Bensington, for the injury inflicted upon our parish, Sir. We hold you responsible."

A firm of solicitors, with a snake of a style—Banghurst, Brown, Flapp, Codlin, Brown, Tedder, and Snoxton, they called themselves, and appeared invariably in the form of a small rufous cunning-looking gentleman with a pointed nose—said vague things about damages, and there was a polished personage, her ladyship's agent, who came in suddenly upon Redwood one day and asked, "Well, Sir, and what do you propose to do?"

To which Redwood answered that he proposed to discontinue supplying the food for the child, if he or Bensington were bothered any further about the matter. "I give it for nothing as it is," he said, "and the child will yell your village to ruins before it dies if you don't let it have the stuff. The child's on your hands, and you have to keep it. Lady Wondershoot can't always be Lady Bountiful and Earthly Providence of her parish without sometimes meeting a responsibility, you know."

"The mischief's done," Lady Wondershoot decided when they told her—with expurgations—what Redwood had said.

"The mischief's done," echoed the Vicar.

Though indeed as a matter of fact the mischief was only beginning.

CHAPTER THE SECOND.
THE BRAT GIGANTIC.

I.

The giant child was ugly—the Vicar would insist. "He always had been ugly—as all excessive things must be." The Vicar's views had carried him out of sight of just judgment in this matter. The child was much subjected to snapshots even in that rustic retirement, and their net testimony is against the Vicar, testifying that the young monster was at first almost pretty, with a copious curl of hair reaching to his brow and a great readiness to smile. Usually Caddles, who was slightly built, stands smiling behind the baby, perspective emphasising his relative smallness.

After the second year the good looks of the child became more subtle and more contestable. He began to grow, as his unfortunate grandfather would no doubt have put it, "rank." He lost colour and developed an increasing effect of being somehow, albeit colossal, yet slight. He was vastly delicate. His eyes and something about his face grew finer—grew, as people say, "interesting." His hair, after one cutting, began to tangle into a mat. "It's the degenerate strain coming out in him," said the parish doctor, marking these things, but just how far he was right in that, and just how far the youngster's lapse from ideal healthfulness was the result of living entirely in a whitewashed barn upon Lady Wondershoot's sense of charity tempered by justice, is open to question.

The photographs of him that present him from three to six show him developing into a round-eyed, flaxen-haired youngster with a truncated nose and a friendly stare. There lurks about his lips that never very remote promise of a smile that all the photographs of the early giant children display. In summer he wears loose garments of ticking tacked together with string; there is usually one of those straw baskets upon his head that workmen use for their tools, and he is barefooted. In one picture he grins broadly and holds a bitten melon. in his hand.

The winter pictures are less numerous and satisfactory. He wears huge sabots—no doubt of beechwoods and (as fragments of the inscription "John Stickells, Iping," show) sacks for socks, and his trousers and jacket are unmistakably cut from the remains of a gaily patterned carpet. Underneath that there were rude swathings of flannel; five or six yards of flannel are tied comforter-fashion about his neck. The thing on his head is probably another sack. He stares, sometimes smiling, sometimes a little ruefully, at the camera. Even when he was only five years old, one sees that half whimsical wrinkling over his soft brown eyes that characterised his face.

He was from the first, the Vicar always declared, a terrible nuisance about the village. He seems to have had a proportionate impulse to play, much curiosity and sociability, and in addition there was a certain craving within him—I grieve to say—for more to eat. In spite of what Mrs. Greenfield called an "excessively generous" allowance of food from Lady Wondershoot, he displayed what the doctor perceived at once was the "Criminal Appetite." It carries out only too completely Lady Wondershoot's worst experiences of the lower classes—that in spite of an allowance of nourishment inordinately beyond what is known to be the maximum necessity even of an adult human being, the creature was found to steal. And what he stole he ate with an inelegant voracity. His great hand would come over garden walls; he would covet the very bread in the bakers' carts. Cheeses went from Marlow's store loft, and never a pig trough was safe from him. Some farmer walking over his field of swedes would find the great spoor of his feet and the evidence of his nibbling hunger—a root picked here, a root picked there, and the holes, with childish cunning, heavily erased. He ate a swede as one devours a radish. He would stand and eat apples from a tree, if no one was about, as normal children eat blackberries from a bush. In one way at any rate this shortness of provisions was good for the peace of Cheasing Eyebright—for many years he ate up every grain very nearly of the Food of the Gods that was given him....

Indisputably the child was troublesome and out of place, "He was always about," the Vicar used to say. He could not go to school; he could not go to church by virtue of the obvious limitations of its cubical content. There was some attempt to satisfy the spirit of that "most foolish and destructive law"—I quote the Vicar—the Elementary Education Act of 1870, by getting him to sit outside the open window while instruction was going on within. But his presence there destroyed the discipline of the other children. They were always popping up and peering at him, and every time he spoke they laughed together. His voice was so odd! So they let him stay away.

Nor did they persist in pressing him to come to church, for his vast proportions were of little help to devotion. Yet there they might have had an easier task; there are good reasons for guessing there were the germs of religious feeling somewhere in that big carcase. The music perhaps drew him. He was often in the churchyard on a Sunday morning, picking his way softly among the graves after the congregation had gone in, and he would sit the whole service out beside the porch, listening as one listens outside a hive of bees.

At first he showed a certain want of tact; the people inside would hear his great feet crunch restlessly round their place of worship, or become aware of his dim face peering in through the stained glass, half curious, half envious, and at times some simple hymn would catch him unawares, and he would howl lugubriously in a gigantic attempt at unison. Whereupon little Sloppet, who was organ-blower and verger and beadle and sexton and bell-ringer on Sundays, besides being postman and chimney-sweep all the week, would go out very briskly and valiantly and send him mournfully away. Sloppet, I am glad to say, felt it—in his more thoughtful moments at any rate. It was like sending a dog home when you start out for a walk, he told me.

But the intellectual and moral training of young Caddles, though fragmentary, was explicit. From the first, Vicar, mother, and all the world, combined to make it clear to him that his giant strength was not for use. It was a misfortune that he had to make the best of. He had to mind what was told him, do what was set him, be careful never to break anything nor hurt anything. Particularly he must not go treading on things or jostling against things or jumping about. He had to salute the gentlefolks respectful and be grateful for the food and clothing they spared him out of their riches. And he learnt all these things submissively, being by nature and habit a teachable creature and only by food and accident gigantic.

For Lady Wondershoot, in these early days, he displayed the profoundest awe. She found she could talk to him best when she was in short skirts and had her dog-whip, and she gesticulated with that and was always a little contemptuous and shrill. But sometimes the Vicar played master—a minute, middle-aged, rather breathless David pelting a childish Goliath with reproof and reproach and dictatorial command. The monster was now so big that it seems it was impossible for any one to remember he was after all only a child of seven, with all a child's desire for notice and amusement and fresh experience, with all a child's craving for response, attention and affection, and all a child's capacity for dependence and unrestricted dulness and misery.

The Vicar, walking down the village road some sunlit morning, would encounter an ungainly eighteen feet of the Inexplicable, as fantastic and unpleasant to him as some new form of Dissent, as it padded fitfully along with craning neck, seeking, always seeking the two primary needs of childhood—something to eat and something with which to play.

There would come a look of furtive respect into the creature's eyes and an attempt to touch the matted forelock.

In a limited way the Vicar had an imagination—at any rate, the remains of one—and with young Caddles it took the line of developing the huge possibilities of personal injury such vast muscles must possess. Suppose a sudden madness—! Suppose a mere lapse into disrespect—! However, the truly brave man is not the man who does not feel fear but the man who overcomes it. Every time and always the Vicar got his imagination under. And he used always to address young Caddles stoutly in a good clear service tenor.

"Being a good boy, Albert Edward?"

And the young giant, edging closer to the wall and blushing deeply, would answer, "Yessir—trying."

"Mind you do," said the Vicar, and would go past him with at most a slight acceleration of his breathing. And out of respect for his manhood he made it a rule, whatever he might fancy, never to look back at the danger, when once it was passed.

In a fitful manner the Vicar would give young Caddles private tuition. He never taught the monster to read—it was not needed; but he taught him the more important points of the Catechism—his duty to his neighbour for example, and of that Deity who would punish Caddles with extreme vindictiveness if ever he ventured to disobey the Vicar and Lady Wondershoot. The lessons would go on in the Vicar's yard, and passers-by would hear that great cranky childish voice droning out the essential teachings of the Established Church.

"To onner 'n 'bey the King and allooer put 'nthority under 'im. To s'bmit meself t'all my gov'ners, teachers, spir'shall pastors an' masters. To order myself lowly 'n rev'rently t'all my betters—"

Presently it became evident that the effect of the growing giant on unaccustomed horses was like that of a camel, and he was told to keep off the highroad, not only near the shrubbery (where the oafish smile over the wall had exasperated her ladyship extremely), but altogether. That law he never completely obeyed, because of the vast interest the highroad had for him. But it turned what had been his constant resort into a stolen pleasure. He was limited at last almost entirely to old pasture and the Downs.

I do not know what he would have done if it had not been for the Downs. There there were spaces where he might wander for miles, and over these spaces he wandered. He would pick branches from trees and make insane vast nosegays there until he was forbidden, take up sheep and put them in neat rows, from which they immediately wandered (at this he invariably laughed very heartily), until he was forbidden, dig away the turf, great wanton holes, until he was forbidden....

He would wander over the Downs as far as the hill above Wreckstone, but not farther, because there he came upon cultivated land, and the people, by reason of his depredations upon their root-crops, and inspired moreover by a sort of hostile timidity his big unkempt appearance frequently evoked, always came out against him with yapping dogs to drive him away. They would threaten him and lash at him with cart whips. I have heard that they would sometimes fire at him with shot guns. And in the other direction he ranged within sight of Hickleybrow. From above Thursley Hanger he could get a glimpse of the London, Chatham, and Dover railway, but ploughed fields and a suspicious hamlet prevented his nearer access.

And after a time there came boards—great boards with red letters that barred him in every direction. He could not read what the letters said: "Out of Bounds," but in a little while he understood. He was often to be seen in those days, by the railway passengers, sitting, chin on knees, perched up on the Down hard by the Thursley chalk pits, where afterwards he was set working. The train seemed to inspire a dim emotion of friendliness in him, and sometimes he would wave an enormous hand at it, and sometimes give it a rustic incoherent hail.

"Big," the peering passenger would say. "One of these Boom children. They say, Sir, quite unable to do anything for itself—little better than an idiot in fact, and a great burden on the locality."

"Parents quite poor, I'm told."

"Lives on the charity of the local gentry."

Every one would stare intelligently at that distant squatting monstrous figure for a space.

"Good thing that was put a stop to," some spacious thinking mind would suggest. "Nice to 'ave a few thousand of them on the rates, eh?"

And usually there was some one wise enough to tell this philosopher:"You're about Right there, Sir," in hearty tones.

II.

He had his bad days.

There was, for example, that trouble with the river.

He made little boats out of whole newspapers, an art he learnt by watching the Spender boy, and he set them sailing down the stream—great paper cocked-hats. When they vanished under the bridge which marks the boundary of the strictly private grounds about Eyebright House, he would give a great shout and run round and across Tormat's new field—Lord! how Tormat's pigs did scamper, to be sure, and turn their good fat into lean muscle!—and so to meet his boats by the ford. Right across the nearer lawns these paper boats of his used to go, right in front of Eyebright House, right under Lady Wondershoot's eyes! Disorganising folded newspapers! A pretty thing!

Gathering enterprise from impunity, he began babyish hydraulic engineering. He delved a huge port for his paper fleets with an old shed door that served him as a spade, and, no one chancing to observe his operations just then, he devised an ingenious canal that incidentally flooded Lady Wondershoot's ice-house, and finally he dammed the river. He dammed it right across with a few vigorous doorfuls of earth—he must have worked like an avalanche—and down came a most amazing spate through the shrubbery and washed away Miss Spinks and her easel and the most promising water-colour sketch she had ever begun, or, at any rate, it washed away her easel and left her wet to the knees and dismally tucked up in flight to the house, and thence the waters rushed through the kitchen garden, and so by the green door into the lane and down into the riverbed again by Short's ditch.

Meanwhile, the Vicar, interrupted in conversation with the blacksmith, was amazed to see distressful stranded fish leaping out of a few residual pools, and heaped green weed in the bed of the stream, where ten minutes before there had been eight feet and more of clear cool water.

After that, horrified at his own consequences, young Caddles fled his home for two days and nights. He returned only at the insistent call of hunger, to bear with stoical calm an amount of violent scolding that was more in proportion to his size than anything else that had ever before fallen to his lot in the Happy Village.

III.

Immediately after that affair Lady Wondershoot, casting about for exemplary additions to the abuse and fastings she had inflicted, issued a Ukase. She issued it first to her butler, and very suddenly, so that she made him jump. He was clearing away the breakfast things, and she was staring out of the tall window on the terrace where the fawns would come to be fed. "Jobbet," she said, in her most imperial voice—"Jobbet, this Thing must work for its living."

And she made it quite clear not only to Jobbet (which was easy), but to every one else in the village, including young Caddles, that in this matter, as in all things, she meant what she said.

"Keep him employed," said Lady Wondershoot. "That's the tip for MasterCaddles."

"It's the Tip, I fancy, for all Humanity," said the Vicar. "The simple duties, the modest round, seed-time and harvest—"

"Exactly," said Lady Wondershoot. "What I always say. Satan finds some mischief still for idle hands to do. At any rate among the labouring classes. We bring up our under-housemaids on that principle, always. What shall we set him to do?"

That was a little difficult. They thought of many things, and meanwhile they broke him in to labour a bit by using him instead of a horse messenger to carry telegrams and notes when extra speed was needed, and he also carried luggage and packing-cases and things of that sort very conveniently in a big net they found for him. He seemed to like employment, regarding it as a sort of game, and Kinkle, Lady Wondershoot's agent, seeing him shift a rockery for her one day, was struck by the brilliant idea of putting him into her chalk quarry at Thursley Hanger, hard by Hickleybrow. This idea was carried out, and it seemed they had settled his problem.

He worked in the chalk pit, at first with the zest of a playing child, and afterwards with an effect of habit—delving, loading, doing all the haulage of the trucks, running the full ones down the lines towards the siding, and hauling the empty ones up by the wire of a great windlass—working the entire quarry at last single-handed.

I am told that Kinkle made a very good thing indeed out of him for Lady Wondershoot, consuming as he did scarcely anything but his food, though that never restrained her denunciation of "the Creature" as a gigantic parasite upon her charity....

At that time he used to wear a sort of smock of sacking, trousers of patched leather, and iron-shod sabots. Over his head was sometimes a queer thing—a worn-out beehive straw chair it was, but usually he went bareheaded. He would be moving about the pit with a powerful deliberation, and the Vicar on his constitutional round would get there about midday to find him shamefully eating his vast need of food with his back to all the world.

His food was brought to him every day, a mess of grain in the husk, in a truck—a small railway truck, like one of the trucks he was perpetually filling with chalk, and this load he used to char in an old limekiln and then devour. Sometimes he would mix with it a bag of sugar. Sometimes he would sit licking a lump of such salt as is given to cows, or eating a huge lump of dates, stones and all, such as one sees in London on barrows. For drink he walked to the rivulet beyond the burnt-out site of the Experimental Farm at Hickleybrow and put down his face to the stream. It was from his drinking in that way after eating that the Food of the Gods did at last get loose, spreading first of all in huge weeds from the river-side, then in big frogs, bigger trout and stranding carp, and at last in a fantastic exuberance of vegetation all over the little valley.

And after a year or so the queer monstrous grub things in the field before the blacksmith's grew so big and developed into such frightful skipjacks and cockchafers—motor cockchafers the boys called them—that they drove Lady Wondershoot abroad.

IV.

But soon the Food was to enter upon a new phase of its work in him. In spite of the simple instructions of the Vicar—instructions intended to round off the modest natural life befitting a giant peasant, in the most complete and final manner—he began to ask questions, to inquire into things, to think. As he grew from boyhood to adolescence it became increasingly evident that his mind had processes of its own—out of the Vicar's control. The Vicar did his best to ignore this distressing phenomenon, but still—he could feel it there.

The young giant's material for thought lay about him. Quite involuntarily, with his spacious views, his constant overlooking of things, he must have seen a good deal of human life, and as it grew clearer to him that he too, save for this clumsy greatness of his, was also human, he must have come to realise more and more just how much was shut against him by his melancholy distinction. The sociable hum of the school, the mystery of religion that was partaken in such finery, and which exhaled so sweet a strain of melody, the jovial chorusing from the Inn, the warmly glowing rooms, candle-lit and fire-lit, into which he peered out of the darkness, or again the shouting excitement, the vigour of flannelled exercise upon some imperfectly understood issue that centred about the cricket-field— all these things must have cried aloud to his companionable heart. It would seem that as his adolescence crept upon him, he began to take a very considerable interest in the proceedings of lovers, in those preferences and pairings, those close intimacies that are so cardinal in life.

One Sunday, just about that hour when the stars and the bats and the passions of rural life come out, there chanced to be a young couple "kissing each other a bit" in Love Lane, the deep hedged lane that runs out back towards the Upper Lodge. They were giving their little emotions play, as secure in the warm still twilight as any lovers could be. The only conceivable interruption they thought possible must come pacing visibly up the lane; the twelve-foot hedge towards the silent Downs seemed to them an absolute guarantee.

Then suddenly—incredibly—they were lifted and drawn apart.

They discovered themselves held up, each with a finger and thumb under the armpits, and with the perplexed brown eyes of young Caddles scanning their warm flushed faces. They were naturally dumb with the emotions of their situation.

"Why do you like doing that?" asked young Caddles.

I gather the embarrassment continued until the swain remembering his manhood, vehemently, with loud shouts, threats, and virile blasphemies, such as became the occasion, bade young Caddles under penalties put them down. Whereupon young Caddles, remembering his manners, did put them down politely and very carefully, and conveniently near for a resumption of their embraces, and having hesitated above them for a while, vanished again into the twilight ...

"But I felt precious silly," the swain confided to me. "We couldn't 'ardly look at one another—bein' caught like that.

"Kissing we was—you know.

"And the cur'ous thing is, she blamed it all on to me," said the swain.

"Flew out something outrageous, and wouldn't 'ardly speak to me all the way 'ome...."

The giant was embarking upon investigations, there could be no doubt. His mind, it became manifest, was throwing up questions. He put them to few people as yet, but they troubled him. His mother, one gathers, sometimes came in for cross-examination.

He used to come into the yard behind his mother's cottage, and, after a careful inspection of the ground for hens and chicks, he would sit down slowly with his back against the barn. In a minute the chicks, who liked him, would be pecking all over him at the mossy chalk-mud in the seams of his clothing, and if it was blowing up for wet, Mrs. Caddles' kitten, who never lost her confidence in him, would assume a sinuous form and start scampering into the cottage, up to the kitchen fender, round, out, up his leg, up his body, right up to his shoulder, meditative moment, and then scat! back again, and so on. Sometimes she would stick her claws in his face out of sheer gaiety of heart, but he never dared to touch her because of the uncertain weight of his hand upon a creature so frail. Besides, he rather liked to be tickled. And after a time he would put some clumsy questions to his mother.

"Mother," he would say, "if it's good to work, why doesn't every one work?"

His mother would look up at him and answer, "It's good for the likes of us."

He would meditate, "Why?"

And going unanswered, "What's work for, mother? Why do I cut chalk and you wash clothes, day after day, while Lady Wondershoot goes about in her carriage, mother, and travels off to those beautiful foreign countries you and I mustn't see, mother?"

"She's a lady," said Mrs. Caddles.

"Oh," said young Caddles, and meditated profoundly.

"If there wasn't gentlefolks to make work for us to do," said Mrs.Caddles, "how should we poor people get a living?"

This had to be digested.

"Mother," he tried again; "if there wasn't any gentlefolks, wouldn't things belong to people like me and you, and if they did—"

"Lord sakes and drat the Boy!" Mrs. Caddles would say—she had with the help of a good memory become quite a florid and vigorous individuality since Mrs. Skinner died. "Since your poor dear grandma was took, there's no abiding you. Don't you arst no questions and you won't be told no lies. If once I was to start out answerin' you serious, y'r father 'd 'ave to go' and arst some one else for 'is supper—let alone finishing the washin'."

"All right, mother," he would say, after a wondering stare at her. "I didn't mean to worry."

And he would go on thinking.

V.

He was thinking too four years after, when the Vicar, now no longer ripe but over-ripe, saw him for the last time of all. You figure the old gentleman visibly a little older now, slacker in his girth, a little coarsened and a little weakened in his thought and speech, with a quivering shakiness in his hand and a quivering shakiness in his convictions, but his eye still bright and merry for all the trouble the Food had caused his village and himself. He had been frightened at times and disturbed, but was he not alive still and the same still? and fifteen long years—a fair sample of eternity—had turned the trouble into use and wont.

"It was a disturbance, I admit," he would say, "and things are different—different in many ways. There was a time when a boy could weed, but now a man must go out with axe and crowbar— in some places down by the thickets at least. And it's a little strange still to us old-fashioned people for all this valley, even what used to be the river bed before they irrigated, to be under wheat—as it is this year—twenty-five feet high. They used the old-fashioned scythe here twenty years ago, and they would bring home the harvest on a wain—rejoicing—in a simple honest fashion. A little simple drunkenness, a little frank love-making, to conclude … poor dear Lady Wondershoot—she didn't like these Innovations. Very conservative, poor dear lady! A touch of the eighteenth century about her, I always Said. Her language for example … Bluff vigour …

"She died comparatively poor. These big weeds got into her garden. She was not one of these gardening women, but she liked her garden in order—things growing where they were planted and as they were planted—under control … The way things grew was unexpected—upset her ideas … She didn't like the perpetual invasion of this young monster—at last she began to fancy he was always gaping at her over her wall … She didn't like his being nearly as high as her house … Jarred with her sense of proportion. Poor dear lady! I had hoped she would last my time. It was the big cockchafers we had for a year or so that decided her. They came from the giant larvae— nasty things as big as rats—in the valley turf …

"And the ants no doubt weighed with her also.

"Since everything was upset and there was no peace and quietness anywhere now, she said she thought she might just as well be at Monte Carlo as anywhere else. And she went.

"She played pretty boldly, I'm told. Died in a hotel there. Very sad end... Exile... Not—not what one considers meet... A natural leader of our English people... Uprooted. So I...

"Yet after all," harped the Vicar, "it comes to very little. A nuisance of course. Children cannot run about so freely as they used to do, what with ant bites and so forth. Perhaps it's as well ... There used to be talk—as though this stuff would revolutionise everything ... But there is something that defies all these forces of the New ... I don't know of course. I'm not one of your modern philosophers—explain everything with ether and atoms. Evolution. Rubbish like that. What I mean is something the 'Ologies don't include. Matter of reason—not understanding. Ripe wisdom. Human nature. Aere perennius. ... Call it what you will."

And so at last it came to the last time.

The Vicar had no intimation of what lay so close upon him. He did his customary walk, over by Farthing Down, as he had done it for more than a score of years, and so to the place whence he would watch young Caddles. He did the rise over by the chalk-pit crest a little puffily—he had long since lost the Muscular Christian stride of early days; but Caddles was not at his work, and then, as he skirted the thicket of giant bracken that was beginning to obscure and overshadow the Hanger, he came upon the monster's huge form seated on the hill—brooding as it were upon the world. Caddles' knees were drawn up, his cheek was on his hand, his head a little aslant. He sat with his shoulder towards the Vicar, so that those perplexed eyes could not be seen. He must have been thinking very intently—at any rate he was sitting very still ...

He never turned round. He never knew that the Vicar, who had played so large a part in shaping his life, looked then at him for the very last of innumerable times—did not know even that he was there. (So it is so many partings happen.) The Vicar was struck at the time by the fact that, after all, no one on earth had the slightest idea of what this great monster thought about when he saw fit to rest from his labours. But he was too indolent to follow up that new theme that day; he fell back from its suggestion into his older grooves of thought.

"Aere-perennius," he whispered, walking slowly homeward by a path that no longer ran straight athwart the turf after its former fashion, but wound circuitously to avoid new sprung tussocks of giant grass. "No! nothing is changed. Dimensions are nothing. The simple round, the common way—"

And that night, quite painlessly, and all unknowing, he himself went the common way—out of this Mystery of Change he had spent his life in denying.

They buried him in the churchyard of Cheasing Eyebright, near to the largest yew, and the modest tombstone bearing his epitaph— it ended with: Ut in Principio, nunc est et semper—was almost immediately hidden from the eye of man by a spread of giant, grey tasselled grass too stout for scythe or sheep, that came sweeping like a fog over the village out of the germinating moisture of the valley meadows in which the Food of the Gods had been working.

BOOK III.
HE HARVEST OF THE FOOD

CHAPTER THE FIRST.
THE ALTERED WORLD.

I.

Change played in its new fashion with the world for twenty years. To most men the new things came little by little and day by day, remarkably enough, but not so abruptly as to overwhelm. But to one man at least the full accumulation of those two decades of the Food's work was to be revealed suddenly and amazingly in one day. For our purpose it is convenient to take him for that one day and to tell something of the things he saw. This man was a convict, a prisoner for life—his crime is no concern of ours—whom the law saw fit to pardon after twenty years. One summer morning this poor wretch, who had left the world a young man of three-and-twenty, found himself thrust out again from the grey simplicity of toil and discipline, that had become his life, into a dazzling freedom. They had put unaccustomed clothes upon him; his hair had been growing for some weeks, and he had parted it now for some days, and there he stood, in a sort of shabby and clumsy newness of body and mind, blinking with his eyes and blinking indeed with his soul, outside again, trying to realise one incredible thing, that after all he was again for a little while in the world of life, and for all other incredible things, totally unprepared. He was so fortunate as to have a brother who cared enough for their distant common memories to come and meet him and clasp his hand—a brother he had left a little lad, and who was now a bearded prosperous man—whose very eyes were unfamiliar. And together he and this stranger from his kindred came down into the town of Dover, saying little to one another and feeling many things.

They sat for a space in a public-house, the one answering the questions of the other about this person and that, reviving queer old points of view, brushing aside endless new aspects and new perspectives, and then it was time to go to the station and take the London train. Their names and the personal things they had to talk of do not matter to our story, but only the changes and all the strangeness that this poor returning soul found in the once familiar world.

In Dover itself he remarked little except the goodness of beer from pewter—never before had there been such a draught of beer, and it brought tears of gratitude to his eyes. "Beer's as good as ever," said he, believing it infinitely better....

It was only as the train rattled them past Folkestone that he could look out beyond his more immediate emotions, to see what had happened to the world. He peered out of the window. "It's sunny," he said for the twelfth time. "I couldn't ha' had better weather." And then for the first time it dawned upon him that there were novel disproportions in the world. "Lord sakes," he cried, sitting up and looking animated for the first time, "but them's mortal great thissels growing out there on the bank by that broom. If so be they be thissels? Or 'ave I been forgetting?" But they were thistles, and what he took for tall bushes of broom was the new grass, and amidst these things a company of British soldiers—red-coated as ever—was skirmishing in accordance with the directions of the drill book that had been partially revised after the Boer War. Then whack! into a tunnel, and then into Sandling Junction, which was now embedded and dark—its lamps were all alight—in a great thicket of rhododendron that had crept out of some adjacent gardens and grown enormously up the valley. There was a train of trucks on the Sandgate siding piled high with rhododendron logs, and here it was the returning citizen heard first of Boomfood.

As they sped out into a country again that seemed absolutely unchanged, the two brothers were hard at their explanations. The one was full of eager, dull questions; the other had never thought, had never troubled to see the thing as a single fact, and he was allusive and difficult to follow. "It's this here Boomfood stuff," he said, touching his bottom rock of knowledge. "Don't you know? 'Aven't they told you—any of 'em? Boomfood! You know—Boomfood. What all the election's about. Scientific sort of stuff. 'Asn't no one ever told you?"

He thought prison had made his brother a fearful duffer not to know that.

They made wide shots at each other by way of question and answer. Between these scraps of talk were intervals of window-gazing. At first the man's interest in things was vague and general. His imagination had been busy with what old so-and-so would say, how so-and-so would look, how he would say to all and sundry certain things that would present his "putting away" in a mitigated light. This Boomfood came in at first as it were a thing in an odd paragraph of the newspapers, then as a source of intellectual difficulty with his brother. But it came to him presently that Boomfood was persistently coming in upon any topic he began.

In those days the world was a patchwork of transition, so that this great new fact came to him in a series of shocks of contrast. The process of change had not been uniform; it had spread from one centre of distribution here and another centre there. The country was in patches: great areas where the Food was still to come, and areas where it was already in the soil and in the air, sporadic and contagious. It was a bold new motif creeping in among ancient and venerable airs.

The contrast was very vivid indeed along the line from Dover to London at that time. For a space they traversed just such a country-side as he had known since his childhood, the small oblongs of field, hedge-lined, of a size for pigmy horses to plough, the little roads three cart-widths wide, the elms and oaks and poplars dotting these fields about, little thickets of willow beside the streams; ricks of hay no higher than a giant's knees, dolls' cottages with diamond panes, brickfields, and straggling village streets, the larger houses of the petty great, flower-grown railway banks, garden-set stations, and all the little things of the vanished nineteenth century still holding out against Immensity. Here and there would be a patch of wind-sown, wind-tattered giant thistle defying the axe; here and there a ten-foot puff-ball or the ashen stems of some burnt-out patch of monster grass; but that was all there was to hint at the coming of the Food.

For a couple of score of miles there was nothing else to foreshadow in any way the strange bigness of the wheat and of the weeds that were hidden from him not a dozen miles from his route just over the hills in the Cheasing Eyebright valley. And then presently the traces of the Food would begin. The first striking thing was the great new viaduct at Tonbridge, where the swamp of the choked Medway (due to a giant variety of Chara) began in those days. Then again the little country, and then, as the petty multitudinous immensity of London spread out under its haze, the traces of man's fight to keep out greatness became abundant and incessant.

In that south-eastern region of London at that time, and all about where Cossar and his children lived, the Food had become mysteriously insurgent at a hundred points; the little life went on amidst daily portents that only the deliberation of their increase, the slow parallel growth of usage to their presence, had robbed of their warning. But this returning citizen peered out to see for the first time the facts of the Food strange and predominant, scarred and blackened areas, big unsightly defences and preparations, barracks and arsenals that this subtle, persistent influence had forced into the life of men.

Here, on an ampler scale, the experience of the first Experimental Farm had been repeated time and again. It had been in the inferior and accidental things of life—under foot and in waste places, irregularly and irrelevantly—that the coming of a new force and new issues had first declared itself. There were great evil-smelling yards and enclosures where some invincible jungle of weed furnished fuel for gigantic machinery (little cockneys came to stare at its clangorous oiliness and tip the men a sixpence); there were roads and tracks for big motors and vehicles—roads made of the interwoven fibres of hypertrophied hemp; there were towers containing steam sirens that could yell at once and warn the world against any new insurgence of vermin, or, what was queerer, venerable church towers conspicuously fitted with a mechanical scream. There were little red-painted refuge huts and garrison shelters, each with its 300-yard rifle range, where the riflemen practised daily with soft-nosed ammunition at targets in the shape of monstrous rats.

Six times since the day of the Skinners there had been outbreaks of giant rats—each time from the south-west London sewers, and now they were as much an accepted fact there as tigers in the delta by Calcutta....

The man's brother had bought a paper in a heedless sort of way at Sandling, and at last this chanced to catch the eye of the released man. He opened the unfamiliar sheets—they seemed to him to be smaller, more numerous, and different in type from the papers of the times before—and he found himself confronted with innumerable pictures about things so strange as to be uninteresting, and with tall columns of printed matter whose headings, for the most part, were as unmeaning as though they had been written in a foreign tongue—"Great Speech by Mr. Caterham"; "The Boomfood Laws."

"Who's this here Caterham?" he asked, in an attempt to make conversation.

"He's all right," said his brother.

"Ah! Sort of politician, eh?"

"Goin' to turn out the Government. Jolly well time he did."

"Ah!" He reflected. "I suppose all the lot I used to know—Chamberlain, Rosebery—all that lot—What?"

His brother had grasped his wrist and pointed out of the window.

"That's the Cossars!" The eyes of the released prisoner followed the finger's direction and saw—

"My Gawd!" he cried, for the first time really overcome with amazement. The paper dropped into final forgottenness between his feet. Through the trees he could see very distinctly, standing in an easy attitude, the legs wide apart and the hand grasping a ball as if about to throw it, a gigantic human figure a good forty feet high. The figure glittered in the sunlight, clad in a suit of woven white metal and belted with a broad belt of steel. For a moment it focussed all attention, and then the eye was wrested to another more distant Giant who stood prepared to catch, and it became apparent that the whole area of that great bay in the hills just north of Sevenoaks had been scarred to gigantic ends.

A hugely banked entrenchment overhung the chalk pit, in which stood the house, a monstrous squat Egyptian shape that Cossar had built for his sons when the Giant Nursery had served its turn, and behind was a great dark shed that might have covered a cathedral, in which a spluttering incandescence came and went, and from out of which came a Titanic hammering to beat upon the ear. Then the attention leapt back to the giant as the great ball of iron-bound timber soared up out of his hand.

The two men stood up and stared. The ball seemed as big as a cask.

"Caught!" cried the man from prison, as a tree blotted out the thrower.

The train looked on these things only for the fraction of a minute and then passed behind trees into the Chislehurst tunnel. "My Gawd!" said the man from prison again, as the darkness closed about them. "Why! that chap was as 'igh as a 'ouse."

"That's them young Cossars," said his brother, jerking his head allusively—"what all this trouble's about...."

They emerged again to discover more siren-surmounted towers, more red huts, and then the clustering villas of the outer suburbs. The art of bill-sticking had lost nothing in the interval, and from countless tall hoardings, from house ends, from palings, and a hundred such points of vantage came the polychromatic appeals of the great Boomfood election. "Caterham," "Boomfood," and "Jack the Giant-killer" again and again and again, and monstrous caricatures and distortions—a hundred varieties of misrepresentations of those great and shining figures they had passed so nearly only a few minutes before....

II.

It had been the purpose of the younger brother to do a very magnificent thing, to celebrate this return to life by a dinner at some restaurant of indisputable quality, a dinner that should be followed by all that glittering succession of impressions the Music Halls of those days were so capable of giving. It was a worthy plan to wipe off the more superficial stains of the prison house by this display of free indulgence; but so far as the second item went the plan was changed. The dinner stood, but there was a desire already more powerful than the appetite for shows, already more efficient in turning the man's mind away from his grim prepossession with his past than any theatre could be, and that was an enormous curiosity and perplexity about this Boomfood and these Boom children—this new portentous giantry that seemed to dominate the world. "I 'aven't the 'ang of 'em," he said. "They disturve me."

His brother had that fineness of mind that can even set aside a contemplated hospitality. "It's your evening, dear old boy," he said. "We'll try to get into the mass meeting at the People's Palace."

And at last the man from prison had the luck to find himself wedged into a packed multitude and staring from afar at a little brightly lit platform under an organ and a gallery. The organist had been playing something that had set boots tramping as the people swarmed in; but that was over now.

Hardly had the man from prison settled into place and done his quarrel with an importunate stranger who elbowed, before Caterham came. He walked out of a shadow towards the middle of the platform, the most insignificant little pigmy, away there in the distance, a little black figure with a pink dab for a face,—in profile one saw his quite distinctive aquiline nose—a little figure that trailed after it most inexplicably—a cheer. A cheer it was that began away there and grew and spread. A little spluttering of voices about the platform at first that suddenly leapt up into a flame of sound and swept athwart the whole mass of humanity within the building and without. How they cheered! Hooray! Hooray!

No one in all those myriads cheered like the man from prison. The tears poured down his face, and he only stopped cheering at last because the thing had choked him. You must have been in prison as long as he before you can understand, or even begin to understand, what it means to a man to let his lungs go in a crowd. (But for all that he did not even pretend to himself that he knew what all this emotion was about.) Hooray! O God!—Hoo-ray!

And then a sort of silence. Caterham had subsided to a conspicuous patience, and subordinate and inaudible persons were saying and doing formal and insignificant things. It was like hearing voices through the noise of leaves in spring. "Wawawawa—-" What did it matter? People in the audience talked to one another. "Wawawawawa—-" the thing went on. Would that grey-headed duffer never have done? Interrupting? Of course they were interrupting. "Wa, wa, wa, wa—-" But shall we hear Caterham any better?

Meanwhile at any rate there was Caterham to stare at, and one could stand and study the distant prospect of the great man's features. He was easy to draw was this man, and already the world had him to study at leisure on lamp chimneys and children's plates, on Anti-Boomfood medals and Anti-Boomfood flags, on the selvedges of Caterham silks and cottons and in the linings of Good Old English Caterham hats. He pervades all the caricature of that time. One sees him as a sailor standing to an old-fashioned gun, a port-fire labelled "New Boomfood Laws" in his hand; while in the sea wallows that huge, ugly, threatening monster, "Boomfood;" or he is cap-a-pie in armour, St. George's cross on shield and helm, and a cowardly titanic Caliban sitting amidst desecrations at the mouth of a horrid cave declines his gauntlet of the "New Boomfood Regulations;" or he comes flying down as Perseus and rescues a chained and beautiful Andromeda (labelled distinctly about her belt as "Civilisation") from a wallowing waste of sea monster bearing upon its various necks and claws "Irreligion," "Trampling Egotism," "Mechanism," "Monstrosity," and the like. But it was as "Jack the Giant-killer" that the popular imagination considered Caterham most correctly cast, and it was in the vein of a Jack the Giant-killer poster that the man from prison, enlarged that distant miniature.

The "Wawawawa" came abruptly to an end.

He's done. He's sitting down. Yes! No! Yes! It's Caterham! "Caterham!""Caterham!" And then came the cheers.

It takes a multitude to make such a stillness as followed that disorder of cheering. A man alone in a wilderness;—it's stillness of a sort no doubt, but he hears himself breathe, he hears himself move, he hears all sorts of things. Here the voice of Caterham was the one single thing heard, a thing very bright and clear, like a little light burning in a black velvet recess. Hear indeed! One heard him as though he spoke at one's elbow.

It was stupendously effective to the man from prison, that gesticulating little figure in a halo of light, in a halo of rich and swaying sounds; behind it, partially effaced as it were, sat its supporters on the platform, and in the foreground was a wide perspective of innumerable backs and profiles, a vast multitudinous attention. That little figure seemed to have absorbed the substance from them all.

Caterham spoke of our ancient institutions. "Earearear," roared the crowd. "Ear! ear!" said the man from prison. He spoke of our ancient spirit of order and justice. "Earearear!" roared the crowd. "Ear! Ear!" cried the man from prison, deeply moved. He spoke of the wisdom of our forefathers, of the slow growth of venerable institutions, of moral and social traditions, that fitted our English national characteristics as the skin fits the hand. "Ear! Ear!" groaned the man from prison, with tears of excitement on his cheeks. And now all these things were to go into the melting pot. Yes, into the melting pot! Because three men in London twenty years ago had seen fit to mix something indescribable in a bottle, all the order and sanctity of things—Cries of "No! No!"—Well, if it was not to be so, they must exert themselves, they must say good-bye to hesitation—Here there came a gust of cheering. They must say good-bye to hesitation and half measures.

"We have heard, gentlemen," cried Caterham, "of nettles that become giant nettles. At first they are no more than other nettles—little plants that a firm hand may grasp and wrench away; but if you leave them—if you leave them, they grow with such a power of poisonous expansion that at last you must needs have axe and rope, you must needs have danger to life and limb, you must needs have toil and distress—men may be killed in their felling, men may be killed in their felling—-"

There came a stir and interruption, and then the man from prison heard Caterham's voice again, ringing clear and strong: "Learn about Boomfood from Boomfood itself and—" He paused—"Grasp your nettle before it is too late!"

He stopped and stood wiping his lips. "A crystal," cried some one, "a crystal," and then came that same strange swift growth to thunderous tumult, until the whole world seemed cheering....

The man from prison came out of the hall at last, marvellously stirred, and with that in his face that marks those who have seen a vision. He knew, every one knew; his ideas were no longer vague. He had come back to a world in crisis, to the immediate decision of a stupendous issue. He must play his part in the great conflict like a man—like a free, responsible man. The antagonism presented itself as a picture. On the one hand those easy gigantic mail-clad figures of the morning—one saw them now in a different light—on the other this little black-clad gesticulating creature under the limelight, that pigmy thing with its ordered flow of melodious persuasion, its little, marvellously penetrating voice, John Caterham—"Jack the Giant-killer." They must all unite to "grasp the nettle" before it was "too late."

III.

The tallest and strongest and most regarded of all the children of the Food were the three sons of Cossar. The mile or so of land near Sevenoaks in which their boyhood passed became so trenched, so dug out and twisted about, so covered with sheds and huge working models and all the play of their developing powers, it was like no other place on earth. And long since it had become too little for the things they sought to do. The eldest son was a mighty schemer of wheeled engines; he had made himself a sort of giant bicycle that no road in the world had room for, no bridge could bear. There it stood, a great thing of wheels and engines, capable of two hundred and fifty miles an hour, useless save that now and then he would mount it and fling himself backwards and forwards across that cumbered work-yard. He had meant to go around the little world with it; he had made it with that intention, while he was still no more than a dreaming boy. Now its spokes were rusted deep red like wounds, wherever the enamel had been chipped away.

"You must make a road for it first, Sonnie," Cossar had said, "before you can do that."

So one morning about dawn the young giant and his brothers had set to work to make a road about the world. They seem to have had an inkling of opposition impending, and they had worked with remarkable vigour. The world had discovered them soon enough, driving that road as straight as a flight of a bullet towards the English Channel, already some miles of it levelled and made and stamped hard. They had been stopped before midday by a vast crowd of excited people, owners of land, land agents, local authorities, lawyers, policemen, soldiers even.

"We're making a road," the biggest boy had explained.

"Make a road by all means," said the leading lawyer on the ground, "but please respect the rights of other people. You have already infringed the private rights of twenty-seven private proprietors; let alone the special privileges and property of an urban district board, nine parish councils, a county council, two gasworks, and a railway company...."

"Goodney!" said the elder boy Cossar.

"You will have to stop it."

"But don't you want a nice straight road in the place of all these rotten rutty little lanes?"

"I won't say it wouldn't be advantageous, but—"

"It isn't to be done," said the eldest Cossar boy, picking up his tools.

"Not in this way," said the lawyer, "certainly."

"How is it to be done?"

The leading lawyer's answer had been complicated and vague.

Cossar had come down to see the mischief his children had done, and reproved them severely and laughed enormously and seemed to be extremely happy over the affair. "You boys must wait a bit," he shouted up to them, "before you can do things like that."

"The lawyer told us we must begin by preparing a scheme, and getting special powers and all sorts of rot. Said it would take us years."

"We'll have a scheme before long, little boy," cried Cossar, hands to his mouth as he shouted, "never fear. For a bit you'd better play about and make models of the things you want to do."

They did as he told them like obedient sons.

But for all that the Cossar lads brooded a little.

"It's all very well," said the second to the first, "but I don't always want just to play about and plan, I want to do something real, you know. We didn't come into this world so strong as we are, just to play about in this messy little bit of ground, you know, and take little walks and keep out of the towns"—for by that time they were forbidden all boroughs and urban districts, "Doing nothing's just wicked. Can't we find out something the little people want done and do it for them— just for the fun of doing it?

"Lots of them haven't houses fit to live in," said the second boy, "Let's go and build 'em a house close up to London, that will hold heaps and heaps of them and be ever so comfortable and nice, and let's make 'em a nice little road to where they all go and do business—nice straight little road, and make it all as nice as nice. We'll make it all so clean and pretty that they won't any of them be able to live grubby and beastly like most of them do now. Water enough for them to wash with, we'll have—you know they're so dirty now that nine out of ten of their houses haven't even baths in them, the filthy little skunks! You know, the ones that have baths spit insults at the ones that haven't, instead of helping them to get them—and call 'em the Great Unwashed—-You know. We'll alter all that. And we'll make electricity light and cook and clean up for them, and all. Fancy! They make their women—women who are going to be mothers—crawl about and scrub floors!

"We could make it all beautifully. We could bank up a valley in that range of hills over there and make a nice reservoir, and we could make a big place here to generate our electricity and have it all simply lovely. Couldn't we, brother? And then perhaps they'd let us do some other things."

"Yes," said the elder brother, "we could do it very nice for them."

"Then let's," said the second brother.

"I don't mind," said the elder brother, and looked about for a handy tool.

And that led to another dreadful bother.

Agitated multitudes were at them in no time, telling them for a thousand reasons to stop, telling them to stop for no reason at all—babbling, confused, and varied multitudes. The place they were building was too high—it couldn't possibly be safe. It was ugly; it interfered with the letting of proper-sized houses in the neighbourhood; it ruined the tone of the neighbourhood; it was unneighbourly; it was contrary to the Local Building Regulations; it infringed the right of the local authority to muddle about with a minute expensive electric supply of its own; it interfered with the concerns of the local water company.

Local Government Board clerks roused themselves to judicial obstruction. The little lawyer turned up again to represent about a dozen threatened interests; local landowners appeared in opposition; people with mysterious claims claimed to be bought off at exorbitant rates; the Trades Unions of all the building trades lifted up collective voices; and a ring of dealers in all sorts of building material became a bar. Extraordinary associations of people with prophetic visions of aesthetic horrors rallied to protect the scenery of the place where they would build the great house, of the valley where they would bank up the water. These last people were absolutely the worst asses of the lot, the Cossar boys considered. That beautiful house of the Cossar boys was just like a walking-stick thrust into a wasps' nest, in no time.

"I never did!" said the elder boy.

"We can't go on," said the second brother.

"Rotten little beasts they are," said the third of the brothers; "we can't do anything!"

"Even when it's for their own comfort. Such a nice place we'd have made for them too."

"They seem to spend their silly little lives getting in each other's way," said the eldest boy, "Rights and laws and regulations and rascalities; it's like a game of spellicans.... Well, anyhow, they'll have to live in their grubby, dirty, silly little houses for a bit longer. It's very evident we can't go on with this."

And the Cossar children left that great house unfinished, a mere hole of foundations and the beginning of a wall, and sulked back to their big enclosure. After a time the hole was filled with water and with stagnation and weeds, and vermin, and the Food, either dropped there by the sons of Cossar or blowing thither as dust, set growth going in its usual fashion. Water voles came out over the country and did infinite havoc, and one day a farmer caught his pigs drinking there, and instantly and with great presence of mind—for he knew: of the great hog of Oakham—slew them all. And from that deep pool it was the mosquitoes came, quite terrible mosquitoes, whose only virtue was that the sons of Cossar, after being bitten for a little, could stand the thing no longer, but chose a moonlight night when law and order were abed and drained the water clean away into the river by Brook.

But they left the big weeds and the big water voles and all sorts of big undesirable things still living and breeding on the site they had chosen—the site on which the fair great house of the little people might have towered to heaven ...

IV.

That had been in the boyhood of the Sons, but now they were nearly men, And the chains had been tightening upon them and tightening with every year of growth. Each year they grew, and the Food spread and great things multiplied, each year the stress and tension rose. The Food had been at first for the great mass of mankind a distant marvel, and now It was coming home to every threshold, and threatening, pressing against and distorting the whole order of life. It blocked this, it overturned that; it changed natural products, and by changing natural products it stopped employments and threw men out of work by the hundred thousands; it swept over boundaries and turned the world of trade into a world of cataclysms: no wonder mankind hated it.

And since it is easier to hate animate than inanimate things, animals more than plants, and one's fellow-men more completely than any animals, the fear and trouble engendered by giant nettles and six-foot grass blades, awful insects and tiger-like vermin, grew all into one great power of detestation that aimed itself with a simple directness at that scattered band of great human beings, the Children of the Food. That hatred had become the central force in political affairs. The old party lines had been traversed and effaced altogether under the insistence of these newer issues, and the conflict lay now with the party of the temporisers, who were for putting little political men to control and regulate the Food, and the party of reaction for whom Caterharn spoke, speaking always with a more sinister ambiguity, crystallising his intention first in one threatening phrase and then another, now that men must "prune the bramble growths," now that they must find a "cure for elephantiasis," and at last upon the eve of the election that they must "Grasp the nettle."

One day the three sons of Cossar, who were now no longer boys but men, sat among the masses of their futile work and talked together after their fashion of all these things. They had been working all day at one of a series of great and complicated trenches their father had bid them make, and now it was sunset, and they sat in the little garden space before the great house and looked at the world and rested, until the little servants within should say their food was ready.

You must figure these mighty forms, forty feet high the least of them was, reclining on a patch of turf that would have seemed a stubble of reeds to a common man. One sat up and chipped earth from his huge boots with an iron girder he grasped in his hand; the second rested on his elbow; the third whittled a pine tree into shape and made a smell of resin in the air. They were clothed not in cloth but in under-garments of woven rope and outer clothes of felted aluminium wire; they were shod with timber and iron, and the links and buttons and belts of their clothing were all of plated steel. The great single-storeyed house they lived in, Egyptian in its massiveness, half built of monstrous blocks of chalk and half excavated from the living rock of the hill, had a front a full hundred feet in height, and beyond, the chimneys and wheels, the cranes and covers of their work sheds rose marvellously against the sky. Through a circular window in the house there was visible a spout from which some white-hot metal dripped and dripped in measured drops into a receptacle out of sight. The place was enclosed and rudely fortified by monstrous banks of earth, backed with steel both over the crests of the Downs above and across the dip of the valley. It needed something of common size to mark the nature of the scale. The train that came rattling from Sevenoaks athwart their vision, and presently plunged into the tunnel out of their sight, looked by contrast with them like some small-sized automatic toy.

"They have made all the woods this side of Ightham out of bounds," said one, "and moved the board that was out by Knockholt two miles and more this way."

"It is the least they could do," said the youngest, after a pause. "They are trying to take the wind out of Caterham's sails."

"It's not enough for that, and—it is almost too much for us," said the third.

"They are cutting us off from Brother Redwood. Last time I went to him the red notices had crept a mile in, either way. The road to him along the Downs is no more than a narrow lane."

The speaker thought. "What has come to our brother Redwood?"

"Why?" said the eldest brother.

The speaker hacked a bough from his pine. "He was like—as though he wasn't awake. He didn't seem to listen to what I had to say. And he said something of—love."

The youngest tapped his girder on the edge of his iron sole and laughed."Brother Redwood," he said, "has dreams."

Neither spoke for a space. Then the eldest brother said, "This cooping up and cooping up grows more than I can bear. At last, I believe, they will draw a line round our boots and tell us to live on that."

The middle brother swept aside a heap of pine boughs with one hand and shifted his attitude. "What they do now is nothing to what they will do when Caterham has power."

"If he gets power," said the youngest brother, smiting the ground with his girder.

"As he will," said the eldest, staring at his feet.

The middle brother ceased his lopping, and his eye went to the great banks that sheltered them about. "Then, brothers," he said, "our youth will be over, and, as Father Redwood said to us long ago, we must quit ourselves like men."

"Yes," said the eldest brother; "but what exactly does that mean? Just what does it mean—when that day of trouble comes?"

He too glanced at those rude vast suggestions of entrenchment about them, looking not so much at them as through them and over the hills to the innumerable multitudes beyond. Something of the same sort came into all their minds—a vision of little people coming out to war, in a flood, the little people, inexhaustible, incessant, malignant....

"They are little," said the youngest brother; "but they have numbers beyond counting, like the sands of the sea."

"They have arms—they have weapons even, that our brothers in Sunderland have made."

"Besides, Brothers, except for vermin, except for little accidents with evil things, what have we seen of killing?"

"I know," said the eldest brother. "For all that—we are what we are.When the day of trouble comes we must do the thing we have to do."

He closed his knife with a snap—the blade was the length of a man—and used his new pine staff to help himself rise. He stood up and turned towards the squat grey immensity of the house. The crimson of the sunset caught him as he rose, caught the mail and clasps about his neck and the woven metal of his arms, and to the eyes of his brother it seemed as though he was suddenly suffused with blood ...

As the young giant rose a little black figure became visible to him against that western incandescence on the top of the embankment that towered above the summit of the down. The black limbs waved in ungainly gestures. Something in the fling of the limbs suggested haste to the young giant's mind. He waved his pine mast in reply, filled the whole valley with his vast Hullo! threw a "Something's up" to his brothers, and set off in twenty-foot strides to meet and help his father.

V.

It chanced too that a young man who was not a giant was delivering his soul about these sons of Cossar just at that same time. He had come over the hills beyond Sevenoaks, he and his friend, and he it was did the talking. In the hedge as they came along they had heard a pitiful squealing, and had intervened to rescue three nestling tits from the attack of a couple of giant ants. That adventure it was had set him talking.

"Reactionary!" he was saying, as they came within sight of the Cossar encampment. "Who wouldn't be reactionary? Look at that square of ground, that space of God's earth that was once sweet and fair, torn, desecrated, disembowelled! Those sheds! That great wind-wheel! That monstrous wheeled machine! Those dykes! Look at those three monsters squatting there, plotting some ugly devilment or other! Look—look at all the land!"

His friend glanced at his face. "You have been listening to Caterham," he said.

"Using my eyes. Looking a little into the peace and order of the past we leave behind. This foul Food is the last shape of the Devil, still set as ever upon the ruin of our world. Think what the world must have been before our days, what it was still when our mothers bore us, and see it now! Think how these slopes once smiled under the golden harvest, how the hedges, full of sweet little flowers, parted the modest portion of this man from that, how the ruddy farmhouses dotted the land, and the voice of the church bells from yonder tower stilled the whole world each Sabbath into Sabbath prayer. And now, every year, still more and more of monstrous weeds, of monstrous vermin, and these giants growing all about us, straddling over us, blundering against all that is subtle and sacred in our world. Why here—Look!"

He pointed, and his friend's eyes followed the line of his white finger.

"One of their footmarks. See! It has smashed itself three feet deep and more, a pitfall for horse and rider, a trap to the unwary. There is a briar rose smashed to death; there is grass uprooted and a teazle crushed aside, a farmer's drain pipe snapped and the edge of the pathway broken down. Destruction! So they are doing all over the world, all over the order and decency the world of men has made. Trampling on all things. Reaction! What else?"

"But—reaction. What do you hope to do?"

"Stop it!" cried the young man from Oxford. "Before it is too late."

"But—-"

"It's not impossible," cried the young man from Oxford, with a jump in his voice. "We want the firm hand; we want the subtle plan, the resolute mind. We have been mealy-mouthed and weak-handed; we have trifled and temporised and the Food has grown and grown. Yet even now—"

He stopped for a moment. "This is the echo of Caterham," said his friend.

"Even now. Even now there is hope—abundant hope, if only we make sure of what we want and what we mean to destroy. The mass of people are with us, much more with us than they were a few years ago; the law is with us, the constitution and order of society, the spirit of the established religions, the customs and habits of mankind are with us—and against the Food. Why should we temporise? Why should we lie? We hate it, we don't want it; why then should we have it? Do you mean to just grizzle and obstruct passively and do nothing—till the sands are out?"

He stopped short and turned about. "Look at that grove of nettles there. In the midst of them are homes—deserted—where once clean families of simple men played out their honest lives!

"And there!" he swung round to where the young Cossars muttered to one another of their wrongs.

"Look at them! And I know their father, a brute, a sort of brute beast with an intolerant loud voice, a creature who has ran amuck in our all too merciful world for the last thirty years and more. An engineer! To him all that we hold dear and sacred is nothing. Nothing! The splendid traditions of our race and land, the noble institutions, the venerable order, the broad slow march from precedent to precedent that has made our English people great and this sunny island free—it is all an idle tale, told and done with. Some claptrap about the Future is worth all these sacred things.... The sort of man who would run a tramway over his mother's grave if he thought that was the cheapest line the tramway could take.... And you think to temporise, to make some scheme of compromise, that will enable you to live in your way while that—that machinery—lives in its. I tell you it is hopeless—hopeless. As well make treaties with a tiger! They want things monstrous—we want them sane and sweet. It is one thing or the other."

"But what can you do?"

"Much! All! Stop the Food! They are still scattered, these giants; still immature and disunited. Chain them, gag them, muzzle them. At any cost stop them. It is their world or ours! Stop the Food. Shut up these men who make it. Do anything to stop Cossar! You don't seem to remember—one generation—only one generation needs holding down, and then—Then we could level those mounds there, fill up their footsteps, take the ugly sirens from our church towers, smash all our elephant guns, and turn our faces again to the old order, the ripe old civilisation for which the soul of man is fitted."

"It's a mighty effort."

"For a mighty end. And if we don't? Don't you see the prospect before us clear as day? Everywhere the giants will increase and multiply; everywhere they will make and scatter the Food. The grass will grow gigantic in our fields, the weeds in our hedges, the vermin in the thickets, the rats in the drains. More and more and more. This is only a beginning. The insect world will rise on us, the plant world, the very fishes in the sea, will swamp and drown our ships. Tremendous growths will obscure and hide our houses, smother our churches, smash and destroy all the order of our cities, and we shall become no more than a feeble vermin under the heels of the new race. Mankind will be swamped and drowned in things of its own begetting! And all for nothing! Size! Mere size! Enlargement and da capo. Already we go picking our way among the first beginnings of the coming time. And all we do is to say 'How inconvenient!' To grumble and do nothing. No!"

He raised his hand.

"Let them do the thing they have to do! So also will I. I am for Reaction—unstinted and fearless Reaction. Unless you mean to take this Food also, what else is there to do in all the world? We have trifled in the middle ways too long. You! Trifling in the middle ways is your habit, your circle of existence, your space and time. So, not I! I am against the Food, with all my strength and purpose against the Food."

He turned on his companion's grunt of dissent. "Where are you?"

"It's a complicated business—-"

"Oh!—Driftwood!" said the young man from Oxford, very bitterly, with a fling of all his limbs. "The middle way is nothingness. It is one thing or the other. Eat or destroy. Eat or destroy! What else is there to do?"

CHAPTER THE SECOND.
THE GIANT LOVERS.

I.

Now it chanced in the days when Caterham was campaigning against the Boom-children before the General Election that was—amidst the most tragic and terrible circumstances—to bring him into power, that the giant Princess, that Serene Highness whose early nutrition had played so great a part in the brilliant career of Doctor Winkles, had come from the kingdom of her father to England, on an occasion that was deemed important. She was affianced for reasons of state to a certain Prince—and the wedding was to be made an event of international significance. There had arisen mysterious delays. Rumour and Imagination collaborated in the story and many things were said. There were suggestions of a recalcitrant Prince who declared he would not be made to look like a fool—at least to this extent. People sympathised with him. That is the most significant aspect of the affair.

Now it may seem a strange thing, but it is a fact that the giant Princess, when she came to England, knew of no other giants whatever. She had lived in a world where tact is almost a passion and reservations the air of one's life. They had kept the thing from her; they had hedged her about from sight or suspicion of any gigantic form, until her appointed coming to England was due. Until she met young Redwood she had no inkling that there was such a thing as another giant in the world.

In the kingdom of the father of the Princess there were wild wastes of upland and mountains where she had been accustomed to roam freely. She loved the sunrise and the sunset and all the great drama of the open heavens more than anything else in the world, but among a people at once so democratic and so vehemently loyal as the English her freedom was much restricted. People came in brakes, in excursion trains, in organised multitudes to see her; they would cycle long distances to stare at her, and it was necessary to rise betimes if she would walk in peace. It was still near the dawn that morning when young Redwood came upon her.

The Great Park near the Palace where she lodged stretched, for a score of miles and more, west and south of the western palace gates. The chestnut trees of its avenues reached high above her head. Each one as she passed it seemed to proffer a more abundant wealth of blossom. For a time she was content with sight and scent, but at last she was won over by these offers, and set herself so busily to choose and pick that she did not perceive young Redwood until he was close upon her.

She moved among the chestnut trees, with the destined lover drawing near to her, unanticipated, unsuspected. She thrust her hands in among the branches, breaking them and gathering them. She was alone in the world. Then—-

She looked up, and in that moment she was mated.

We must needs put our imaginations to his stature to see the beauty he saw. That unapproachable greatness that prevents our immediate sympathy with her did not exist for him. There she stood, a gracious girl, the first created being that had ever seemed a mate for him, light and slender, lightly clad, the fresh breeze of the dawn moulding the subtly folding robe upon her against the soft strong lines of her form, and with a great mass of blossoming chestnut branches in her hands. The collar of her robe opened to show the whiteness of her neck and a soft shadowed roundness that passed out of sight towards her shoulders. The breeze had stolen a strand or so of her hair too, and strained its red-tipped brown across her cheek. Her eyes were open blue, and her lips rested always in the promise of a smile as she reached among the branches.

She turned upon him with a start, saw him, and for a space they regarded one another. For her, the sight of him was so amazing, so incredible, as to be, for some moments at least, terrible. He came to her with the shock of a supernatural apparition; he broke all the established law of her world. He was a youth of one-and-twenty then, slenderly built, with his father's darkness and his father's gravity. He was clad in a sober soft brown leather, close-fitting easy garments, and in brown hose, that shaped him bravely. His head went uncovered in all weathers. They stood regarding one another—she incredulously amazed, and he with his heart beating fast. It was a moment without a prelude, the cardinal meeting of their lives.

For him there was less surprise. He had been seeking her, and yet his heart beat fast. He came towards her, slowly, with his eyes upon her face.

"You are the Princess," he said. "My father has told me. You are thePrincess who was given the Food of the Gods."

"I am the Princess—yes," she said, with eyes of wonder. "But—what are you?"

"I am the son of the man who made the Food of the Gods."

"The Food of the Gods!"

"Yes, the Food of the Gods."

"But—"

Her face expressed infinite perplexity.

"What? I don't understand. The Food of the Gods?"

"You have not heard?"

"The Food of the Gods! No!"

She found herself trembling violently. The colour left her face. "I did not know," she said. "Do you mean—?"

He waited for her.

"Do you mean there are other—giants?"

He repeated, "Did you not know?"

And she answered, with the growing amazement of realisation, "No!"

The whole world and all the meaning of the world was changing for her. A branch of chestnut slipped from her hand. "Do you mean to say," she repeated stupidly, "that there are other giants in the world? That some food—?"

He caught her amazement.

"You know nothing?" he cried. "You have never heard of us? You, whom theFood has made akin to us!"

There was terror still in the eyes that stared at him. Her hand rose towards her throat and fell again. She whispered, "No."

It seemed to her that she must weep or faint. Then in a moment she had rule over herself and she was speaking and thinking clearly. "All this has been kept from me," she said. "It is like a dream. I have dreamt—have dreamt such things. But waking—No. Tell me! Tell me! What are you? What is this Food of the Gods? Tell me slowly—and clearly. Why have they kept it from me, that I am not alone?"

II.

"Tell me," she said, and young Redwood, tremulous and excited, set himself to tell her—it was poor and broken telling for a time—of the Food of the Gods and the giant children who were scattered over the world.

You must figure them both, flushed and startled in their bearing; getting at one another's meaning through endless half-heard, half-spoken phrases, repeating, making perplexing breaks and new departures—a wonderful talk, in which she awakened from the ignorance of all her life. And very slowly it became clear to her that she was no exception to the order of mankind, but one of a scattered brotherhood, who had all eaten the Food and grown for ever out of the little limits of the folk beneath their feet. Young Redwood spoke of his father, of Cossar, of the Brothers scattered throughout the country, of the great dawn of wider meaning that had come at last into the history of the world. "We are in the beginning of a beginning," he said; "this world of theirs is only the prelude to the world the Food will make.

"My father believes—and I also believe—that a time will come when littleness will have passed altogether out of the world of man,—when giants shall go freely about this earth—their earth—doing continually greater and more splendid things. But that—that is to come. We are not even the first generation of that—we are the first experiments."

"And of these things," she said, "I knew nothing!"

"There are times when it seems to me almost as if we had come too soon. Some one, I suppose, had to come first. But the world was all unprepared for our coming and for the coming of all the lesser great things that drew their greatness from the Food. There have been blunders; there have been conflicts. The little people hate our kind....

"They are hard towards us because they are so little.... And because our feet are heavy on the things that make their lives. But at any rate they hate us now; they will have none of us—only if we could shrink back to the common size of them would they begin to forgive....

"They are happy in houses that are prison cells to us; their cities are too small for us; we go in misery along their narrow ways; we cannot worship in their churches....

"We see over their walls and over their protections; we look inadvertently into their upper windows; we look over their customs; their laws are no more than a net about our feet....

"Every time we stumble we hear them shouting; every time we blunder against their limits or stretch out to any spacious act....

"Our easy paces are wild flights to them, and all they deem great and wonderful no more than dolls' pyramids to us. Their pettiness of method and appliance and imagination hampers and defeats our powers. There are no machines to the power of our hands, no helps to fit our needs. They hold our greatness in servitude by a thousand invisible bands. We are stronger, man for man, a hundred times, but we are disarmed; our very greatness makes us debtors; they claim the land we stand upon; they tax our ampler need of food and shelter, and for all these things we must toil with the tools these dwarfs can make us—and to satisfy their dwarfish fancies ...

"They pen us in, in every way. Even to live one must cross their boundaries. Even to meet you here to-day I have passed a limit. All that is reasonable and desirable in life they make out of bounds for us. We may not go into the towns; we may not cross the bridges; we may not step on their ploughed fields or into the harbours of the game they kill. I am cut off now from all our Brethren except the three sons of Cossar, and even that way the passage narrows day by day. One could think they sought occasion against us to do some more evil thing ..."

"But we are strong," she said.

"We should be strong—yes. We feel, all of us—you too I know must feel—that we have power, power to do great things, power insurgent in us. But before we can do anything—"

He flung out a hand that seemed to sweep away a world.

"Though I thought I was alone in the world," she said, after a pause, "I have thought of these things. They have taught me always that strength was almost a sin, that it was better to be little than great, that all true religion was to shelter the weak and little, encourage the weak and little, help them to multiply and multiply until at last they crawled over one another, to sacrifice all our strength in their cause. But ... always I have doubted the thing they taught."

"This life," he said, "these bodies of ours, are not for dying."

"No."

"Nor to live in futility. But if we would not do that, it is already plain to all our Brethren a conflict must come. I know not what bitterness of conflict must presently come, before the little folks will suffer us to live as we need to live. All the Brethren have thought of that. Cossar, of whom I told you: he too has thought of that."

"They are very little and weak."

"In their way. But you know all the means of death are in their hands, and made for their hands. For hundreds of thousands of years these little people, whose world we invade, have been learning how to kill one another. They are very able at that. They are able in many ways. And besides, they can deceive and change suddenly.... I do not know.... There comes a conflict. You—you perhaps are different from us. For us, assuredly, the conflict comes.... The thing they call War. We know it. In a way we prepare for it. But you know—those little people!—we do not know how to kill, at least we do not want to kill—"

"Look," she interrupted, and he heard a yelping horn.

He turned at the direction of her eyes, and found a bright yellow motor car, with dark goggled driver and fur-clad passengers, whooping, throbbing, and buzzing resentfully at his heel. He moved his foot, and the mechanism, with three angry snorts, resumed its fussy way towards the town. "Filling up the roadway!" floated up to him.

Then some one said, "Look! Did you see? There is the monster Princess over beyond the trees!" and all their goggled faces came round to stare.

"I say," said another. "That won't do ..."

"All this," she said, "is more amazing than I can tell."

"That they should not have told you," he said, and left his sentence incomplete.

"Until you came upon me, I had lived in a world where I was great—alone. I had made myself a life—for that. I had thought I was the victim of some strange freak of nature. And now my world has crumbled down, in half an hour, and I see another world, other conditions, wider possibilities—fellowship—"

"Fellowship," he answered.

"I want you to tell me more yet, and much more," she said. "You know this passes through my mind like a tale that is told. You even ... In a day perhaps, or after several days, I shall believe in you. Now— Now I am dreaming.... Listen!"

The first stroke of a clock above the palace offices far away had penetrated to them. Each counted mechanically "Seven."

"This," she said, "should be the hour of my return. They will be taking the bowl of my coffee into the hall where I sleep. The little officials and servants—you cannot dream how grave they are—will be stirring about their little duties."

"They will wonder ... But I want to talk to you."

She thought. "But I want to think too. I want now to think alone, and think out this change in things, think away the old solitude, and think you and those others into my world.... I shall go. I shall go back to-day to my place in the castle, and to-morrow, as the dawn comes, I shall come again—here."

"I shall be here waiting for you."

"All day I shall dream and dream of this new world you have given me.Even now, I can scarcely believe—"

She took a step back and surveyed him from the feet to the face. Their eyes met and locked for a moment.

"Yes," she said, with a little laugh that was half a sob. "You are real. But it is very wonderful! Do you think—indeed—? Suppose to-morrow I come and find you—a pigmy like the others... Yes, I must think. And so for to-day—as the little people do—"

She held out her hand, and for the first time they touched one another. Their hands clasped firmly and their eyes met again.

"Good-bye," she said, "for to-day. Good-bye! Good-bye, Brother Giant!"

He hesitated with some unspoken thing, and at last he answered her simply, "Good-bye."

For a space they held each other's hands, studying each the other's face. And many times after they had parted, she looked back half doubtfully at him, standing still in the place where they had met....

She walked into her apartments across the great yard of the Palace like one who walks in a dream, with a vast branch of chestnut trailing from her hand.

III.

These two met altogether fourteen times before the beginning of the end. They met in the Great Park or on the heights and among the gorges of the rusty-roaded, heathery moorland, set with dusky pine-woods, that stretched to the south-west. Twice they met in the great avenue of chestnuts, and five times near the broad ornamental water the king, her great-grandfather, had made. There was a place where a great trim lawn, set with tall conifers, sloped graciously to the water's edge, and there she would sit, and he would lie at her knees and look up in her face and talk, telling of all the things that had been, and of the work his father had set before him, and of the great and spacious dream of what the giant people should one day be. Commonly they met in the early dawn, but once they met there in the afternoon, and found presently a multitude of peering eavesdroppers about them, cyclists, pedestrians, peeping from the bushes, rustling (as sparrows will rustle about one in the London parks) amidst the dead leaves in the woods behind, gliding down the lake in boats towards a point of view, trying to get nearer to them and hear.

It was the first hint that offered of the enormous interest the countryside was taking in their meetings. And once—it was the seventh time, and it precipitated the scandal—they met out upon the breezy moorland under a clear moonlight, and talked in whispers there, for the night was warm and still.

Very soon they had passed from the realisation that in them and through them a new world of giantry shaped itself in the earth, from the contemplation of the great struggle between big and little, in which they were clearly destined to participate, to interests at once more personal and more spacious. Each time they met and talked and looked on one another, it crept a little more out of their subconscious being towards recognition, that something more dear and wonderful than friendship was between them, and walked between them and drew their hands together. And in a little while they came to the word itself and found themselves lovers, the Adam and Eve of a new race in the world.

They set foot side by side into the wonderful valley of love, with its deep and quiet places. The world changed about them with their changing mood, until presently it had become, as it were, a tabernacular beauty about their meetings, and the stars were no more than flowers of light beneath the feet of their love, and the dawn and sunset the coloured hangings by the way. They ceased to be beings of flesh and blood to one another and themselves; they passed into a bodily texture of tenderness and desire. They gave it first whispers and then silence, and drew close and looked into one another's moonlit and shadowy faces under the infinite arch of the sky. And the still black pine-trees stood about them like sentinels.

The beating steps of time were hushed into silence, and it seemed to them the universe hung still. Only their hearts were audible, beating. They seemed to be living together in a world where there is no death, and indeed so it was with them then. It seemed to them that they sounded, and indeed they sounded, such hidden splendours in the very heart of things as none have ever reached before. Even for mean and little souls, love is the revelation of splendours. And these were giant lovers who had eaten the Food of the Gods ...

* * * * *

You may imagine the spreading consternation in this ordered world when it became known that the Princess who was affianced to the Prince, the Princess, Her Serene Highness! with royal blood in her veins! met,—frequently met,—the hypertrophied offspring of a common professor of chemistry, a creature of no rank, no position, no wealth, and talked to him as though there were no Kings and Princes, no order, no reverence—nothing but Giants and Pigmies in the world, talked to him and, it was only too certain, held him as her lover.

"If those newspaper fellows get hold of it!" gasped Sir Arthur PoodleBootlick ...

"I am told—" whispered the old Bishop of Frumps.

"New story upstairs," said the first footman, as he nibbled among the dessert things. "So far as I can make out this here giant Princess—"

"They say—" said the lady who kept the stationer's shop by the main entrance to the Palace, where the little Americans get their tickets for the State Apartments ...

And then:

"We are authorised to deny—" said "Picaroon" in Gossip.

And so the whole trouble came out.

IV.

"They say that we must part," the Princess said to her lover.

"But why?" he cried. "What new folly have these people got into their heads?"

"Do you know," she asked, "that to love me—is high treason?"

"My dear," he cried; "but does it matter? What is their right—right without a shadow of reason—and their treason and their loyalty to us?"

"You shall hear," she said, and told him of the things that had been told to her.

"It was the queerest little man who came to me with a soft, beautifully modulated voice, a softly moving little gentleman who sidled into the room like a cat and put his pretty white hand up so, whenever he had anything significant to say. He is bald, but not of course nakedly bald, and his nose and face are chubby rosy little things, and his beard is trimmed to a point in quite the loveliest way. He pretended to have emotions several times and made his eyes shine. You know he is quite a friend of the real royal family here, and he called me his dear young lady and was perfectly sympathetic even from the beginning. 'My dear young lady,' he said, 'you know—you mustn't,' several times, and then, 'You owe a duty.'"

"Where do they make such men?"

"He likes it," she said.

"But I don't see—"

"He told me serious things."

"You don't think," he said, turning on her abruptly, "that there's anything in the sort of thing he said?"

"There's something in it quite certainly," said she.

"You mean—?"

"I mean that without knowing it we have been trampling on the most sacred conceptions of the little folks. We who are royal are a class apart. We are worshipped prisoners, processional toys. We pay for worship by losing—our elementary freedom. And I was to have married that Prince—You know nothing of him though. Well, a pigmy Prince. He doesn't matter.... It seems it would have strengthened the bonds between my country and another. And this country also was to profit. Imagine it!—strengthening the bonds!"

"And now?"

"They want me to go on with it—as though there was nothing between us two."

"Nothing!"

"Yes. But that isn't all. He said—"

"Your specialist in Tact?"

"Yes. He said it would be better for you, better for all the giants, if we two—abstained from conversation. That was how he put it."

"But what can they do if we don't?"

"He said you might have your freedom."

"I!"

"He said, with a stress, 'My dear young lady, it would be better, it would be more dignified, if you parted, willingly.' That was all he said. With a stress on willingly."

"But—! What business is it of these little wretches, where we love, how we love? What have they and their world to do with us?"

"They do not think that."

"Of course," he said, "you disregard all this."

"It seems utterly foolish to me."

"That their laws should fetter us! That we, at the first spring of life, should be tripped by their old engagements, their aimless institutions! Oh—! We disregard it."

"I am yours. So far—yes."

"So far? Isn't that all?"

"But they—If they want to part us—"

"What can they do?"

"I don't know. What can they do?"

"Who cares what they can do, or what they will do? I am yours and you are mine. What is there more than that? I am yours and you are mine—for ever. Do you think I will stop for their little rules, for their little prohibitions, their scarlet boards indeed!—and keep from you?"

"Yes. But still, what can they do?"

"You mean," he said, "what are we to do?"

"Yes."

"We? We can go on."

"But if they seek to prevent us?"

He clenched his hands. He looked round as if the little people were already coming to prevent them. Then turned away from her and looked about the world. "Yes," he said. "Your question was the right one. What can they do?"

"Here in this little land," she said, and stopped.He seemed to survey it all. "They are everywhere."

"But we might—"

"Whither?"

"We could go. We could swim the seas together. Beyond the seas—"

"I have never been beyond the seas."

"There are great and desolate mountains amidst which we should seem no more than little people, there are remote and deserted valleys, there are hidden lakes and snow-girdled uplands untrodden by the feet of men. There—"

"But to get there we must fight our way day after day through millions and millions of mankind."

"It is our only hope. In this crowded land there is no fastness, no shelter. What place is there for us among these multitudes? They who are little can hide from one another, but where are we to hide? There is no place where we could eat, no place where we could sleep. If we fled—night and day they would pursue our footsteps."

A thought came to him.

"There is one place," he said, "even in this island."

"Where?"

"The place our Brothers have made over beyond there. They have made great banks about their house, north and south and east and west; they have made deep pits and hidden places, and even now—one came over to me quite recently. He said—I did not altogether heed what he said then. But he spoke of arms. It may be—there—we should find shelter....

"For many days," he said, after a pause, "I have not seen our Brothers... Dear! I have been dreaming, I have been forgetting! The days have passed, and I have done nothing but look to see you again ... I must go to them and talk to them, and tell them of you and of all the things that hang over us. If they will help us, they can help us. Then indeed we might hope. I do not know how strong their place is, but certainly Cossar will have made it strong. Before all this—before you came to me, I remember now—there was trouble brewing. There was an election—when all the little people settle things, by counting heads. It must be over now. There were threats against all our race—against all our race, that is, but you. I must see our Brothers. I must tell them all that has happened between us, and all that threatens now."

V.

He did not come to their next meeting until she had waited some time. They were to meet that day about midday in a great space of park that fitted into a bend of the river, and as she waited, looking ever southward under her hand, it came to her that the world was very still, that indeed it was broodingly still. And then she perceived that, spite of the lateness of the hour, her customary retinue of voluntary spies had failed her. Left and right, when she came to look, there was no one in sight, and there was never a boat upon the silver curve of the Thames. She tried to find a reason for this strange stillness in the world....

Then, a grateful sight for her, she saw young Redwood far away over a gap in the tree masses that bounded her view.

Immediately the trees hid him, and presently he was thrusting through them and in sight again. She could see there was something different, and then she saw that he was hurrying unusually and then that he limped. He gestured to her, and she walked towards him. His face became clearer, and she saw with infinite concern that he winced at every stride.

She ran towards him, her mind full of questions and vague fear. He drew near to her and spoke without a greeting.

"Are we to part?" he panted.

"No," she answered. "Why? What is the matter?"

"But if we do not part—! It is now."

"What is the matter?"

"I do not want to part," he said. "Only—" He broke off abruptly to ask, "You will not part from me?"

She met his eyes with a steadfast look. "What has happened?" she pressed.

"Not for a time?"

"What time?"

"Years perhaps."

"Part! No!"

"You have thought?" he insisted.

"I will not part." She took his hand. "If this meant death, now, I would not let you go."

"If it meant death," he said, and she felt his grip upon her fingers.

He looked about him as if he feared to see the little people coming as he spoke. And then: "It may mean death."

"Now tell me," she said.

"They tried to stop my coming."

"How?"

"And as I came out of my workshop where I make the Food of the Gods for the Cossars to store in their camp, I found a little officer of police—a man in blue with white clean gloves—who beckoned me to stop. 'This way is closed!' said he. I thought little of that; I went round my workshop to where another road runs west, and there was another officer. 'This road is closed!' he said, and added: 'All the roads are closed!'"

"And then?"

"I argued with him a little. 'They are public roads!' I said.

"'That's it,' said he. 'You spoil them for the public.'

"'Very well,' said I, 'I'll take the fields,' and then, up leapt others from behind a hedge and said, 'These fields are private.'

"'Curse your public and private,' I said, 'I'm going to my Princess,' and I stooped down and picked him up very gently—kicking and shouting—and put him out of my way. In a minute all the fields about me seemed alive with running men. I saw one on horseback galloping beside me and reading something as he rode—shouting it. He finished and turned and galloped away from me—head down. I couldn't make it out. And then behind me I heard the crack of guns."

"Guns!"

"Guns—just as they shoot at the rats. The bullets came through the air with a sound like things tearing: one stung me in the leg."

"And you?"

"Came on to you here and left them shouting and running and shooting behind me. And now—"

"Now?"

"It is only the beginning. They mean that we shall part. Even now they are coming after me."

"We will not."

"No. But if we will not part—then you must come with me to ourBrothers."

"Which way?" she said.

"To the east. Yonder is the way my pursuers will be coming. This then is the way we must go. Along this avenue of trees. Let me go first, so that if they are waiting—"

He made a stride, but she had seized his arm.

"No," cried she. "I come close to you, holding you. Perhaps I am royal, perhaps I am sacred. If I hold you—Would God we could fly with my arms about you!—it may be, they will not shoot at you—"

She clasped his shoulder and seized his hand as she spoke; she pressed herself nearer to him. "It may be they will not shoot you," she repeated, and with a sudden passion of tenderness he took her into his arms and kissed her cheek. For a space he held her.

"Even if it is death," she whispered.

She put her hands about his neck and lifted her face to his.

"Dearest, kiss me once more."

He drew her to him. Silently they kissed one another on the lips, and for another moment clung to one another. Then hand in hand, and she striving always to keep her body near to his, they set forward if haply they might reach the camp of refuge the sons of Cossar had made, before the pursuit of the little people overtook them.

And as they crossed the great spaces of the park behind the castle there came horsemen galloping out from among the trees and vainly seeking to keep pace with their giant strides. And presently ahead of them were houses, and men with guns running out of the houses. At the sight of that, though he sought to go on and was even disposed to fight and push through, she made him turn aside towards the south.

As they fled a bullet whipped by them overhead.

CHAPTER THE THIRD.
YOUNG CADDLES IN LONDON.

I.

All unaware of the trend of events, unaware of the laws that were closing in upon all the Brethren, unaware indeed that there lived a Brother for him on the earth, young Caddles chose this time to come out of his chalk pit and see the world. His brooding came at last to that. There was no answer to all his questions in Cheasing Eyebright; the new Vicar was less luminous even than the old, and the riddle of his pointless labour grew at last to the dimensions of exasperation. "Why should I work in this pit day after day?" he asked. "Why should I walk within bounds and be refused all the wonders of the world beyond there? What have I done, to be condemned to this?"

And one day he stood up, straightened his back, and said in a loud voice, "No!

"I won't," he said, and then with great vigour cursed the pit.

Then, having few words, he sought to express his thought in acts. He took a truck half filled with chalk, lifted it, and flung it, smash, against another. Then he grasped a whole row of empty trucks and spun them down a bank. He sent a huge boulder of chalk bursting among them, and then ripped up a dozen yards of rail with a mighty plunge of his foot. So he commenced the conscientious wrecking of the pit.

"Work all my days," he said, "at this!"

It was an astonishing five minutes for the little geologist he had, in his preoccupation, overlooked. This poor little creature having dodged two boulders by a hairbreadth, got out by the westward corner and fled athwart the hill, with flapping rucksack and twinkling knicker-bockered legs, leaving a trail of Cretaceous echinoderms behind him;

while young Caddles, satisfied with the destruction he had achieved, came striding out to fulfil his purpose in the world.

"Work in that old pit, until I die and rot and stink!... What worm did they think was living in my giant body? Dig chalk for God knows what foolish purpose! Not I!"

The trend of road and railway perhaps, or mere chance it was, turned his face to London, and thither he came striding; over the Downs and athwart the meadows through the hot afternoon, to the infinite amazement of the world. It signified nothing to him that torn posters in red and white bearing various names flapped from every wall and barn; he knew nothing of the electoral revolution that had flung Caterham, "Jack the Giant-killer," into power. It signified nothing to him that every police station along his route had what was known as Caterham's ukase upon its notice board that afternoon, proclaiming that no giant, no person whatever over eight feet in height, should go more than five miles from his "place of location" without a special permission. It signified nothing to him that on his wake belated police officers, not a little relieved to find themselves belated, shook warning handbills at his retreating back. He was going to see what the world had to show him, poor incredulous blockhead, and he did not mean that occasional spirited persons shouting "Hi!" at him should stay his course. He came on down by Rochester and Greenwich towards an ever-thickening aggregation of houses, walking rather slowly now, staring about him and swinging his huge chopper.

People in London had heard something of him before, how that he was idiotic but gentle, and wonderfully managed by Lady Wondershoot's agent and the Vicar; how in his dull way he revered these authorities and was grateful to them for their care of him, and so forth. So that when they learnt from the newspaper placards that afternoon that he also was "on strike," the thing appeared to many of them as a deliberate, concerted act.

"They mean to try our strength," said the men in the trains going home from business.

"Lucky we have Caterham."

"It's in answer to his proclamation."

The men in the clubs were better informed. They clustered round the tape or talked in groups in their smoking-rooms.

"He has no weapons. He would have gone to Sevenoaks if he had been put up to it."

"Caterham will handle him...."

The shopmen told their customers. The waiters in restaurants snatched a moment for an evening paper between the courses. The cabmen read it immediately after the betting news....

The placards of the chief government evening paper were conspicuous with "Grasping the Nettle." Others relied for effect on: "Giant Redwood continues to meet the Princess." The Echo struck a line of its own with: "Rumoured Revolt of Giants in the North of England. The Sunderland Giants start for Scotland." The, Westminster Gazette sounded its usual warning note. "Giants Beware," said the Westminster Gazette, and tried to make a point out of it that might perhaps serve towards uniting the Liberal party—at that time greatly torn between seven intensely egotistical leaders. The later newspapers dropped into uniformity. "The Giant in the New Kent Road," they proclaimed.

"What I want to know," said the pale young man in the tea shop, "is why we aren't getting any news of the young Cossars. You'd think they'd be in it most of all ..."

"They tell me there's another of them young giants got loose," said the barmaid, wiping out a glass. "I've always said they was dangerous things to 'ave about. Right away from the beginning ... It ought to be put a stop to. Any'ow, I 'ope 'e won't come along 'ere."

"I'd like to 'ave a look at 'im," said the young man at the bar recklessly, and added, "I seen the Princess."

"D'you think they'll 'urt 'im?" said the barmaid.

"May 'ave to," said the young man at the bar, finishing his glass.

Amidst a hum of ten million such sayings young Caddles came to London...

II.

I think of young Caddles always as he was seen in the New Kent Road, the sunset warm upon his perplexed and staring face. The Road was thick with its varied traffic, omnibuses, trams, vans, carts, trolleys, cyclists, motors, and a marvelling crowd—loafers, women, nurse-maids, shopping women, children, venturesome hobble-dehoys—

gathered behind his gingerly moving feet. The hoardings were untidy everywhere with the tattered election paper. A babblement of voices surged about him. One sees the customers and shopmen crowding in the doorways of the shops, the faces that came and went at the windows, the little street boys running and shouting, the policemen taking it all quite stiffly and calmly, the workmen knocking off upon scaffoldings, the seething miscellany of the little folks. They shouted to him, vague encouragement, vague insults, the imbecile catchwords of the day, and he stared down at them, at such a multitude of living creatures as he had never before imagined in the world.

Now that he had fairly entered London he had had to slacken his pace more and more, the little folks crowded so mightily upon him. The crowd grew denser at every step, and at last, at a corner where two great ways converged, he came to a stop, and the multitude flowed about him and closed him in.

There he stood, with his feet a little apart, his back to a big corner gin palace that towered twice his height and ended In a sky sign, staring down at the pigmies and wondering—trying, I doubt not, to collate it all with the other things of his life, with the valley among the downlands, the nocturnal lovers, the singing in the church, the chalk he hammered daily, and with instinct and death and the sky, trying to see it all together coherent and significant. His brows were knit. He put up his huge paw to scratch his coarse hair, and groaned aloud.

"I don't see It," he said.

His accent was unfamiliar. A great babblement went across the open space—a babblement amidst which the gongs of the trams, ploughing their obstinate way through the mass, rose like red poppies amidst corn. "What did he say?" "Said he didn't see." "Said, where is the sea?" "Said, where is a seat?" "He wants a seat." "Can't the brasted fool sit on a 'ouse or somethin'?"

"What are ye for, ye swarming little people? What are ye all doing, what are ye all for?"

"What are ye doing up here, ye swarming little people, while I'm a-cuttin' chalk for ye, down in the chalk pits there?"

His queer voice, the voice that had been so bad for school discipline at Cheasing Eyebright, smote the multitude to silence while it sounded and splashed them all to tumult at the end. Some wit was audible screaming "Speech, speech!" "What's he saying?" was the burthen of the public mind, and an opinion was abroad that he was drunk. "Hi, hi, hi," bawled the omnibus-drivers, threading a dangerous way. A drunken American sailor wandered about tearfully inquiring, "What's he want anyhow?" A leathery-faced rag-dealer upon a little pony-drawn cart soared up over the tumult by virtue of his voice. "Garn 'ome, you Brasted Giant!" he brawled, "Garn 'Ome! You Brasted Great Dangerous Thing! Can't you see you're a-frightening the 'orses? Go 'ome with you! 'Asn't any one 'ad the sense to tell you the law?" And over all this uproar young Caddles stared, perplexed, expectant, saying no more.

Down a side road came a little string of solemn policemen, and threaded itself ingeniously into the traffic. "Stand back," said the little voices; "keep moving, please."

Young Caddles became aware of a little dark blue figure thumping at his shin. He looked down, and perceived two white hands gesticulating. "What?" he said, bending forward.

"Can't stand about here," shouted the inspector.

"No! You can't stand about here," he repeated.

"But where am I to go?"

"Back to your village. Place of location. Anyhow, now—you've got to move on. You're obstructing the traffic."

"What traffic?"

"Along the road."

"But where is it going? Where does it come from? What does it mean? They're all round me. What do they want? What are they doin'? I want to understand. I'm tired of cuttin' chalk and bein' all alone. What are they doin' for me while I'm a-cuttin' chalk? I may just as well understand here and now as anywhere."

"Sorry. But we aren't here to explain things of that sort. I must arst you to move on."

"Don't you know?"

"I must arst you to move on—if you please ... I'd strongly advise you to get off 'ome. We've 'ad no special instructions yet—but it's against the law ... Clear away there. Clear away."

The pavement to his left became invitingly bare, and young Caddles went slowly on his way. But now his tongue was loosened.

"I don't understand," he muttered. "I don't understand." He would appeal brokenly to the changing crowd that ever trailed beside him and behind. "I didn't know there were such places as this. What are all you people doing with yourselves? What's it all for? What is it all for, and where do I come in?"

He had already begotten a new catchword. Young men of wit and spirit addressed each other in this manner, "Ullo 'Arry O'Cock. Wot's it all for? Eh? Wot's it all bloomin' well for?"

To which there sprang up a competing variety of repartees, for the most part impolite. The most popular and best adapted for general use appears to have been "Shut it," or, in a voice of scornful detachment—"Garn!"

There were others almost equally popular.

III.

What was he seeking? He wanted something the pigmy world did not give, some end which the pigmy world prevented his attaining, prevented even his seeing clearly, which he was never to see clearly. It was the whole gigantic social side of this lonely dumb monster crying out for his race, for the things akin to him, for something he might love and something he might serve, for a purpose he might comprehend and a command he could obey. And, you know, all this was dumb, raged dumbly within him, could not even, had he met a fellow giant, have found outlet and expression in speech. All the life he knew was the dull round of the village, all the speech he knew was the talk of the cottage, that failed and collapsed at the bare outline of his least gigantic need. He knew nothing of money, this monstrous simpleton, nothing of trade, nothing of the complex pretences upon which the social fabric of the little folks was built. He needed, he needed—Whatever he needed, he never found his need.

All through the day and the summer night he wandered, growing hungry but as yet untired, marking the varied traffic of the different streets, the inexplicable businesses of all these infinitesimal beings. In the aggregate it had no other colour than confusion for him....

He is said to have plucked a lady from her carriage in Kensington, a lady in evening dress of the smartest sort, to have scrutinised her closely, train and shoulder blades, and to have replaced her—a little carelessly—with the profoundest sigh. For that I cannot vouch. For an hour or so he watched people fighting for places in the omnibuses at the end of Piccadilly. He was seen looming over Kennington Oval for some moments in the afternoon, but when he saw these dense thousands were engaged with the mystery of cricket and quite regardless of him he went his way with a groan.

He came back to Piccadilly Circus between eleven and twelve at night and found a new sort of multitude. Clearly they were very intent: full of things they, for inconceivable reasons, might do, and of others they might not do. They stared at him and jeered at him and went their way. The cabmen, vulture-eyed, followed one another continually along the edge of the swarming pavement. People emerged from the restaurants or entered them, grave, intent, dignified, or gently and agreeably excited or keen and vigilant—beyond the cheating of the sharpest waiter born. The great giant, standing at his corner, peered at them all. "What is it all for?" he murmured in a mournful vast undertone, "What is it all for? They are all so earnest. What is it I do not understand?"

And none of them seemed to see, as he could do, the drink-sodden wretchedness of the painted women at the corner, the ragged misery that sneaked along the gutters, the infinite futility of all this employment. The infinite futility! None of them seemed to feel the shadow of that giant's need, that shadow of the future, that lay athwart their paths...

Across the road high up mysterious letters flamed and went, that might, could he have read them, have measured for him the dimensions of human interest, have told him of the fundamental needs and features of life as the little folks conceived it. First would come a flaming

T;

Then U would follow,

TU;

Then P,

TUP;

Until at last there stood complete, across the sky, this cheerful message to all who felt the burthen of life's earnestness:

TUPPER'S TONIC WINE FOR VIGOUR.

Snap! and it had vanished into night, to be followed in the same slow development by a second universal solicitude:

BEAUTY SOAP.

Not, you remark, mere cleansing chemicals, but something, as they say, "ideal;" and then, completing the tripod of the little life:

TANKER'S YELLOW PILLS.

After that there was nothing for it but Tupper again, in naming crimson letters, snap, snap, across the void.

T U P P....

Early in the small hours it would seem that young Caddles came to the shadowy quiet of Regent's Park, stepped over the railings and lay down on a grassy slope near where the people skate in winter time, and there he slept an hour or so. And about six o'clock in the morning, he was talking to a draggled woman he had found sleeping in a ditch near Hampstead Heath, asking her very earnestly what she thought she was for....

IV.

The wandering of Caddles about London came to a head on the second day in the morning. For then his hunger overcame him. He hesitated where the hot-smelling loaves were being tossed into a cart, and then very quietly knelt down and commenced robbery. He emptied the cart while the baker's man fled for the police, and then his great hand came into the shop and cleared counter and cases. Then with an armful, still eating, he went his way looking for another shop to go on with his meal. It happened to be one of those seasons when work is scarce and food dear, and the crowd in that quarter was sympathetic even with a giant who took the food they all desired. They applauded the second phase of his meal, and laughed at his stupid grimace at the policeman.

"I woff hungry," he said, with his mouth full.

"Brayvo!" cried the crowd. "Brayvo!"

Then when he was beginning his third baker's shop, he was stopped by half a dozen policemen hammering with truncheons at his shins. "Look here, my fine giant, you come along o' me," said the officer in charge. "You ain't allowed away from home like this. You come off home with me." They did their best to arrest him. There was a trolley, I am told, chasing up and down streets at that time, bearing rolls of chain and ship's cable to play the part of handcuffs in that great arrest. There was no intention then of killing him. "He is no party to the plot," Caterham had said. "I will not have innocent blood upon my hands." And added: "—until everything else has been tried."

At first Caddles did not understand the import of these attentions. When he did, he told the policemen not to be fools, and set off in great strides that left them all behind. The bakers' shops had been in the Harrow Road, and he went through canal London to St. John's Wood, and sat down in a private garden there to pick his teeth and be speedily assailed by another posse of constables.

"You lea' me alone," he growled, and slouched through the gardens—spoiling several lawns and kicking down a fence or so, while the energetic little policemen followed him up, some through the gardens, some along the road in front of the houses. Here there were one or two with guns, but they made no use of them. When he came out into the Edgware Road there was a new note and a new movement in the crowd, and a mounted policeman rode over his foot and got upset for his pains.

"You lea' me alone," said Caddles, facing the breathless crowd. "I ain't done anything to you." At that time he was unarmed, for he had left his chalk chopper in Regent's Park. But now, poor wretch, he seems to have felt the need of some weapon. He turned back towards the goods yard of the Great Western Railway, wrenched up the standard of a tall arc light, a formidable mace for him, and flung it over his shoulder. And finding the police still turning up to pester him, he went back along the Edgware Road, towards Cricklewood, and struck off sullenly to the north.

He wandered as far as Waltham, and then turned back westward and then again towards London, and came by the cemeteries and over the crest of Highgate about midday into view of the greatness of the city again. He turned aside and sat down in a garden, with his back to a house that overlooked all London. He was breathless, and his face was lowering, and now the people no longer crowded upon him as they had done when first he came to London, but lurked in the adjacent garden, and peeped from cautious securities. They knew by now the thing was grimmer than they had thought. "Why can't they lea' me alone?" growled young Caddles. "I mus' eat. Why can't they lea' me alone?"

He sat with a darkling face, gnawing at his knuckles and looking down over London. All the fatigue, worry, perplexity, and impotent wrath of his wanderings was coming to a head in him. "They mean nothing," he whispered. "They mean nothing. And they won't let me alone, and they will get in my way." And again, over and over to himself, "Meanin' nothing.

"Ugh! the little people!"

He bit harder at his knuckles and his scowl deepened. "Cuttin' chalk for 'em," he whispered. "And all the world is theirs! I don't come in—nowhere."

Presently with a spasm of sick anger he saw the now familiar form of a policeman astride the garden wall.

"Lea' me alone," grunted the giant. "Lea' me alone."

"I got to do my duty," said the little policeman, with a face that was white and resolute.

"You lea' me alone. I got to live as well as you. I got to think. I got to eat. You lea' me alone."

"It's the Law," said the little policeman, coming no further. "We never made the Law."

"Nor me," said young Caddles. "You little people made all that before I was born. You and your Law! What I must and what I mustn't! No food for me to eat unless I work a slave, no rest, no shelter, nothin', and you tell me—"

"I ain't got no business with that," said the policeman. "I'm not one to argue. All I got to do is to carry out the Law." And he brought his second leg over the wall and seemed disposed to get down. Other policemen appeared behind him.

"I got no quarrel with you—mind," said young Caddles, with his grip tight upon his huge mace of iron, his face pale, and a lank explanatory great finger to the policeman. "I got no quarrel with you. But—You lea' me alone."

The policeman tried to be calm and commonplace, with a monstrous tragedy clear before his eyes. "Give me the proclamation," he said to some unseen follower, and a little white paper was handed to him.

"Lea' me alone," said Caddles, scowling, tense, and drawn together.

"This means," said the policeman before he read, "go 'ome. Go 'ome to your chalk pit. If not, you'll be hurt."

Caddles gave an inarticulate growl.

Then when the proclamation had been read, the officer made a sign. Four men with rifles came into view and took up positions of affected ease along the wall. They wore the uniform of the rat police. At the sight of the guns, young Caddles blazed into anger. He remembered the sting of the Wreckstone farmers' shot guns. "You going to shoot off those at me?" he said, pointing, and it seemed to the officer he must be afraid.

"If you don't march back to your pit—"

Then in an instant the officer had slung himself back over the wall, and sixty feet above him the great electric standard whirled down to his death. Bang, bang, bang, went the heavy guns, and smash! the shattered wall, the soil and subsoil of the garden flew. Something flew with it, that left red drops on one of the shooter's hands. The riflemen dodged this way and that and turned valiantly to fire again. But young Caddles, already shot twice through the body, had spun about to find who it was had hit him so heavily in the back. Bang! Bang! He had a vision of houses and greenhouses and gardens, of people dodging at windows, the whole swaying fearfully and mysteriously. He seems to have made three stumbling strides, to have raised and dropped his huge mace, and to have clutched his chest. He was stung and wrenched by pain.

What was this, warm and wet, on his hand?

One man peering from a bedroom window saw his face, saw him staring, with a grimace of weeping dismay, at the blood upon his hand, and then his knees bent under him, and he came crashing to the earth, the first of the giant nettles to fall to Caterham's resolute clutch, the very last that he had reckoned would come into his hand.

CHAPTER THE FOURTH.
REDWOOD'S TWO DAYS.

I.

So soon as Caterham knew the moment for grasping his nettle had come, he took the law into his own hands and sent to arrest Cossar and Redwood.

Redwood was there for the taking. He had been undergoing an operation in the side, and the doctors had kept all disturbing things from him until his convalescence was assured. Now they had released him. He was just out of bed, sitting in a fire-warmed room, with a heap of newspapers about him, reading for the first time of the agitation that had swept the country into the hands of Caterham, and of the trouble that was darkening over the Princess and his son. It was in the morning of the day when young Caddles died, and when the policeman tried to stop young Redwood on his way to the Princess. The latest newspapers Redwood had did but vaguely prefigure these imminent things. He was re-reading these first adumbrations of disaster with a sinking heart, reading the shadow of death more and more perceptibly into them, reading to occupy his mind until further news should come. When the officers followed the servant into his room, he looked up eagerly.

"I thought it was an early evening paper," he said. Then standing up, and with a swift change of manner: "What's this?"

After that Redwood had no news of anything for two days.

They had come with a vehicle to take him away, but when it became evident that he was ill, it was decided to leave him for a day or so until he could be safely removed, and his house was taken over by the police and converted into a temporary prison. It was the same house in which Giant Redwood had been born and in which Herakleophorbia had for the first time been given to a human being, and Redwood had now been a widower and had lived alone in it eight years.

He had become an iron-grey man, with a little pointed grey beard and still active brown eyes. He was slender and soft-voiced, as he had ever been, but his features had now that indefinable quality that comes of brooding over mighty things. To the arresting officer his appearance was in impressive contrast to the enormity of his offences. "Here's this feller," said the officer in command, to his next subordinate, "has done his level best to bust up everything, and 'e's got a face like a quiet country gentleman; and here's Judge Hangbrow keepin' everything nice and in order for every one, and 'e's got a 'ead like a 'og. Then their manners! One all consideration and the other snort and grunt. Which just shows you, doesn't it, that appearances aren't to be gone upon, whatever else you do."

But his praise of Redwood's consideration was presently dashed. The officers found him troublesome at first until they had made it clear that it was useless for him to ask questions or beg for papers. They made a sort of inspection of his study indeed, and cleared away even the papers he had. Redwood's voice was high and expostulatory. "But don't you see," he said over and over again, "it's my Son, my only Son, that is in this trouble. It isn't the Food I care for, but my Son."

"I wish indeed I could tell you, Sir," said the officer. "But our orders are strict."

"Who gave the orders?" cried Redwood.

"Ah! that, Sir—-" said the officer, and moved towards the door....

"'E's going up and down 'is room," said the second officer, when his superior came down. "That's all right. He'll walk it off a bit."

"I hope 'e will," said the chief officer. "The fact is I didn't see it in that light before, but this here Giant what's been going on with the Princess, you know, is this man's son."

The two regarded one another and the third policeman for a space.

"Then it is a bit rough on him," the third policeman said.

It became evident that Redwood had still imperfectly apprehended the fact that an iron curtain had dropped between him and the outer world. They heard him go to the door, try the handle and rattle the lock, and then the voice of the officer who was stationed on the landing telling him it was no good to do that. Then afterwards they heard him at the windows and saw the men outside looking up. "It's no good that way," said the second officer. Then Redwood began upon the bell. The senior officer went up and explained very patiently that it could do no good to ring the bell like that, and if it was rung for nothing now it might have to be disregarded presently when he had need of something. "Any reasonable attendance, Sir," the officer said. "But if you ring it just by way of protest we shall be obliged, Sir, to disconnect."

The last word the officer heard was Redwood's high-pitched, "But at least you might tell me if my Son—"

II.

After that Redwood spent most of his time at the windows.

But the windows offered him little of the march of events outside. It was a quiet street at all times, and that day it was unusually quiet: scarcely a cab, scarcely a tradesman's cart passed all that morning. Now and then men went by—without any distinctive air of events— now and then a little group of children, a nursemaid and a woman going shopping, and so forth. They came on to the stage right or left, up or down the street, with an exasperating suggestion of indifference to any concerns more spacious than their own; they would discover the police-guarded house with amazement and exit in the opposite direction, where the great trusses of a giant hydrangea hung across the pavement, staring back or pointing. Now and then a man would come and ask one of the policemen a question and get a curt reply ...

Opposite the houses seemed dead. A housemaid appeared once at a bedroom window and stared for a space, and it occurred to Redwood to signal to her. For a time she watched his gestures as if with interest and made a vague response to them, then looked over her shoulder suddenly and turned and went away. An old man hobbled out of Number 37 and came down the steps and went off to the right, altogether without looking up. For ten minutes the only occupant of the road was a cat....

With such events that interminable momentous morning lengthened out.

About twelve there came a bawling of newsvendors from the adjacent road; but it passed. Contrary to their wont they left Redwood's street alone, and a suspicion dawned upon him that the police were guarding the end of the street. He tried to open the window, but this brought a policeman into the room forthwith....

The clock of the parish church struck twelve, and after an abyss of time—one.

They mocked him with lunch.

He ate a mouthful and tumbled the food about a little in order to get it taken away, drank freely of whisky, and then took a chair and went back to the window. The minutes expanded into grey immensities, and for a time perhaps he slept....

He woke with a vague impression of remote concussions. He perceived a rattling of the windows like the quiver of an earthquake, that lasted for a minute or so and died away. Then after a silence it returned.... Then it died away again. He fancied it might be merely the passage of some heavy vehicle along the main road. What else could it be?

After a time he began to doubt whether he had heard this sound.

He began to reason interminably with himself. Why, after all, was he seized? Caterham had been in office two days—just long enough—to grasp his Nettle! Grasp his Nettle! Grasp his Giant Nettle! The refrain once started, sang through his mind, and would not be dismissed.

What, after all, could Caterham do? He was a religious man. He was bound in a sort of way by that not to do violence without a cause.

Grasp his Nettle! Perhaps, for example, the Princess was to be seized and sent abroad. There might be trouble with his son. In which case—! But why had he been arrested? Why was it necessary to keep him in ignorance of a thing like that? The thing suggested—something more extensive.

Perhaps, for example—they meant to lay all the giants by the heels! They were all to be arrested together. There had been hints of that in the election speeches. And then?

No doubt they had got Cossar also?

Caterham was a religious man. Redwood clung to that. The back of his mind was a black curtain, and on that curtain there came and went a word—a word written in letters of fire. He struggled perpetually against that word. It was always as it were beginning to get written on the curtain and never getting completed.

He faced it at last. "Massacre!" There was the word in its full brutality.

No! No! No! It was impossible! Caterham was a religious man, a civilised man. And besides after all these years, after all these hopes!

Redwood sprang up; he paced the room. He spoke to himself; he shouted.

"No!"

Mankind was surely not so mad as that—surely not! It was impossible, it was incredible, it could not be. What good would it do to kill the giant human when the gigantic in all the lower things had now inevitably come? They could not be so mad as that! "I must dismiss such an idea," he said aloud; "dismiss such an idea! Absolutely!"

He pulled up short. What was that?

Certainly the windows had rattled. He went to look out into the street. Opposite he saw the instant confirmation of his ears. At a bedroom at Number 35 was a woman, towel in hand, and at the dining-room of Number 37 a man was visible behind a great vase of hypertrophied maidenhair fern, both staring out and up, both disquieted and curious. He could see now too, quite clearly, that the policeman on the pavement had heard it also. The thing was not his imagination.

He turned to the darkling room.

"Guns," he said.

He brooded.

"Guns?"

They brought him in strong tea, such as he was accustomed to have. It was evident his housekeeper had been taken into consultation. After drinking it, he was too restless to sit any longer at the window, and he paced the room. His mind became more capable of consecutive thought.

The room had been his study for four-and-twenty years. It had been furnished at his marriage, and all the essential equipment dated from then, the large complex writing-desk, the rotating chair, the easy chair at the fire, the rotating bookcase, the fixture of indexed pigeon-holes that filled the further recess. The vivid Turkey carpet, the later Victorian rugs and curtains had mellowed now to a rich dignity of effect, and copper and brass shone warm about the open fire. Electric lights had replaced the lamp of former days; that was the chief alteration in the original equipment. But among these things his connection with the Food had left abundant traces. Along one wall, above the dado, ran a crowded array of black-framed photographs and photogravures, showing his son and Cossar's sons and others of the Boom-children at various ages and amidst various surroundings. Even young Caddles' vacant visage had its place in that collection. In the corner stood a sheaf of the tassels of gigantic meadow grass from Cheasing Eyebright, and on the desk there lay three empty poppy heads as big as hats. The curtain rods were grass stems. And the tremendous skull of the great hog of Oakham hung, a portentous ivory overmantel, with a Chinese jar in either eye socket, snout down above the fire....

It was to the photographs that Redwood went, and in particular to the photographs of his son.

They brought back countless memories of things that had passed out of his mind, of the early days of the Food, of Bensington's timid presence, of his cousin Jane, of Cossar and the night work at the Experimental Farm. These things came to him now very little and bright and distinct, like things seen through a telescope on a sunny day. And then there was the giant nursery, the giant childhood, the young giant's first efforts to speak, his first clear signs of affection.

Guns?

It flowed in on him, irresistibly, overwhelmingly, that outside there, outside this accursed silence and mystery, his son and Cossar's sons, and all these glorious first-fruits of a greater age were even now—fighting. Fighting for life! Even now his son might be in some dismal quandary, cornered, wounded, overcome....

He swung away from the pictures and went up and down the room gesticulating. "It cannot be," he cried, "it cannot be. It cannot end like that!"

"What was that?"

He stopped, stricken rigid.

The trembling of the windows had begun again, and then had come a thud—a vast concussion that shook the house. The concussion seemed to last for an age. It must have been very near. For a moment it seemed that something had struck the house above him—an enormous impact that broke into a tinkle of falling glass, and then a stillness that ended at last with a minute clear sound of running feet in the street below.

Those feet released him from his rigor. He turned towards the window, and saw it starred and broken.

His heart beat high with a sense of crisis, of conclusive occurrence, of release. And then again, his realisation of impotent confinement fell about him like a curtain!

He could see nothing outside except that the small electric lamp opposite was not lighted; he could hear nothing after the first suggestion of a wide alarm. He could add nothing to interpret or enlarge that mystery except that presently there came a reddish fluctuating brightness in the sky towards the south-east.

This light waxed and waned. When it waned he doubted if it had ever waxed. It had crept upon him very gradually with the darkling. It became the predominant fact in his long night of suspense. Sometimes it seemed to him it had the quiver one associates with dancing flames, at others he fancied it was no more than the normal reflection of the evening lights. It waxed and waned through the long hours, and only vanished at last when it was submerged altogether under the rising tide of dawn. Did it mean—? What could it mean? Almost certainly it was some sort of fire, near or remote, but he could not even tell whether it was smoke or cloud drift that streamed across the sky. But about one o'clock there began a flickering of searchlights athwart that ruddy tumult, a flickering that continued for the rest of the night. That too might mean many things? What could it mean? What did it mean? Just this stained unrestful sky he had and the suggestion of a huge explosion to occupy his mind. There came no further sounds, no further running, nothing but a shouting that might have been only the distant efforts of drunken men...

He did not turn up his lights; he stood at his draughty broken window, a distressful, slight black outline to the officer who looked ever and again into the room and exhorted him to rest.

All night Redwood remained at his window peering up at the ambiguous drift of the sky, and only with the coming of the dawn did he obey his fatigue and lie down upon the little bed they had prepared for him between his writing-desk and the sinking fire in the fireplace under the great hog's skull.

III.

For thirty-six long hours did Redwood remain imprisoned, closed in and shut off from the great drama of the Two Days, while the little people in the dawn of greatness fought against the Children of the Food. Then abruptly the iron curtain rose again, and he found himself near the very centre of the struggle. That curtain rose as unexpectedly as it fell. In the late afternoon he was called to the window by the clatter of a cab, that stopped without. A young man descended, and in another minute stood before him in the room, a slightly built young man of thirty perhaps, clean shaven, well dressed, well mannered.

"Mr. Redwood, Sir," he began, "would you be willing to come to Mr.Caterham? He needs your presence very urgently."

"Needs my presence!" There leapt a question into Redwood's mind, that for a moment he could not put. He hesitated. Then in a voice that broke he asked: "What has he done to my Son?" and stood breathless for the reply.

"Your Son, Sir? Your Son is doing well. So at least we gather."

"Doing well?"

"He was wounded, Sir, yesterday. Have you not heard?"

Redwood smote these pretences aside. His voice was no longer coloured by fear, but by anger. "You know I have not heard. You know I have heard nothing."

"Mr. Caterham feared, Sir—It was a time of upheaval. Every one—taken by surprise. He arrested you to save you, Sir, from any misadventure—"

"He arrested me to prevent my giving any warning or advice to my son. Go on. Tell me what has happened. Have you succeeded? Have you killed them all?"

The young man made a pace or so towards the window, and turned.

"No, Sir," he said concisely.

"What have you to tell me?"

"It's our proof, Sir, that this fighting was not planned by us. They found us ... totally unprepared."

"You mean?"

"I mean, Sir, the Giants have—to a certain extent—held their own."

The world changed, for Redwood. For a moment something like hysteria had the muscles of his face and throat. Then he gave vent to a profound "Ah!" His heart bounded towards exultation. "The Giants have held their own!"

"There has been terrible fighting—terrible destruction. It is all a most hideous misunderstanding ... In the north and midlands Giants have been killed ... Everywhere."

"They are fighting now?"

"No, Sir. There was a flag of truce."

"From them?"

"No, Sir. Mr. Caterham sent a flag of truce. The whole thing is a hideous misunderstanding. That is why he wants to talk to you, and put his case before you. They insist, Sir, that you should intervene—"

Redwood interrupted. "Do you know what happened to my Son?" he asked.

"He was wounded."

"Tell me! Tell me!"

"He and the Princess came—before the—the movement to surround the Cossar camp was complete—the Cossar pit at Chislehurst. They came suddenly, Sir, crashing through a dense thicket of giant oats, near River, upon a column of infantry ... Soldiers had been very nervous all day, and this produced a panic."

"They shot him?"

"No, Sir. They ran away. Some shot at him—wildly—against orders."

Redwood gave a note of denial. "It's true, Sir. Not on account of your son, I won't pretend, but on account of the Princess."

"Yes. That's true."

"The two Giants ran shouting towards the encampment. The soldiers ran this way and that, and then some began firing. They say they saw him stagger—"

"Ugh!"

"Yes, Sir. But we know he is not badly hurt."

"How?"

"He sent the message, Sir, that he was doing well!"

"To me?"

"Who else, Sir?"

Redwood stood for nearly a minute with his arms tightly folded, taking this in. Then his indignation found a voice.

"Because you were fools in doing the thing, because you miscalculated and blundered, you would like me to think you are not murderers in intention. And besides—The rest?"

The young man looked interrogation.

"The other Giants?"

The young man made no further pretence of misunderstanding. His tone fell. "Thirteen, Sir, are dead."

"And others wounded?"

"Yes, Sir."

"And Caterham," he gasped, "wants to meet me! Where are the others?"

"Some got to the encampment during the fighting, Sir ... They seem to have known—"

"Well, of course they did. If it hadn't been for Cossar—Cossar is there?"

"Yes, Sir. And all the surviving Giants are there—the ones who didn't get to the camp in the fighting have gone, or are going now under the flag of trace."

"That means," said Redwood, "that you are beaten."

"We are not beaten. No, Sir. You cannot say we are beaten. But your sons have broken the rules of war. Once last night, and now again. After our attack had been withdrawn. This afternoon they began to bombard London—"

"That's legitimate!"

"They have been firing shells filled with—poison."

"Poison?"

"Yes. Poison. The Food—"

"Herakleophorbia?"

"Yes, Sir. Mr. Caterham, Sir—"

"You are beaten! Of course that beats you. It's Cossar! What can you hope to do now? What good is it to do anything now? You will breathe it in the dust of every street. What is there to fight for more? Rules of war, indeed! And now Caterham wants to humbug me to help him bargain. Good heavens, man! Why should I come to your exploded windbag? He has played his game ... murdered and muddled. Why should I?"

The young man stood with an air of vigilant respect.

"It is a fact, Sir," he interrupted, "that the Giants insist that they shall see you. They will have no ambassador but you. Unless you come to them, I am afraid, Sir, there will be more bloodshed."

"On your side, perhaps."

"No, Sir—on both sides. The world is resolved the thing must end."

Redwood looked about the study. His eyes rested for a moment on the photograph of his boy. He turned and met the expectation of the young man. "Yes," he said at last, "I will come."

IV.

His encounter with Caterham was entirely different from his anticipation. He had seen the man only twice in his life, once at dinner and once in the lobby of the House, and his imagination had been active not with the man but with the creation of the newspapers and caricaturists, the legendary Caterham, Jack the Giant-killer, Perseus, and all the rest of it. The element of a human personality came in to disorder all that.

Here was not the face of the caricatures and portraits, but the face of a worn and sleepless man, lined and drawn, yellow in the whites of the eyes, a little weakened about the mouth. Here, indeed, were the red-brown eyes, the black hair, the distinctive aquiline profile of the great demagogue, but here was also something else that smote any premeditated scorn and rhetoric aside. This man was suffering; he was suffering acutely; he was under enormous stress. From the beginning he had an air of impersonating himself. Presently, with a single gesture, the slightest movement, he revealed to Redwood that he was keeping himself up with drugs. He moved a thumb to his waistcoat pocket, and then, after a few sentences more, threw concealment aside, and slipped the little tabloid to his lips.

Moreover, in spite of the stresses upon him, in spite of the fact that he was in the wrong, and Redwood's junior by a dozen years, that strange quality in him, the something—personal magnetism one may call it for want of a better name—that had won his way for him to this eminence of disaster was with him still. On that also Redwood had failed to reckon. From the first, so far as the course and conduct of their speech went, Caterham prevailed over Redwood. All the quality of the first phase of their meeting was determined by him, all the tone and procedure were his. That happened as if it was a matter of course. All Redwood's expectations vanished at his presence. He shook hands before Redwood remembered that he meant to parry that familiarity; he pitched the note of their conference from the outset, sure and clear, as a search for expedients under a common catastrophe.

If he made any mistake it was when ever and again his fatigue got the better of his immediate attention, and the habit of the public meeting carried him away. Then he drew himself up—through all their interview both men stood—and looked away from Redwood, and began to fence and justify. Once even he said "Gentlemen!"

Quietly, expandingly, he began to talk....

There were moments when Redwood ceased even to feel himself an interlocutor, when he became the mere auditor of a monologue. He became the privileged spectator of an extraordinary phenomenon. He perceived something almost like a specific difference between himself and this being whose beautiful voice enveloped him, who was talking, talking. This mind before him was so powerful and so limited. From its driving energy, its personal weight, its invincible oblivion to certain things, there sprang up in Redwood's mind the most grotesque and strange of images. Instead of an antagonist who was a fellow-creature, a man one could hold morally responsible, and to whom one could address reasonable appeals, he saw Caterham as something,

something like a monstrous rhinoceros, as it were, a civilised rhinoceros begotten of the jungle of democratic affairs, a monster of irresistible onset and invincible resistance. In all the crashing conflicts of that tangle he was supreme. And beyond? This man was a being supremely adapted to make his way through multitudes of men. For him there was no fault so important as self-contradiction, no science so significant as the reconciliation of "interests." Economic realities, topographical necessities, the barely touched mines of scientific expedients, existed for him no more than railways or rifled guns or geographical literature exist for his animal prototype. What did exist were gatherings, and caucuses, and votes—above all, votes. He was votes incarnate—millions of votes.

And now in the great crisis, with the Giants broken but not beaten, this vote-monster talked.

It was so evident that even now he had everything to learn. He did not know there were physical laws and economic laws, quantities and reactions that all humanity voting nemine contradicente cannot vote away, and that are disobeyed only at the price of destruction. He did not know there are moral laws that cannot be bent by any force of glamour, or are bent only to fly back with vindictive violence. In the face of shrapnel or the Judgment Day, it was evident to Redwood that this man would have sheltered behind some curiously dodged vote of the House of Commons.

What most concerned his mind now was not the powers that held the fastness away there to the south, not defeat and death, but the effect of these things upon his Majority, the cardinal reality in his life. He had to defeat the Giants or go under. He was by no means absolutely despairful. In this hour of his utmost failure, with blood and disaster upon his hands, and the rich promise of still more horrible disaster, with the gigantic destinies of the world towering and toppling over him, he was capable of a belief that by sheer exertion of his voice, by explaining and qualifying and restating, he might yet reconstitute his power. He was puzzled and distressed no doubt, fatigued and suffering, but if only he could keep up, if only he could keep talking—

As he talked he seemed to Redwood to advance and recede, to dilate and contract. Redwood's share of the talk was of the most subsidiary sort, wedges as it were suddenly thrust in. "That's all nonsense." "No." "It's no use suggesting that." "Then why did you begin?"

It is doubtful if Caterham really heard him at all. Round such interpolations Caterham's speech flowed indeed like some swift stream about a rock. There this incredible man stood, on his official hearthrug, talking, talking with enormous power and skill, talking as though a pause in his talk, his explanations, his presentation of standpoints and lights, of considerations and expedients, would permit some antagonistic influence to leap into being—into vocal being, the only being he could comprehend. There he stood amidst the slightly faded splendours of that official room in which one man after another had succumbed to the belief that a certain power of intervention was the creative control of an empire....

The more he talked the more certain Redwood's sense of stupendous futility grew. Did this man realise that while he stood and talked there, the whole great world was moving, that the invincible tide of growth flowed and flowed, that there were any hours but parliamentary hours, or any weapons in the hands of the Avengers of Blood? Outside, darkling the whole room, a single leaf of giant Virginian creeper tapped unheeded on the pane.

Redwood became anxious to end this amazing monologue, to escape to sanity and judgment, to that beleaguered camp, the fastness of the future, where, at the very nucleus of greatness, the Sons were gathered together. For that this talking was endured. He had a curious impression that unless this monologue ended he would presently find himself carried away by it, that he must fight against Caterham's voice as one fights against a drug. Facts had altered and were altering beneath that spell.

What was the man saying?

Since Redwood had to report it to the Children of the Food, in a sort of way he perceived it did matter. He would have to listen and guard his sense of realities as well as he could.

Much about bloodguiltiness. That was eloquence. That didn't matter.Next?

He was suggesting a convention!

He was suggesting that the surviving Children of the Food should capitulate and go apart and form a community of their own. There were precedents, he said, for this. "We would assign them territory—"

"Where?" interjected Redwood, stooping to argue.

Caterham snatched at that concession. He turned his face to Redwood's, and his voice fell to a persuasive reasonableness. That could be determined. That, he contended, was a quite subsidiary question. Then he went on to stipulate: "And except for them and where they are we must have absolute control, the Food and all the Fruits of the Food must be stamped out—"

Redwood found himself bargaining: "The Princess?"

"She stands apart."

"No," said Redwood, struggling to get back to the old footing. "That's absurd."

"That afterwards. At any rate we are agreed that the making of the Food must stop—"

"I have agreed to nothing. I have said nothing—"

"But on one planet, to have two races of men, one great, one small! Consider what has happened! Consider that is but a little foretaste of what might presently happen if this Food has its way! Consider all you have already brought upon this world! If there is to be a race of Giants, increasing and multiplying—"

"It is not for me to argue," said Redwood. "I must go to our sons. I want to go to my son. That is why I have come to you. Tell me exactly what you offer."

Caterham made a speech upon his terms.

The Children of the Food were to be given a great reservation—in North America perhaps or Africa—in which they might live out their lives in their own fashion.

"But it's nonsense," said Redwood. "There are other Giants now abroad. All over Europe—here and there!"

"There could be an international convention. It's not impossible. Something of the sort indeed has already been spoken of … But in this reservation they can live out their own lives in their own way. They may do what they like; they may make what they like. We shall be glad if they will make us things. They may be happy. Think!"

"Provided there are no more Children."

"Precisely. The Children are for us. And so, Sir, we shall save the world, we shall save it absolutely from the fruits of your terrible discovery. It is not too late for us. Only we are eager to temper expediency with mercy. Even now we are burning and searing the places their shells hit yesterday. We can get it under. Trust me we shall get it under. But in that way, without cruelty, without injustice—"

"And suppose the Children do not agree?"

For the first time Caterham looked Redwood fully in the face.

"They must!"

"I don't think they will."

"Why should they not agree?" he asked, in richly toned amazement.

"Suppose they don't?"

"What can it be but war? We cannot have the thing go on. We cannot. Sir. Have you scientific men no imagination? Have you no mercy? We cannot have our world trampled under a growing herd of such monsters and monstrous growths as your Food has made. We cannot and we cannot! I ask you, Sir, what can it be but war? And remember—this that has happened is only a beginning! This was a skirmish. A mere affair of police. Believe me, a mere affair of police. Do not be cheated by perspective, by the immediate bigness of these newer things. Behind us is the nation—is humanity. Behind the thousands who have died there are millions. Were it not for the fear of bloodshed, Sir, behind our first attacks there would be forming other attacks, even now. Whether we can kill this Food or not, most assuredly we can kill your sons! You reckon too much on the things of yesterday, on the happenings of a mere score of years, on one battle. You have no sense of the slow course of history. I offer this convention for the sake of lives, not because it can change the inevitable end. If you think that your poor two dozen of Giants can resist all the forces of our people and of all the alien peoples who will come to our aid; if you think you can change Humanity at a blow, in a single generation, and alter the nature and stature of Man—"

He flung out an arm. "Go to them now, Sir. I see them, for all the evil they have done, crouching among their wounded—"

He stopped, as though he had glanced at Redwood's son by chance.

There came a pause.

"Go to them," he said.

"That is what I want to do."

"Then go now...."

He turned and pressed the button of a bell; without, in immediate response, came a sound of opening doors and hastening feet.

The talk was at an end. The display was over. Abruptly Caterham seemed to contract, to shrivel up into a yellow-faced, fagged-out, middle-sized, middle-aged man. He stepped forward, as if he were stepping out of a picture, and with a complete assumption of that friendliness that lies behind all the public conflicts of our race, he held out his hand to Redwood.

As if it were a matter of course, Redwood shook hands with him for the second time.

CHAPTER THE FIFTH.
THE GIANT LEAGUER.

I.

Presently Redwood found himself in a train going south over the Thames. He had a brief vision of the river shining under its lights, and of the smoke still going up from the place where the shell had fallen on the north bank, and where a vast multitude of men had been organised to burn the Herakleophorbia out of the ground. The southern bank was dark, for some reason even the streets were not lit, all that was clearly visible was the outlines of the tall alarm-towers and the dark bulks of flats and schools, and after a minute of peering scrutiny he turned his back on the window and sank into thought. There was nothing more to see or do until he saw the Sons....

He was fatigued by the stresses of the last two days; it seemed to him that his emotions must needs be exhausted, but he had fortified himself with strong coffee before starting, and his thoughts ran thin and clear. His mind touched many things. He reviewed again, but now in the enlightenment of accomplished events, the manner in which the Food had entered and unfolded itself in the world.

"Bensington thought it might be an excellent food for infants," he whispered to himself, with a faint smile. Then there came into his mind as vivid as if they were still unsettled his own horrible doubts after he had committed himself by giving it to his own son. From that, with a steady unfaltering expansion, in spite of every effort of men to help and hinder, the Food had spread through the whole world of man. And now?

"Even if they kill them all," Redwood whispered, "the thing is done."

The secret of its making was known far and wide. That had been his own work. Plants, animals, a multitude of distressful growing children would conspire irresistibly to force the world to revert again to the Food, whatever happened in the present struggle. "The thing is done," he said, with his mind swinging round beyond all his controlling to rest upon the present fate of the Children and his son. Would he find them exhausted by the efforts of the battle, wounded, starving, on the verge of defeat, or would he find them still stout and hopeful, ready for the still grimmer conflict of the morrow? His son was wounded! But he had sent a message!

His mind came back to his interview with Caterham.

He was roused from his thoughts by the stopping of his train in Chislehurst station. He recognised the place by the huge rat alarm-tower that crested Camden Hill, and the row of blossoming giant hemlocks that lined the road....

Caterham's private secretary came to him from the other carriage and told him that half a mile farther the line had been wrecked, and that the rest of the journey was to be made in a motor car. Redwood descended upon a platform lit only by a hand lantern and swept by the cool night breeze. The quiet of that derelict, wood-set, weed-embedded suburb—for all the inhabitants had taken refuge in London at the outbreak of yesterday's conflict—became instantly impressive. His conductor took him down the steps to where a motor car was waiting with blazing lights—the only lights to be seen—handed him over to the care of the driver and bade him farewell.

"You will do your best for us," he said, with an imitation of his master's manner, as he held Redwood's hand.

So soon as Redwood could be wrapped about they started out into the night. At one moment they stood still, and then the motor car was rushing softly and swiftly down the station incline. They turned one corner and another, followed the windings of a lane of villas, and then before them stretched the road. The motor droned up to its topmost speed, and the black night swept past them. Everything was very dark under the starlight, and the whole world crouched mysteriously and was gone without a sound. Not a breath stirred the flying things by the wayside; the deserted, pallid white villas on either hand, with their black unlit windows, reminded him of a noiseless procession of skulls. The driver beside him was a silent man, or stricken into silence by the conditions of his journey. He answered

Redwood's brief questions in monosyllables, and gruffly. Athwart the southern sky the beams of searchlights waved noiseless passes; the sole strange evidences of life they seemed in all that derelict world about the hurrying machine.

The road was presently bordered on either side by gigantic blackthorn shoots that made it very dark, and by tail grass and big campions, huge giant dead-nettles as high as trees, flickering past darkly in silhouette overhead. Beyond Keston they came to a rising hill, and the driver went slow. At the crest he stopped. The engine throbbed and became still. "There," he said, and his big gloved finger pointed, a black misshapen thing before Redwood's eyes.

Far away as it seemed, the great embankment, crested by the blaze from which the searchlights sprang, rose up against the sky. Those beams went and came among the clouds and the hilly land about them as if they traced mysterious incantations.

"I don't know," said the driver at last, and it was clear he was afraid to go on.

Presently a searchlight swept down the sky to them, stopped as it were with a start, scrutinised them, a blinding stare confused rather than mitigated by an intervening monstrous weed stem or so. They sat with their gloves held over their eyes, trying to look under them and meet that light.

"Go on," said Redwood after a while.

The driver still had his doubts; he tried to express them, and died down to "I don't know" again.

At last he ventured on. "Here goes," he said, and roused his machinery to motion again, followed intently by that great white eye.

To Redwood it seemed for a long time they were no longer on earth, but in a state of palpitating hurry through a luminous cloud. Teuf, teuf, teuf, teuf, went the machine, and ever and again—obeying I know not what nervous impulse—the driver sounded his horn.

They passed into the welcome darkness of a high-fenced lane, and down into a hollow and past some houses into that blinding stare again. Then for a space the road ran naked across a down, and they seemed to hang throbbing in immensity. Once more giant weeds rose about them and whirled past. Then quite abruptly close upon them loomed the figure of a giant, shining brightly where the searchlight caught him below, and black against the sky above. "Hullo there!" he cried, and "stop! There's no more road beyond ... Is that Father Redwood?"

Redwood stood up and gave a vague shout by way of answer, and then Cossar was in the road beside him, gripping both hands with both of his and pulling him out of the car.

"What of my son?" asked Redwood.

"He's all right," said Cossar. "They've hurt nothing serious in him."

"And your lads?"

"Well. All of them, well. But we've had to make a fight for it."

The Giant was saying something to the motor driver. Redwood stood aside as the machine wheeled round, and then suddenly Cossar vanished, everything vanished, and he was in absolute darkness for a space. The glare was following the motor back to the crest of the Keston hill. He watched the little conveyance receding in that white halo. It had a curious effect, as though it was not moving at all and the halo was. A group of war-blasted Giant elders flashed into gaunt scarred gesticulations and were swallowed again by the night ... Redwood turned to Cossar's dim outline again and clasped his hard. "I have been shut up and kept in ignorance," he said, "for two whole days."

"We fired the Food at them," said Cossar. "Obviously! Thirty shots. Eh!"

"I come from Caterham."

"I know you do." He laughed with a note of bitterness. "I suppose he's wiping it up."

II.

"Where is my son?" said Redwood.

"He is all right. The Giants are waiting for your message."

"Yes, but my son—..."

He passed with Cossar down a long slanting tunnel that was lit red for a moment and then became dark again, and came out presently into the great pit of shelter the Giants had made.

Redwood's first impression was of an enormous arena bounded by very high cliffs and with its floor greatly encumbered. It was in darkness save for the passing reflections of the watchman's searchlights that whirled perpetually high overhead, and for a red glow that came and went from a distant corner where two Giants worked together amidst a metallic clangour. Against the sky, as the glare came about, his eye caught the familiar outlines of the old worksheds and playsheds that were made for the Cossar boys. They were hanging now, as it were, at a cliff brow, and strangely twisted and distorted with the guns of Caterham's bombardment. There were suggestions of huge gun emplacements above there, and nearer were piles of mighty cylinders that were perhaps ammunition. All about the wide space below, the forms of great engines and incomprehensible bulks were scattered in vague disorder. The Giants appeared and vanished among these masses and in the uncertain light; great shapes they were, not disproportionate to the things amidst which they moved. Some were actively employed, some sitting and lying as if they courted sleep, and one near at hand, whose body was bandaged, lay on a rough litter of pine boughs and was certainly asleep. Redwood peered at these dim forms; his eyes went from one stirring outline to another.

"Where is my son, Cossar?"

Then he saw him.

His son was sitting under the shadow of a great wall of steel. He presented himself as a black shape recognisable only by his pose, — his features were invisible. He sat chin upon hand, as though weary or lost in thought. Beside him Redwood discovered the figure of the Princess, the dark suggestion of her merely, and then, as the glow from the distant iron returned, he saw for an instant, red lit and tender, the infinite kindliness of her shadowed face. She stood looking down upon her lover with her hand resting against the steel. It seemed that she whispered to him.

Redwood would have gone towards them.

"Presently," said Cossar. "First there is your message."

"Yes," said Redwood, "but—"

He stopped. His son was now looking up and speaking to the Princess, but in too low a tone for them to hear. Young Redwood raised his face, and she bent down towards him, and glanced aside before she spoke.

"But if we are beaten," they heard the whispered voice of young Redwood.

She paused, and the red blaze showed her eyes bright with unshed tears. She bent nearer him and spoke still lower. There was something so intimate and private in their bearing, in their soft tones, that Redwood—Redwood who had thought for two whole days of nothing but his son—felt himself intrusive there. Abruptly he was checked. For the first time in his life perhaps he realised how much more a son may be to his father than a father can ever be to a son; he realised the full predominance of the future over the past. Here between these two he had no part. His part was played. He turned to Cossar, in the instant realisation. Their eyes met. His voice was changed to the tone of a grey resolve.

"I will deliver my message now," he said. "Afterwards—... It will be soon enough then."

The pit was so enormous and so encumbered that it was a long and tortuous route to the place from which Redwood could speak to them all.

He and Cossar followed a steeply descending way that passed beneath an arch of interlocking machinery, and so came into a vast deep gangway that ran athwart the bottom of the pit. This gangway, wide and vacant, and yet relatively narrow, conspired with everything about it to enhance Redwood's sense of his own littleness. It became, as it were, an excavated gorge. High overhead, separated from him by cliffs of darkness, the searchlights wheeled and blazed, and the shining shapes went to and fro. Giant voices called to one another above there, calling the Giants together to the Council of War, to hear the terms that Caterham had sent. The gangway still inclined downward towards black vastnesses, towards shadows and mysteries and inconceivable things, into which Redwood went slowly with reluctant footsteps and Cossar with a confident stride....

Redwood's thoughts were busy. The two men passed into the completest darkness, and Cossar took his companion's wrist. They went now slowly perforce.

Redwood was moved to speak. "All this," he said, "is strange."

"Big," said Cossar.

"Strange. And strange that it should be strange to me—I, who am, in a sense, the beginning of it all. It's—"

He stopped, wrestling with his elusive meaning, and threw an unseen gesture at the cliff.

"I have not thought of it before. I have been busy, and the years have passed. But here I see—It is a new generation, Cossar, and new emotions and new needs. All this, Cossar—"

Cossar saw now his dim gesture to the things about them.

"All this is Youth."

Cossar made no answers and his irregular footfalls went striding on.

"It isn't our youth, Cossar. They are taking things over. They arebeginning upon their own emotions, their own experiences, their own way.We have made a new world, and it isn't ours. It isn't even—sympathetic.This great place—"

"I planned it," said Cossar, his face close.

"But now?"

"Ah! I have given it to my sons."

Redwood could feel the loose wave of the arm that he could not see.

"That is it. We are over—or almost over."

"Your message!"

"Yes. And then—"

"We're over."

"Well—?"

"Of course we are out of it, we two old men," said Cossar, with his familiar note of sudden anger. "Of course we are. Obviously. Each man for his own time. And now—it's their time beginning. That's all right. Excavator's gang. We do our job and go. See? That is what death is for. We work out all our little brains and all our little emotions, and then this lot begins afresh. Fresh and fresh! Perfectly simple. What's the trouble?"

He paused to guide Redwood to some steps.

"Yes," said Redwood, "but one feels—"

He left his sentence incomplete.

"That is what Death is for." He heard Cossar below him insisting, "How else could the thing be done? That is what Death is for."

III.

After devious windings and ascents they came out upon a projecting ledge from which it was possible to see over the greater extent of the Giants' pit, and from which Redwood might make himself heard by the whole of their assembly. The Giants were already gathered below and about him at different levels, to hear the message he had to deliver. The eldest son of Cossar stood on the bank overhead watching the revelations of the searchlights, for they feared a breach of the truce. The workers at the great apparatus in the corner stood out clear in their own light; they were near stripped; they turned their faces towards Redwood, but with a watchful reference ever and again to the castings that they could not leave. He saw these nearer figures with a fluctuating indistinctness, by lights that came and went, and the remoter ones still less distinctly. They came from and vanished again into the depths of great obscurities. For these Giants had no more light than they could help in the pit, that their eyes might be ready to see effectually any attacking force that might spring upon them out of the darknesses around.

Ever and again some chance glare would pick out and display this group or that of tall and powerful forms, the Giants from Sunderland clothed in overlapping metal plates, and the others clad in leather, in woven rope or in woven metal, as their conditions had determined. They sat amidst or rested their hands upon, or stood erect among machines and weapons as mighty as themselves, and all their faces, as they came and went from visible to invisible, had steadfast eyes.

He made an effort to begin and did not do so. Then for a moment his son's face glowed out in a hot insurgence of the fire, his son's face looking up to him, tender as well as strong; and at that he found a voice to reach them all, speaking across a gulf, as it were, to his son.

"I come from Caterham," he said. "He sent me to you, to tell you the terms he offers."

He paused. "They are impossible terms, I know, now that I see you here all together; they are impossible terms, but I brought them to you, because I wanted to see you all—and my son. Once more ... I wanted to see my son...."

"Tell them the terms," said Cossar.

"This is what Caterham offers. He wants you to go apart and leave his world!"

"Where?"

"He does not know. Vaguely somewhere in the world a great region is to be set apart.... And you are to make no more of the Food, to have no children of your own, to live in your own way for your own time, and then to end for ever."

He stopped.

"And that is all?"

"That is all."

There followed a great stillness. The darkness that veiled the Giants seemed to look thoughtfully at him.

He felt a touch at his elbow, and Cossar was holding a chair for him—a queer fragment of doll's furniture amidst these piled immensities. He sat down and crossed his legs, and then put one across the knee of the other, and clutched his boot nervously, and felt small and self-conscious and acutely visible and absurdly placed.

Then at the sound of a voice he forgot himself again.

"You have heard, Brothers," said this voice out of the shadows.

And another answered, "We have heard."

"And the answer, Brothers?"

"To Caterham?"

"Is No!"

"And then?"

There was a silence for the space of some seconds.

Then a voice said: "These people are right. After their lights, that is. They have been right in killing all that grew larger than its kind—beast and plant and all manner of great things that arose. They were right in trying to massacre us. They are right now in saying we must not marry our kind. According to their lights they are right. They know—it is time that we also knew—that you cannot have pigmies and giants in one world together. Caterham has said that again and again—clearly—their world or ours."

"We are not half a hundred now," said another, "and they are endless millions."

"So it may be. But the thing is as I have said."

Then another long silence.

"And are we to die then?"

"God forbid!"

"Are they?"

"No."

"But that is what Caterham says! He would have us live out our lives, die one by one, till only one remains, and that one at last would die also, and they would cut down all the giant plants and weeds, kill all the giant under-life, burn out the traces of the Food—make an end to us and to the Food for ever. Then the little pigmy world would be safe. They would go on—safe for ever, living their little pigmy lives, doing pigmy kindnesses and pigmy cruelties each to the other; they might even perhaps attain a sort of pigmy millennium, make an end to war, make an end to over-population, sit down in a world-wide city to practise pigmy arts, worshipping one another till the world begins to freeze...."

In the corner a sheet of iron fell in thunder to the ground.

"Brothers, we know what we mean to do."

In a spluttering of light from the searchlights Redwood saw earnest youthful faces turning to his son.

"It is easy now to make the Food. It would be easy for us to make Food for all the world."

"You mean, Brother Redwood," said a voice out of the darkness, "that it is for the little people to eat the Food."

"What else is there to do?"

"We are not half a hundred and they are many millions."

"But we held our own."

"So far."

"If it is God's will, we may still hold our own."

"Yes. But think of the dead!"

Another voice took up the strain. "The dead," it said. "Think of the unborn...."

"Brothers," came the voice of young Redwood, "what can we do but fight them, and if we beat them, make them take the Food? They cannot help but take the Food now. Suppose we were to resign our heritage and do this folly that Caterham suggests! Suppose we could! Suppose we give up this great thing that stirs within us, repudiate this thing our fathers did for us—that you, Father, did for us—and pass, when our time has come, into decay and nothingness! What then? Will this little world of theirs be as it was before? They may fight against greatness in us who are the children of men, but can they conquer? Even if they should destroy us every one, what then? Would it save them? No! For greatness is abroad, not only in us, not only in the Food, but in the purpose of all things! It is in the nature of all things; it is part of space and time. To grow and still to grow: from first to last that is Being—that is the law of life. What other law can there be?"

"To help others?"

"To grow. It is still, to grow. Unless we help them to fail...."

"They will fight hard to overcome us," said a voice.

And another, "What of that?"

"They will fight," said young Redwood. "If we refuse these terms, I doubt not they will fight. Indeed I hope they will be open and fight. If after all they offer peace, it will be only the better to catch us unawares. Make no mistake, Brothers; in some way or other they will fight. The war has begun, and we must fight, to the end. Unless we are wise, we may find presently we have lived only to make them better weapons against our children and our kind. This, so far, has been only the dawn of battle. All our lives will be a battle. Some of us will be killed in battle, some of us will be waylaid. There is no easy victory—no victory whatever that is not more than half defeat for us. Be sure of that. What of that? If only we keep a foothold, if only we leave behind us a growing host to fight when we are gone!"

"And to-morrow?"

"We will scatter the Food; we will saturate the world with the Food."

"Suppose they come to terms?"

"Our terms are the Food. It is not as though little and great could live together in any perfection of compromise. It is one thing or the other. What right have parents to say, My child shall have no light but the light I have had, shall grow no greater than the greatness to which I have grown? Do I speak for you, Brothers?"

Assenting murmurs answered him.

"And to the children who will be women as well as to the children who will be men," said a voice from the darkness.

"Even more so—to be mothers of a new race ..."

"But for the next generation there must be great and little," saidRedwood, with his eyes on his son's face.

"For many generations. And the little will hamper the great and the great press upon the little. So it must needs be, father."

"There will be conflict."

"Endless conflict. Endless misunderstanding. All life is that. Great and little cannot understand one another. But in every child born of man, Father Redwood, lurks some seed of greatness—waiting for the Food."

"Then I am to go to Caterham again and tell him—"

"You will stay with us, Father Redwood. Our answer goes to Caterham at dawn."

"He says that he will fight...."

"So be it," said young Redwood, and his brethren murmured assent.

"The iron waits," cried a voice, and the two giants who were working in the corner began a rhythmic hammering that made a mighty music to the scene. The metal glowed out far more brightly than it had done before, and gave Redwood a clearer view of the encampment than had yet come to him. He saw the oblong space to its full extent, with the great engines of warfare ranged ready to hand. Beyond, and at a higher level, the house of the Cossars stood.

About him were the young giants, huge and beautiful, glittering in their mail, amidst the preparations for the morrow. The sight of them lifted his heart. They were so easily powerful! They were so tall and gracious! They were so steadfast in their movements! There was his son amongst them, and the first of all giant women, the Princess....

There leapt into his mind the oddest contrast, a memory of Bensington, very bright and little—Bensington with his hand amidst the soft breast feathers of that first great chick, standing in that conventionally furnished room of his, peering over his spectacles dubiously as cousin Jane banged the door....

It had all happened in a yesterday of one-and-twenty years.

Then suddenly a strange doubt took hold of him: that this place and present greatness were but the texture of a dream; that he was dreaming, and would in an instant wake to find himself in his study again, the Giants slaughtered, the Food suppressed, and himself a prisoner locked in. What else indeed was life but that—always to be a prisoner locked in! This was the culmination and end of his dream. He would wake through bloodshed and battle, to find his Food the most foolish of fancies, and his hopes and faith of a greater world to come no more than the coloured film upon a pool of bottomless decay. Littleness invincible!

So strong and deep was this wave of despondency, this suggestion of impending disillusionment, that he started to his feet. He stood and pressed his clenched fists into his eyes, and so for a moment remained, fearing to open them again and see, lest the dream should already have passed away....

The voice of the giant children spoke to one another, an undertone to that clangorous melody of the smiths. His tide of doubt ebbed. He heard the giant voices; he heard their movements about him still. It was real, surely it was real—as real as spiteful acts! More real, for these great things, it may be, are the coming things, and the littleness, bestiality, and infirmity of men are the things that go. He opened his eyes. "Done," cried one of the two ironworkers, and they flung their hammers down.

A voice sounded above. The son of Cossar, standing on the great embankment, had turned and was now speaking to them all.

"It is not that we would oust the little people from the world," he said, "in order that we, who are no more than one step upwards from their littleness, may hold their world for ever. It is the step we fight for and not ourselves.... We are here, Brothers, to what end? To serve the spirit and the purpose that has been breathed into our lives. We fight not for ourselves—for we are but the momentary hands and eyes of the Life of the World. So you, Father Redwood, taught us. Through us and through the little folk the Spirit looks and learns. From us by word and birth and act it must pass—to still greater lives. This earth is no resting place; this earth is no playing place, else indeed we might put our throats to the little people's knife, having no greater right to live than they. And they in their turn might yield to the ants and vermin. We fight not for ourselves but for growth—growth that goes on for ever. To-morrow, whether we live or die, growth will conquer through us. That is the law of the spirit for ever more. To grow according to the will of God! To grow out of these cracks and crannies, out of these shadows and darknesses, into greatness and the light! Greater," he said, speaking with slow deliberation, "greater, my Brothers! And then—still greater. To grow, and again—to grow. To grow at last into the fellowship and understanding of God. Growing.... Till the earth is no more than a footstool.... Till the spirit shall have driven fear into nothingness, and spread...." He swung his arm heavenward:— "There!" His voice ceased. The white glare of one of the searchlights wheeled about, and for a moment fell upon him, standing out gigantic with hand upraised against the sky.

For one instant he shone, looking up fearlessly into the starry deeps, mail-clad, young and strong, resolute and still. Then the light had passed, and he was no more than a great black outline against the starry sky—a great black outline that threatened with one mighty gesture the firmament of heaven and all its multitude of stars.

THE END.